LOVE AT PEBBLE CREEK

behind her, the lock clicked into place. The wreath she'd made for her mother was hanging on its holder for dear life, so she quickly unhooked it, opened the front door, and set the decoration just inside.

She closed the door again and stepped out on the front porch. To her surprise, the hot summer temperature had taken a sudden dip since early this morning, and an unusually cold breeze for the second week in July cooled her cheeks.

Her *daed* followed the weather closely, and he would have prepared and warned her if this storm had been in the forecast. But her keen instincts noted the red flags that indicated one was coming: the suddenly dark sky and the loud, eerie-sounding wind.

For a brief moment, she imagined grabbing a phone from her pocket and dialing her *eltern*. She gave a quick shake of her head.

That wasn't about to happen. The Amish didn't use cell phones, not in this neck of the woods anyway, and the wall phone was out in the barn, so getting things done was all up to her.

Without help, no doubt, closing things up so fast would be a challenge. Still, there was plenty to smile about. The clipping she'd found while cleaning up at King's Bakery that morning. A customer had left a St. Louis newspaper on a *tisch*.

She'd picked it up from the table and torn off the part of interest and stuffed it in her satchel. And the clipping would stay her secret. This entry could give her long-time dream a chance to come true. Which she wanted

PIF
Baker

ZEBRA BOOKS are published by

Kensington Publishing Corp.
119 West 40th Street
New York, NY 10018

All Kensington titles, imprints, and distributed lines are available at special quantity discounts for bulk purchases for sales promotion, premiums, fund-raising, educational, or institutional use.

Special book excerpts or customized printings can also be created to fit specific needs. For details, write or phone the office of the Kensington Sales Manager: Attn.: Sales Department. Kensington Publishing Corp., 119 West 40th Street, New York, NY 10018. Phone: 1-800-221-2647.

First Printing: September 2019
ISBN-13: 978-1-4201-4746-9
ISBN-10: 1-4201-4746-3

ISBN-13: 978-1-4201-4747-6 (eBook)
ISBN-10: 1-4201-4747-1 (eBook)

10 9 8 7 6 5 4 3 2 1

Printed in the United States of America

LOVE AT
PEBBLE CREEK

Lisa Jones Baker

ZEBRA BOOKS
KENSINGTON PUBLISHING CORP.
www.kensingtonbooks.com

*To my loving parents,
John and Marcia Baker,
and to my beloved late grandparents,
Anna and Louis Jones and Edna and Merle Baker,
who are the epitome of hard work and honesty,
and whom I can only aspire to emulate in this life*

My appreciation to Brittany Yoder, Village Square Real Estate, Arthur, Illinois, for helping me to fact check my real estate transaction between the Norrises and the Beilers.

To Sadie Preston, Sales Coordinator, St. Louis Marriott Grand, for acquainting me with the Majestic Ballroom, where the story's art contest takes place.

To Lori Manning, Aquatics Director at the Decatur, Illinois, YMCA for taking time to discuss the scene that takes place at the Conrads' pond.

To the Bloomington Geek Squad, thanks!

To hundreds of writers within the RWA who have reviewed my books and offered valuable feedback, THANK YOU!

To agent of the year Tamela Hancock Murray, who spent numerous hours helping me to hone *Rebecca's Bouquet*, my first Amish story, before it was even contracted. You invested in me when publication was no guarantee.

To Joan Wester Anderson, thank you for helping me to launch my writing career. You're my role model.

Selena James, my brilliant editor, you're the best.

My sincere gratitude to publicist Jane Nutter and Kensington Books, and to everyone in Arthur, Illinois, who have so kindly answered my questions for the past decade. I went to many sources for information for this book. Any mistakes are mine alone.

Last but not least, much appreciation to my Amish go-to friend, who inspires me and who helps me to make my stories consistent with how the Amish live in Arthur, Illinois. You are why it's a great honor to write in this particular genre, about wondrous faith-driven people who have my utmost fascination and admiration.

Acknowledgments

First of all, thanks to my Creator for blessing me with this amazing opportunity to write inspirational stories. Nearly three decades of prayers were answered, and my wait time was definitely worth the reward.

To Marcia, my reading specialist mother and my biggest fan for over thirty years, who has listened to me read thirty-something books out loud. Mom, you are the most patient person in the world!

Beth Zehr, sister extraordinaire. I don't know what I would do without your technical expertise and your full support. Having a business teacher in the family has its advantages.

Aunt Velda Baker, you're another blessing. I don't take for granted the time you spent reviewing this story for accuracy. I truly believe you'd make a great investigator.

Lisa Norato, true friend and critique partner for thirty years, I was fortunate to have met you years ago at my very first writing conference. From the commencement of our friendship, you've offered unconditional support while we both sought publication. Also, huge thanks for clarifying my questions about the Catholic faith for this book.

Chapter One

A storm was about to hit. Thunder crackled, forcing twenty-year-old Anna King to work faster. As the wind howled and oak branches brushed against the sides of her family's home in the countryside of Arthur, Illinois, she looked around and mentally ticked off her to-do list before the rain came.

The windows are closed. Fertig. The horse tied outside needs to be taken to the stall. As soon as the livestock are inside, close the barn doors. At least, the front ones. The wheelbarrow's by the garden; put it in the shed. The hoe, too. If time permits, put mesh over the garden plants.

She looked down. *And change aprons.* With one quick motion, she removed the one she was wearing and replaced it with her bigger work apron. Her parents were at King's Bakery so no one was home but her. Anna's adrenaline revved to an urgent speed as she considered everything needed to be done before the unforecasted downpour.

As she pulled the large front door of her home

behind her, the lock clicked into place. The wreath she'd made for her mother was hanging on its holder for dear life, so she quickly unhooked it, opened the front door, and set the decoration just inside.

She closed the door again and stepped out on the front porch. To her surprise, the hot summer temperature had taken a sudden dip since early this morning, and an unusually cold breeze for the second week in July lifted her bangs.

Her *daed* followed the weather closely, and he would have prepared and warned her if this storm had been in the forecast. But her keen instincts noted the red flags that indicated one was coming: the suddenly dark sky and the loud, eerie-sounding wind.

For a brief moment, she imagined grabbing a phone from her pocket and dialing her *eltern*. She gave a quick shake of her head.

That wasn't about to happen. The Amish didn't use cell phones, not in this neck of the woods anyway, and the wall phone was out in the barn, so getting things done was all up to her.

Without help, no doubt, closing things up so fast would be a challenge. Still, there was plenty to smile about. The clipping she'd found while cleaning up at King's Bakery that morning. A customer had left a St. Louis newspaper on a *tisch*.

She'd picked it up from the table and torn off the part of interest and stuffed it in her satchel. The clipping would stay her secret. This entry could give her long-time dream a chance to come true. ... she wanted

more than anything. The number-one thing on the list she kept inside her hope chest.

Outside, a few unruly tendrils of jet-black hair broke free from her *kapp*, and she didn't bother to shove them back under her tight head covering. By the fierce-looking sky, she was sure there wasn't much time to act.

The old chain that held the painted, light-blue wooden front porch swing to the ceiling creaked as the wind moved it back and forth in an uneven motion. Automatically, she grabbed the metal and hiked up one side to hook the middle part to the ceiling and stepped to the other side to repeat the action.

It came automatically to her because she and *Maemm* routinely did this together after any weather advisory in order to prevent the swing from being blown against the front of the house or, even worse, from colliding with and breaking the large front window. She lifted the heavy bench on one side as high as she could. Just enough for the chain to hook.

Fertig. As she caught her breath, she took in the sky in the distance, which had quickly become an uglier shade of dark gray. The color reminded her of charcoals in her *daed*'s grill after they'd burned.

The air smelled of rain. She pressed her lips together in a straight line, realizing that time was of the essence. She hiked up her dress and rushed down the front porch stairs. At the bottom, she continued to hold both sides to avoid tripping and falling.

She glimpsed Blaze, their beloved horse, tied to a post. Automatically, her eyes followed the path to the

large, open barn doors. A drop of cold rain landed on her forehead, and she ran a hand over it.

As the ruthless, unforgiving wind continued to pick up speed, tall oak branches banged the roof of the two-story family dwelling. Bolts of lightning sparked in the sky. Some let out a loud crack, while others were silent.

Ominous-sounding thunder. She could hear loud neighs, whinnies, and moos as their livestock proceeded into the barn's back entrance.

As she took in the healthy distance that needed covering fast, she straightened and let out a determined sigh before traversing the long stretch of jade-colored grass that her *daed* kept mowed short. She took quick, small steps, fully aware that her sturdy black shoes and her long navy dress weren't conducive for running.

As she made her way to Blaze, she passed her summer garden, filled with produce that Anna would freeze for the winter. Bright red tomatoes. Red and green peppers. Green beans. Zucchini. Pumpkin plants.

Cucumber vines lined the ground like a map of the world. Tall stalks of corn stood in the back, accompanied by a row of large, yellow sunflowers. The wind moved the faux snake across the yard.

As Anna stepped around a dip in the lawn, she felt sorry for the plants. Because right now, they fought for survival against Mother Nature as they swayed back and forth and dipped helplessly with the wind. Anna hoped that their stems would be able to withstand the power of the storm that, by the sound of it, was only getting started.

The urgent noises of livestock competed with a loose

shutter banging against the house. Metal pans tied throughout the garden to scare off birds made a light, tinny sound as they bumped one another.

As dirt blew into her eyes, she stopped for a moment to cover her face with her hands. She blinked at the sting and teared up. She blinked again, uncovered her eyes, and continued forward.

The fake owl perched on top of the clothesline post fell to the ground. From her peripheral vision, she glimpsed the empty *dawdy* house. Two brown and white goats skipped across the large backyard to the barn, where they entered with three chickens through the large front doors that had blown open.

Blaze clomped his right hoof and let out a loud whinny. Not long after, he repeated the action.

"I'm coming!"

As she got closer to the horse, she remembered that she'd left her satchel on the buggy, which was parked next to the house. Losing the satchel to the brewing storm didn't worry her, but what was inside of it did. The newspaper clipping. But it would have to wait.

A rooster darted in front of her, and Anna made an abrupt stop to avoid tripping over it. The bird eventually made his way into the hen coop. As charcoal-gray clouds moved toward the west, a duo of light raindrops hit the back of her neck.

No rain yet, please. On both sides of her, purple coneheads dipped in the direction the wind blew them. Tin pans tied to wooden posts in the garden jumped up and down with the breeze, making a light sound as they met with the metal stakes they were attached to.

When she dropped the sides of her dress, she quickly yanked them up again to avoid tripping. Finally, she reached Blaze and untied him. "C'mon, Blaze. Let's get you inside." She grabbed his lead.

As she and the family horse approached the large, old structure, rain came down. First, at a light dose. Then, the volume increased.

She blinked open and closed to avoid getting dirt and debris in her eyes. As rain dampened her clothes, a chill swept up her spine, and she shivered, realizing how very cold it had gotten. Between the rain and the wind, it was becoming increasingly difficult to see. And to breathe.

Sounds of protest floated through the air. A loud chorus from the cattle eventually morphed into one solid sound, competing with whinnies from their field horses.

As they got closer, Blaze jerked his long, *braun* neck up. Anna struggled to catch her breath, but the wind was against her, and she still had quite a distance to cover.

She started to lose her balance and stopped for a moment. When a large bolt of lightning crackled, a downpour started, and Anna tasted dirt on her lips. Smelled it. Her eyes felt gritty, and the speed of the wind became so fierce, it took her *kapp*. "C'mon, boy. Let's get inside." She could feel her long mass of thick hair drop to her shoulders.

As Anna and Blaze hurried to the barn, all sounds became one: rain, thunder, the animal chorus, and her own breathing. It became so difficult to see, she held on tightly to the lead and slowed her pace, moving in the

direction of the clanging of heavy doors being blown open and shut.

For a moment, the rain let up just enough for her to glimpse the barn. "C'mon, boy! We're almost there!" Just then, something hit her with such great force, it knocked her down. Jagged ends of a heavy broken oak limb that had cracked in the middle stuck in the ground on both sides of her and pinned her entire body.

As she closed her eyes a moment, she tasted blood and realized it was coming from her forehead. *I have to get Blaze inside and close the doors to protect the animals.*

"Dear Lord, please keep us safe. Amen."

The moment she whispered her prayer, there was an additional sound that she hadn't noticed before. She heard the whinny of a new horse in the distance. Surely her parents hadn't attempted to make it home from the bakery in this storm. When the clomp-clomping of hooves and another loud whinny sounded, Blaze responded with his own and made his way into the barn.

At that moment, the sky opened up even more and drenched her. Clumps of leaves covered her face as she tried to move the tree parts off of her. But it was impossible. Between the fierce wind and the heavy downpour, Anna struggled to get her breath.

She was drenched. She coughed. It was hard to believe that just a short time ago, she'd enjoyed the sun's warm rays, which had beaten down on her face.

But now, thanks to the branch that pinned her, she couldn't get up, and there was a severe pain in her head. Warm blood oozed from the place she'd been pierced. Yet even with her injury, all she could think about was getting

to the barn and closing the doors so the animals would be safe from blowing debris. But would it happen?

It was Jesse Beiler's first day of work for one of the owners of King's Bakery. Never had he imagined that the morning would start like this. He'd pictured his initial task as having something to do in the large barn. Like sharpening tools. Or raking animal stalls. Or working in the hayloft. Or, best of all, farming the one hundred and some acres behind Paul King's home.

But it was nothing of the sort. To his surprise, John King's brother had assigned him the responsibility of ensuring that his only daughter was safe, which, to Jesse's mind, was a far cry from farming.

But here he was, in the countryside of Arthur, Illinois. He leaned forward as Serene, his beloved Standardbred, which had been adopted from Dr. Jared Zimmerman, picked up speed, pulling him and his buggy down the desolate blacktop that led to the two-story dwelling of Paul King, his wife Naomi, and his only child, Anna. And according to the sky, the gusty wind, and the severe temperature drop, time was of the essence.

In the past half hour, Jesse had given his word that he'd ensure Anna was inside the house, safe and sound, from the unexpected storm. Now, he was second-guessing his promise.

When he'd committed, he hadn't known that the storm would progress so quickly. Unfortunately, its unexpected nature hadn't given him much time.

But he was almost there. The combination of fierce

wind and rain made it difficult to see. Fortunately, he and Serene were familiar with the blacktop they traveled. And from where they were, it was a straight shot to their destination.

To his relief, the rain let up just long enough to offer enough time to check his whereabouts. A quick, clear glance at the familiar landscape told him that he was within close range of the King farm.

Even so, as the downpour restarted, Jesse was fully aware that the remaining half mile to the farm wouldn't be easy. It was still late morning, yet the sky was as dark as it would be after sunset.

He straightened, praying to get there in time to make sure Anna was okay. As he said "Amen," a large bolt of lightning charged the sky. To Jesse's dismay, Serene reacted by rearing her front legs in the air.

"Whoa!"

Jesse gritted his teeth, still determined to keep his word. Although today was his first day as a farmhand, he and the Kings had been friends and fellow church members for years, and he couldn't count the number of times they'd gotten together here.

So, the layout wasn't a mystery. He knew where to find the garden, the house, and the large, old barn where Paul loved to spend time. The three made a triangle, with the garden nearest the road.

Still, despite the fact that Jesse knew their place like the back of his hand, what needed to be done wouldn't be easy. Not in this storm. Thankful he was closer, he was fully aware that being outside in these conditions wasn't safe. For him. Or Serene. As they headed up the long, dirt drive, flying debris filled the air.

"Whoa, girl." The moment he reached the barn, he jumped off and quickly led Serene inside the building. As he did so, he heard a call for help.

Outside, he followed the sound of the voice. "I'm coming!"

Finally, he looked down at Anna, who was pinned to the ground by a large, broken oak limb.

Even as he asked, he could see she wasn't all right. Her head was bleeding. "I'll get you inside." With all of his strength, he pulled the heavy limb that trapped her out of the ground, scooped her into his arms, and carried her inside the barn.

He could hear her soft, tired voice. "Jesse . . . How . . . how did you know? What are you doing here?"

He didn't respond. Right now, he needed to get her to a safe place. Then he'd explain.

As he took quick steps, he held on to her tightly and focused on his footing as he searched for where she'd be most comfortable. It didn't take long to decide on the best spot. Her arms encircled his waist. He could hear small coughs coming from her throat.

He stopped to catch his own breath. "You okay?"

The only response was a cough.

He eyed several bales of straw that touched the wall nearest the stalls. "I'll put you down." He bent, careful to support her neck. She wasn't light, but she wasn't heavy either.

Thunder rumbled as he frowned at the large gash on her forehead and the blood oozing from the injury.

"Jesse? What are you doing here?" Before he could answer, she went on. "I . . . I'm okay," she said to the bishop's son.

He frowned, fully aware that the first thing he had to do was to stop the flow of blood. He kneeled so he was eye-to-eye with her before glancing at the nearest wall. With one fluid motion, he made his way to a hook with a clean, oversize rag. As he returned to Anna and pressed the cloth gently against her forehead, a cold shiver swept up his spine.

A faint smile of appreciation lifted the corners of her lips as she met his gaze. "How did you know I needed help?"

Relief swept up his arms and landed in his shoulders. "Right now, I'm just glad you're conscious." He leaned over her, gently using the cotton to absorb the blood. "By the looks of your forehead, that limb hit you pretty hard. Just try to stay still while I stop the blood."

For a moment, she closed her eyes. He bent so his face was near hers. With great care not to hurt her, he took strands of loose, jet-black hair and, using his most gentle, careful touch, pulled them, one by one, off her face.

He heard the cadence of her breathing change. "Ouch."

He lowered the pitch of his voice so that it was barely more than a whisper. "Sorry."

When she opened her eyes, it was impossible not to notice the mesmerizing jade color. The deep shade reminded him of a beautiful yard after a fresh mow.

Circumstances warranted their closeness. He'd never seen her with her hair down, and the fullness and beauty of the wet, jet-black waves took him by surprise.

He wasn't sure why; he supposed it was just because

he'd never seen Anna King without her *kapp*. Or any other girl who went to church with him, for that matter.

As he continued pulling her hair away from her face, he folded the rag and touched the dry side to her forehead. "It looks like you'll need stitches."

He pressed. She winced.

He gritted his teeth in agony. The last thing he wanted to do was put her in more pain than she already was. "Sorry. I don't have much practice with this sort of thing."

As she closed her eyes, he tried to keep her talking to make sure she stayed awake. Not sure what to ask, he said the first thing that came to his mind. "What's your favorite color?"

When she opened her lids, he was quick to catch the expression of disbelief.

"Blue." The corners of her lips lifted in amusement. "Like your eyes."

As soon as she closed her lids again, he smiled a little in satisfaction. She'd always been spunky. And unafraid. But right now, her verbal reaction wasn't all he sought.

He needed more evidence to convince him that she was okay. The gash on her forehead looked wicked, and the knot over it was growing. She might have a concussion.

"My next question will tell me whether or not you're on your toes." He cleared his throat and pitched his question with an odd combination of hopefulness and confidence. "What's King's Bakery famous for?"

While he awaited a response, he removed the material from her wound to fold it again to find a dry spot.

When he did, he continued dabbing the cotton fabric against the ominous-looking cut.

He frowned and snapped his fingers. "Anna, answer my question."

"What?"

"What's King's Bakery famous for?"

When she opened her eyes and grinned, a great sense of relief swept through him.

"Cinnamon rolls."

He laughed.

"What's so funny?"

He considered her question but didn't have an answer. To his dismay, she continued looking at him with an expression of expectation. Curiosity. Finally, he acknowledged that she expected an answer, so he had to come up with one.

He lifted his chin a notch as words came to him. "There's nothing funny about this situation. Nothing at all. But my laugh . . . I think it was a reaction of relief. I was worried that you couldn't remember."

He blew out a deep breath and shook his head before locking gazes with her again. "You had me worried. The gash on your forehead . . . it's wicked-looking."

After a slight pause, he went on. "But as soon as the storm lets up . . ." He lifted a brow and straightened. "We're gonna get you to a doctor."

When she sat up, he steadied her with his hand and used as much persuasion as he could to convince her. "Easy does it, Anna. You're not goin' anywhere soon."

She closed her eyes a moment. As she did so, he took advantage of the opportunity to get a better look at her face. To his relief, color had started to return to her

cheeks. Her long, thick lashes were as black as her thick head of hair.

Even though he'd been around her most of his life, through school and church, he admitted he didn't really know much about the *tochter* of Paul and Naomi. Just that she had been adopted as a baby. And that she could be a bit determined. Not in a bad way.

In school, she'd stuck up for what was right. He automatically recalled one incident when Israel Schmucker, the orneriest kid around, had stolen her homework. Anna hadn't said a word to their teacher, Mrs. Graber.

But, to Jesse's surprise, Anna had returned the favor after Mrs. Graber had asked Israel the answer to a math problem. The prankster answered correctly, but when Anna had followed up with her own question about how he'd gotten that response, Israel had been surprised. And unknowledgeable.

Jesse had seen the slight smile after their teacher began asking Israel more follow-ups. It had quickly become obvious that the homework on his desk wasn't his own.

But personally, he knew so little about her, this new realization prompted his jaw to drop in surprise. He was aware that Naomi had made numerous unsuccessful attempts to conceive. He also was fully aware that this dark-haired girl loved to draw.

She'd never said so. But he'd sat behind her in school often enough to know that she'd sketched whenever the opportunity had arisen. It had always amused him when he'd watched her open her textbook and quickly slip a piece of paper in between the pages.

Most likely, Mrs. Graber had thought the girl was

taking notes. Because when posed questions, Anna rarely missed an answer. But while she sketched, she'd done mostly landscapes. And, humorously, she'd captured the expression on Israel's face when Mrs. Graber had taken away his stolen answers.

What had stunned Jesse even more than her uncanny ability to pretend note-taking was that her sketches had been incredibly good. In his eyes anyway.

As her words came out, she smiled a little. The color continued to return to her cheeks. Inside, he sighed relief.

"*Denki*, Jesse."

For some reason, the way she spoke with such gratitude softened his heart. He swallowed an emotional knot. Her words came out filled with adulation.

He could feel warm blood rush to his cheeks, and he silently scolded himself. "God planted me in your yard at the right time and the right place. And I'm glad He did."

"By the way, you never said what you were doing here. But you must have come to talk to *Daed*."

A wide smile revealed a row of straight white teeth. "Not exactly. I work here now, Anna. Your *daed* . . . he hired me . . . for the summer. Since the addition at the bakery has become more of a project than anticipated. And there's no need to worry about your parents . . . they're both at the bakery, safe and sound. In fact, they sent me to warn you of the storm and to make sure you were inside, safe and sound."

She lifted her chin a notch in sudden recollection. "I wasn't aware that he'd actually hired someone." She paused and then added in a light voice, "You."

When she opened her eyes, he took in the expression on her face that indicated urgency.

"What is it?"

She frowned. "I just remembered something." She sighed with regret. "My satchel." She started to get up, but he stopped her with his hand.

"Uh-oh. Not so fast. When your *daed* asked me to make sure you were safe, I'm sure he expected me to follow through. Besides, you've got to be freezing in those wet clothes."

"Right now, there's really no option until I get back to the house. But you're drenched, too."

"I'll survive. Like you said, there's no option."

She smiled a little and expressed her gratitude. "*Ich bin dankbar* to be in here. But my satchel . . . I left it on the buggy. Something important's inside."

He considered the two statements. And frowned. "The wind . . . Anna, I don't want to sound like the voice of doom, but you and I both know how strong the storm is. And unless that satchel of yours has a heavy stone inside it, only heaven knows where it is now." After clearing his throat, he lowered his tone to a more serious pitch. "What's inside can surely be replaced."

He was quick to note the tension in her shoulders. She wrapped her arms around her waist and straightened. And when their gazes locked, he caught her expression's deep concern. He could see it in her set jaw. In the way her lips parted.

"I've got to go . . ."

Lightning illuminated the area for a quick second. He waited for her to explain what was in her satchel that was so important, but to his surprise, she didn't.

"Tell you what . . . As soon as I'm convinced it's safe to leave you, I'll try to find your satchel."

She gave him an abashed smile. "No. I can't ask you to do that. You've already done so much."

As he listened, he noticed the sudden lessening of the wind. The rain had lightened significantly, although he could still hear drops on the roof. To his relief, she hadn't closed her eyes for some time now.

"Tell you what, the wind has let up . . ." He lifted one corner of his lips in amusement. "A little water never hurt anyone, now did it?" Before she could respond, he went on. "Besides . . ."

He pointed to his wet clothes. "How much worse can it get?"

They laughed. He stood. And stopped. "By the way, to help me find it . . . what's the color?"

"*Braun.*"

He bobbed his head toward the front doors and spoke during his stride to them. "I'll do my best, Miss King. Wish me luck."

At the doors, he turned back and darted an encouraging wink. "If it's in the near vicinity, I might have a shot at finding it. But considering the strength of the storm . . ." He lifted an uncertain brow. "No promises, Anna."

Before stepping outside, he drew in a deep breath. Right now, he was fairly sure he could safely look for the satchel. However, he wasn't certain how long the lull would last.

Outside, quick steps took him to the Kings' spare buggy. He looked closely. Not expecting to find the satchel, he arched a surprised brow when he glimpsed it.

With the strong speed of the winds, he'd expected the satchel to have traveled to the state of Texas by now. But it was stuck in the buggy's wheel, wrapped around a spoke.

He kneeled and retrieved it with both hands. The satchel was soaked. But Anna hadn't seemed concerned with the satchel itself, rather with what was inside it. *What could be so important?*

As the barn doors slammed, Anna's head ached. She squeezed her eyes closed and continued to hold the large rag to the gash. The pounding in her head wasn't as fierce as it had been; still, the pain was there.

Only now, it was duller. And all she wanted was to close her eyes and fall into a deep slumber. But the pain wouldn't let her. And neither would her conscience. She breathed relief that she was alone.

Not that she wasn't grateful to Jesse; she was. Because he had rescued her, picked her up off the ground, in the wind and the rain, and had carried her into the barn, then placed her on this bale of straw . . . she looked down at the loose pieces that stuck to her wet clothes . . . where he had been tending to her like a mother would take care of a child.

Only, to her dismay, in her vulnerable condition, she was fully aware that this unexpected interaction with Jesse was far from that of a *maemm* caring for a little one. When he had lifted her and taken her into the tall shelter, she'd been conscious enough to recognize the feel of his strong arms around her body.

As he'd lifted her, she'd glimpsed the small freckle

beside his nose. The gray flecks she'd never noticed on his deep blue eyes. The shade reminded her of the beautiful pictures she'd seen of the Bahamas in the window of a travel agency when she'd gone to the city to shop with friends last Christmas.

As she began to realize how close she'd been to him physically, she tensed. Even though the circumstances had led to this happening, she was fully aware that their closeness had made her pulse pick up. *Dear Lord, I know that all that counts is what's inside a person's heart. Please stop me from feeling like this around him. Amen.*

She breathed in, opened her eyes, and tried to make sense of how she felt. She finally reasoned that her inappropriate reaction had been caused by the shock of having lost a lot of blood.

She'd tried to keep her eyes closed in order to avoid his gaze, but now that she was thinking through everything that had happened since his arrival, a rush of heat flooded her cheeks.

Not because what he did was wrong. But her reaction certainly was. Finally, she let out a sigh of acceptance and reasoned that the odd circumstances of the afternoon were affecting her emotions in strong ways. *Jah, that has to be it.*

She remembered the cut on her forehead and resumed the strict instructions Jesse had given her before stepping outside the barn to retrieve her satchel.

Leaning her head back against the wall, she gently continued to press the material to her wound. Her head still pounded. As she sat up, she looked down at her disheveled appearance and suddenly recalled the livestock. She wondered if all the animals had made it into the barn, safe and sound.

The whinnies from the horses and the constant mooing from the cattle reassured her that they were okay, although, just from the sounds, she couldn't account for each individual animal.

As she thought of Jesse Beiler, she smiled a little. And as she observed the blood-covered rag, she expelled a sigh, acknowledging how very fortunate she was that he'd arrived when he had.

The fierce throbbing in her head forced her to close her eyes again. As she did so, automatically, Jesse came back in to her thoughts, and she arched a brow, wondering how she could have known him for so long yet not know him at all.

Of course, Anna was fully aware that she hadn't been the most outgoing child. She'd been interested mainly in art. Sketching landscapes and people on paper.

The wind picked up speed again. The livestock reacted strongly to the rumbling of thunder and the crackle of lightning by increasing their volume. She wiped her hands together to get rid of the loose straw that stuck to her skin.

But what was most important now was making sure Jesse made it back inside. *Is he okay?*

Outside, Jesse assessed the obvious damage from the storm. *This will require lots of cleanup.* By the looks of it, gutters had been swept from the house and strewn about the large country yard. Some of the old oaks were missing nearly half of their branches.

Thank goodness the livestock had made it inside.

And his buggy . . . amazingly, it was still in one piece, which was a miracle because it had been outside. The Kings' spare buggy looked okay, too. Jesse knew that Paul and Naomi's other mode of transportation was parked outside King's Bakery in town.

He sensed that the storm wasn't over. Jesse enjoyed following the weather. He looked up at the light-gray clouds that hovered precariously in the sky and narrowed his brows in skepticism.

But his uncanny knack to forecast, along with his keen instincts, told him to get back inside the building. Right away. Besides, he didn't want to leave Anna alone for too long.

Even though she seemed to be recovering, her gash would most likely need medical attention. She was fortunate that the huge limb that had struck her and had trapped her hadn't done more damage. And he worried about a concussion. As soon as the storm was over and the Kings were home, he'd offer to get someone to take their daughter to the hospital. And he'd go, too.

He was fairly sure that one of his *Englisch* neighbors would drive her to the closest emergency room. But for some reason, he wanted to be with her. He was aware that to others, it might seem odd for him to accompany her, being that they weren't courting or married; still, considering the circumstances, he felt responsible for her safety.

Clutching the drenched satchel, Jesse made his way back to the barn. Just as he'd guessed, the storm wasn't over. But the lull had given him enough time to complete his mission.

As he slammed the front barn doors and barred them closed, the loud crack of lightning made him sigh in relief that he was back inside. Another heavy downpour started up again.

A smile tugged at his lips. This morning, when he'd awakened, he'd never dreamed that he'd be here at Paul King's farm, in the barn, alone with his only daughter.

He considered the girl he'd always referred to, in his mind, as "the artist." The softness of her voice prompted Jesse to look at her like never before. Chaos flitted throughout his mind and his heart as he tried to figure out what was going on inside him.

To his surprise, he wasn't sure what he was feeling. He finally ascertained that he didn't have to. That the events of the morning had been so unexpected and so unusual . . . that the oddness of what had occurred in such a short amount of time alone would play havoc with his emotions.

She was where he'd left her. Sitting up and leaning against the wall.

She lifted her chin in surprise. "You found it! *Gut!* Where was it?"

"Caught in the spoke of a buggy wheel."

"I shouldn't have let you go outside," she said in an apologetic voice. "I'm sorry, Jesse. I wasn't thinking."

As she eyed him, he handed her the satchel. But somewhere in between his hands and hers, it dropped to the cement floor.

As thunder rumbled, she looked down at the news-paper entry that was soaking wet. Amazingly, the slightly faded ink was still readable. Jesse's gaze followed

Anna's to the clip, and he glimpsed her eyes widening in regret as he took in the large black print. "ART CONTEST AUGUST 25. WINNER TO GET FULL SCHOLARSHIP TO WASHINGTON UNIVERSITY, ST. LOUIS."

Chapter Two

The moment it fell out of the leather satchel, a loud, bold bolt of lightning popped, and Anna jumped. But to her surprise, the weather didn't scare her nearly as much as the fact that the bishop's son now knew what she was up to.

In her mind, there was nothing wrong with studying and teaching art. She had dreamed of it since childhood. And since that time, it had remained at the top of her list. But she acknowledged why she'd kept her desire a secret. And the look on Jesse's face only reinforced the reason she'd never dared to tell anyone about her dream.

As she tried for the right words, she wondered what would become of her life if her Amish community became aware of her goal. Her parents might suffer because of her. If she moved out of state for four years to go to college, everyone in their church would know that Anna couldn't adhere to the *Ordnung* away from their community for that amount of time. And the Amish stayed pretty much within the confines of their tightly knit community to avoid temptations that they'd otherwise be exposed to.

As they stared at each other, he arched a curious brow. "So, this is what's so important?"

His questions subdued her for a few moments. While she thought of the most appropriate response she could, she took in the gray flecks dancing with interest on his blue irises. But the way they moved indicated disapproval more than curiosity. At that very moment, she realized that the explanation she now owed Jesse was much more painful than her injury.

While Anna eyed Jesse's shocked expression, she was sure she should never have mentioned her satchel. Now she had some serious explaining to do that otherwise wouldn't have needed to be done. But she'd be honest. It wasn't in her nature to avoid difficult subjects.

He bent to retrieve the soaking-wet newspaper clipping. Other than being wet, the print was still easily readable. He held it between his fingers before slowly handing it to her before dragging his hand over his mouth and chin. He leaned back against the wall and crossed his arms over his waist.

As he did so, she reasoned that the circumstances of what had happened in the storm and her injury were affecting her more than she'd like to admit. As thunder rumbled, and the livestock reacted, Anna wondered how much worse the day could get. Deciding that direct honesty was the only approach, she swung her legs over the side of the straw and looked up at him.

She pointed to the empty space next to her on the bale and motioned for him to sit down. "Please let me explain, Jesse. I don't want you to think badly of me. You're the only one who knows this."

"What?" Uncertainty edged his voice. He took a deep,

steadying breath. "That you plan to pursue a four-year degree? Out of state?"

She looked down at the cement floor and carefully considered her response before allowing words to spill out of her mouth, fully aware that whatever came out could not be undone.

"Please."

He responded with a gruff "okay" as he plopped down next to her.

As he skirted closer to her, she started her explanation. "Studying and sharing my art has always been my dream." She paused to consider the right words. "It's been at the top of my list since I was a kid. But in all honesty, I never thought I'd even have a chance at it. Jesse, all I know about my birth mother is that she was an artist. Maybe that's why I love to draw. I know nothing else about my heritage."

After an emotional sigh, she went on. "Surely God gave me this talent for a reason. I'm sure He wouldn't want me to waste it."

Jesse tapped his fingers against his thighs and remained in thoughtful silence. "So, you want to win this contest to feel connected to your *maemm*?"

She considered his question and finally offered a nod. "That's part of it. I know it's a long shot, but I believe in the power of prayer, Jesse. I'm trusting God to guide me. For years, I've asked Him for something like this to happen."

When he still didn't respond, she edged her voice with genuine compassion. "Finally, here's my opportunity. I want to share my passion with others. To show them beautiful landscapes on paper. And people. To capture emotions on paper. Of course, there's no guarantee I'll win."

Her smile widened with great hope. "But God is offering me a chance." She lifted her shoulders. "That's all I can ask from Him."

Jesse looked away, and an expression that was a strong combination of uncertainty and deep thought crossed his face. "If you win, obviously, you'll move to St. Louis . . ."

He hesitated, as if carefully considering his words. "In the city, you won't be able to live like we do. You'll be exposed to a lifestyle that will tempt you to do things that are wrong."

She offered a firm nod. "I'm aware of the challenges I would face."

As the rain continued beating down on the roof, he lowered his tone and edged it with great curiosity. "Do your *eltern* know about this?"

She gave a firm shake of her head. "No. And I'm not ready to say anything. To anybody. Not yet. And if I don't win, I won't even mention it." She lowered her pitch. "I don't have a backup plan."

The way he looked at her made her heart race. She'd known Jesse her entire life, yet she didn't know him at all, and here she was trying to explain something to the bishop's *sohn* that she was fully aware her community would disapprove of.

The Amish believed in staying away from the temptations of the *Englisch* world. Because of that, residing in the city would definitely be something they would disapprove of. She'd had good reason to hide her dream, but now Jesse awaited a response. *How do I further explain? I haven't even figured things out myself.*

But first things first. She lowered her voice for emphasis. "Jesse, please . . . would you not say anything to anyone?"

A tense silence passed between them while the rain beat down on the roof. She looked at him, hoping he'd keep her secret. Wishing she hadn't asked him to find her satchel. Thinking of how the church would react if he didn't keep what he knew confidential, and how her parents would suffer.

When he finally spoke, the sound of his voice prompted a surge of relief that ran up her arms and landed in her shoulders. She didn't know what he'd say, but just the mere soft, understanding tone helped her to relax.

"So you want me to keep your secret?"

Suddenly, she couldn't find her voice. So she offered a quick, decisive nod.

A long silence ensued while she clenched her fingers into her palms. She sat very still and held her breath. Finally, he lifted a brow and locked gazes with her.

The thunder banged, and she startled. Loud noises came from the livestock.

His voice was measured and reasonable. He rubbed his palms together and smiled a little. "Looks like we're going to be in here a while. Why don't you tell me the whole story?"

When she parted her lips in surprise, he motioned toward the doors. "Neither of us can go anywhere until the rain lets up. We've got a lot to cover and plenty of time to do it."

He surprised her by moving closer to get a close look at the wound. He nodded approval as thunder rumbled again. "It looks better than it did. How d'you feel?"

"Better, thanks." She brought her legs up to her chest and wrapped her hands around them. At the same time, she leaned back against the barn's wall.

He did the same.

He turned to her with a lazy smile. "I always knew you loved to sketch."

She lifted a curious brow. "You did? How . . ."

He laughed. "Don't forget, Miss King, I sat behind you in school." The amused curve of the corners of his lips claimed her attention.

Finally, she realized he'd seen what she'd been doing during math class. When she looked at him, he responded with a slow nod.

She could feel the warm blood of embarrassment rush to her cheeks. In a more uncertain voice, she spoke. "I didn't know you were watching."

"I didn't make a point to intrude on your privacy, but math was pretty boring, and I had a full view to your desk."

She acknowledged that she couldn't change what he already knew, so she smiled a little. "So you've been aware of my secret all along. At least partially."

He dipped his head in agreement.

"I figured it really didn't matter if Mrs. Graber caught me. She never did like me."

He arched a skeptical brow. "No? I have a hard time believing that because you were the smartest kid in class."

Anna shrugged. She didn't feel like explaining that

she'd overheard her teacher comment at church that she wasn't a true Amish, so she stayed silent on the subject and instead focused on her dream.

"For years, I've known what I wanted, but there wasn't a means to make it materialize." She shrugged. "It seemed impossible. But all the while, I still prayed for it to happen."

"And that prayer was answered when you found out about the contest and scholarship."

She nodded, and her voice picked up to an excited speed as she talked about finding the clip. "I came upon it at the bakery early this morning while I was cleaning tables; I work there when someone can't make it. The ad was hard to miss because of the bold print at the top of the page. And as you already know, of course, the winner gets a full scholarship to a prestigious art school in St. Louis."

What she yearned for wasn't simple. Because if she won the contest, she would leave her Amish upbringing and all that accompanied it. And she was prepared to do that. Not because she didn't like the Amish faith; she fully respected it.

But in Anna's mind, she was fairly sure that on Judgment Day, God wouldn't judge a person by which church they attended. To her, being a Christian was mostly about a belief in God and showing His love. *Jesse must not tell.*

A combination of guilt and fear swept through her. Guilt because she loved her family as well as her Amish community. Loved and respected them with all her heart. And fear because now the bishop's son knew her plan, which was highly unlikely to win approval from her church.

If he told of her contest entry, the truth could harm her parents. In fact, the community might very well blame her *maemm* and *daed* for her even thinking of going so far as to pursue an extended education. To consider leaving what they had. The only life she'd ever known.

For long moments, silence ensued between them until Anna couldn't stand the tension. The worst was over. Now, she may as well finish.

As she watched the thoughtful expression on Jesse's face, reality hit her. Here she was, baring her soul to someone who couldn't possibly understand how much she wanted her dream. That she'd yearned for an opportunity like this for years.

Judging by what she knew about Jesse Beiler, he was undoubtedly satisfied living here and working on the farm. Forever. So it was probably a good guess that he didn't have an inkling of how much this opportunity meant to her.

Of course, she would give him the benefit of the doubt. He deserved that. But the real crux of the matter hit her until her shoulders tensed. He hadn't promised to keep her secret.

The speed of the wind picked up, and she automatically clutched her satchel tightly against her chest for reassurance. Thunder rumbled. The wind whistled as it came through the front doors.

A goat wandered over to them and eyed them with curiosity before moving in the opposite direction. A chicken that belonged in the coop clucked from a clean pile of straw in the corner of the building.

"Anna, have you considered how the outcome might affect your parents if you win this contest?"

The question made her swallow an emotional knot. "*Jah*. I've given it a lot of thought. And Jesse . . . I know to you this might sound like something risky."

She waited for him to respond, but he only looked at her, waiting to continue.

"But I know my own heart. What I feel. And my life . . ." Before she went on, she nixed any further thought. "I'm sure I'm a bit different from most of the women around here. Maybe it's good; maybe it's bad."

Finally, he nodded and slapped his palms against his thighs as if a big decision had been made. "Anna, I respect your wishes. I want you to be happy. But I'm curious . . ."

"What?"

He gave a dismissive roll of his eyes. "Never mind."

She motioned with her hand. "No. Go on. What were you going to say?"

"It was what I was going to ask. Not to undermine your talent, but there's only one winner, right?"

She nodded.

"So I think it's safe to assume that the competition will be fierce." He turned a bit to better face her. "Especially with a prize like that."

"*Jah*."

"The last thing I want to do is to discourage you. But . . ." He lowered his tone to a more sympathetic pitch. "We might very well be having this conversation for no reason at all."

When she started to retort, he raised a hand to stop

her. "Like I said, I am not in any way undermining your talent, and obviously, you have a chance to win. In fact, even with a slew of entries, I think you stand a good chance."

She smiled widely.

"I don't know much about art, but your work . . . what I saw sitting behind you . . ." He winked and smiled a little. "It looked so real."

The softness of her voice seemed to float through the air. "I've prayed for years, every night, for God to let my dream come true. I know what you're thinking . . . that I'm an amateur. And I am. And there will undoubtedly be many, many submissions."

After a slight pause, she went on. "And if you look at just that part of it, I'm sure my chances of winning are a long shot. I mean, I have no formal training. However, what I do have is the God-given ability to draw and what I've learned from books in the public library. And a strong faith. I believe that God handed me this contest entry for a reason."

She lifted her palms to the ceiling. "It's like He planted that contest entry on the table, right in front of me, so I'd find it. And Jesse, as you're aware, nothing can compete with the power of prayer. Please promise me you won't say anything."

She expelled a sigh.

"Will you do that for me?"

As Jesse considered Anna's question, the ringing of the phone startled him. At the same time, they both turned in the direction of the sound. Anna responded. "It's probably *Daed* checking to see if I'm okay."

Jesse stood, and quick steps took him to the wall phone. He lifted the receiver from its holder. "Hello."

She watched as he tapped the toe of his boot against the floor. Then he glanced at her.

"No need to worry. We're here in the barn. And she's okay." He went on to briefly explain what had happened. After reassuring his new boss that his daughter was fine, Jesse hung up and stepped back to Anna.

Huge bolts of lightning flickered throughout the large area, and rain continued hard against the barn's roof. Jesse considered his brief conversation with Anna's *daed* as slow, thoughtful steps took him back to her.

He considered the irony of the call. Paul had asked if everything was okay. Anna seemed to be doing fine, and Paul and Naomi planned to get her to the nearest emergency room for stitches as soon as they got home.

Jesse let out a breath and took in the innocent expression on Anna's face as he rejoined her on the bale of straw. He couldn't stop amusement from tugging up the corners of his lips. Because the far more serious issue was what Anna's *eltern* didn't know.

Later that evening, Jesse stepped up the porch steps and into his home. As soon as he opened the door, two of his young nephews, Stephen and Thomas, rushed to him. The aroma of delicious-smelling chicken soup filled the air. A pile of dinner plates was stacked next to the kitchen sink.

"*Hallo!*"

Jesse's heart warmed with that all too familiar joy

that only a family could offer. After big hugs, he gently released the boys and held them at arm's length. Two-year-old Jacob joined the trio, throwing his small arms around Jesse's thighs.

To Jesse's surprise, the little guy bit his leg. Of course, what teeth he had were small, so Jesse barely felt the contact.

"Jacob!" his *maemm* scolded. "I told you not to do that."

The child grinned mischievously and looked up eagerly at Jesse.

Jesse laughed.

Jacob's mother threw her hands in the air in a help-less gesture. "I don't know where he got that. There's so much to teach them these days!"

Jesse threw Jacob up on his shoulders, and the child screamed with excitement. Stephen and Thomas, Gabriel's boys, followed them, laughing and screaming as they stepped from room to room.

Finally, when Jesse put Jacob down, the two older boys begged him to tell them a story.

Jesse lifted a thoughtful brow as the boys looked up at him with pleading expressions on their faces.

"On one condition . . ."

They looked at him to go on.

"That you let me wash up first."

When he returned to the dining room, the trio awaited him. Their eyes were wide with excitement. Jesse was fully aware that their expectations were high. Each time, his story was unique.

In their particular community, kids learned German first, and at about five years of age, they went on to learn English. Stephen and Thomas spoke English, and small Jacob seemed to already know quite a bit. With a wave of his hand, Jesse motioned them to make a circle around him on the dining room floor next to the table. He pulled a handwoven rug from nearby and they sat on it.

As always, he started in a low, serious voice, looking around the circle and meeting each boy's gaze. After he started, he found himself recounting the story of him rescuing Anna in the storm, with a change of names, of course, to Hannah and David.

As he went on, he imagined himself back in the storm. "David and Hannah were on a farm when a big storm hit. Lightning bolts lit up the sky. The thunder was so loud, the ground jumped."

The kids' eyes grew larger, and they all looked at Jesse, waiting for him to go on.

"The rain was coming down so hard, David could barely see. Fierce winds blew debris through the air. All of a sudden, David heard a cry for help."

The group was silent. The adults had stepped outside, and the room was so quiet, you could have heard a pin drop.

Jesse raised the pitch of his voice to an exciting tone. "As the wind blew dirt into David's eyes, he followed the sound of the voice to a large tree limb that had cracked in the middle and had appeared to have stuck in the wet ground. He heard a scream.

"As he got closer, he saw Hannah trapped underneath. Her forehead was bleeding. As the rain continued to come down and the wind continued to blow, David used all his strength to lift Hannah and carry her into the barn, where they were both safe from the storm."

A simultaneous sound came from their mouths. For emphasis, Jesse looked around the circle and again lowered his pitch. "Inside the barn, David lay her on a bale of straw and tended to her cut with a clean rag he'd found on a hook. But she'd been hurt pretty badly. And he knew that he couldn't get her to the nearest emergency room by horse and buggy."

After a long pause, he continued. "The cattle and horses in the back of the large barn made loud sounds when it thundered. I suppose they must've been scared. And Hannah's face was white. He was worried. But soon, her color started returning to her face. And within a matter of time, he knew she was going to be okay."

The questions started. "Did she still have to go to the doctor? Did they have to stay in the barn all night? Did her cut hurt? Did she cry?"

After answering their questions, Jesse narrowed his brows. The women came back inside, and his *maemm* pointed to the round kitchen wall clock. Jesse knew that meant to wind things up and get ready for dinner. Somehow, he needed to end the story with a line that would start his next one to keep the kids interested.

Finally, he smiled a little. "Hannah and David started talking. And before they both knew it, they'd become close friends. But to David's surprise, there was something Hannah was hiding. It was something she made him promise not to tell."

"Did he?"

Jesse nodded. "But you'd never believe what it was. It was a secret."

* * *

He's going to keep my secret. Early the next morning, Anna sighed with relief as she held on to the rail that led down the steep stairwell to the basement in her home. In the other hand, she carried an empty plastic container and a small flashlight that she aimed in front of her.

Last night, she had convinced her parents not to take her to a doctor. Even if the cut did leave a scar, it wouldn't stand out for long. Her cuts always healed quickly. And anyhow, what did a little scar matter?

Halfway down the stairs, she stopped and smiled a little. Not because her contest dilemma was over; it certainly wasn't. But at least nothing would set her back . . . yet. Because no one would hear about the event or her plan to enter it.

Each wooden step creaked as she put her weight down. As she walked, she was careful not to knock anything off the hooks placed above the rail. While she descended, she considered yesterday and her long conversation with Jesse.

If she won the contest, was there anything she could do to lessen the repercussions of the church community against her family?

To her left, she eyed the outside flower bed from the small window that allowed in a small amount of light. At least now she could sigh with relief that the bishop's son wasn't going to say anything.

She always tried to focus on the positive. On the fact that God protected her and her family. But to her dismay, she found herself imagining the hot gossip and what affect it would have on her parents. Anna King, turning into an *Englischer.*

She considered her longtime dream and frowned.

Because amid the talk that she imagined, she was sure the true reason behind her entry would be sure to be overlooked. *But how do you make others understand what's in your heart? That not knowing where you came from is missing from your life and that you want to hold on to the one thing you know. Surely everyone must have a goal they think of the moment they wake up in the morning. Something that drives them to get out of bed.*

As she took in the large potato bin and the four legs that supported it, she smiled a little and remembered her purpose. For some reason, the holder had always fascinated her. Not because there was anything fancy about it. In fact, that was hardly the case. If a person who'd never seen one glimpsed it, she was sure they would probably view the pile as a heap of unwashed vegetables. But to her, it was much more than that.

She grinned and quickly reasoned that it was due to the fact that potatoes were her second favorite garden produce, mashed with gravy. The way *Maemm* made them. They were just behind tomatoes.

And the vision of the bin created an image in her own mind of one very large crock of hot, buttery mashed potatoes. She enjoyed pulling the brown-skinned baking potatoes from the large holder that was supported by four sturdy legs.

Their dirt didn't bother her. Of course, any produce dug from the ground would need to be cleaned. She would wash and peel each one in the kitchen sink.

She stepped closer to the bin and, using her flashlight, began selecting her potatoes. As always, she chose the largest first. Size was her most important criteria. Because the bigger the vegetable, the more bites.

One by one, she plucked each from the massive pile and began placing them into her large plastic container. As the weight became too much for one arm, she set the holder down next to the bin. And when the container filled, she used both hands to hold it and turned it toward the stairs.

As she did so, she barely glimpsed the side of the basement she was on. But she knew it by heart. She was only about a foot away from the old wringer she'd gotten her arm caught in once while trying to rid wet clothes of water. The days of getting thick towels through prompted a frown.

Things had changed a lot over the years. Now, most of the Amish in her area, including her and her mother, used air-powered washers. The Amish who lived close enough to town could tap into natural gas. Her home was too far out; still, their appliances, including the freezer to her right, ran off propane.

On her left, a long clothesline ran from one side of the wall to the other. Usually they hung wet garments outside, but when it rained, she and *Maemm* used the line downstairs.

Just around the corner, a small room housed shelves and shelves of quarts of canned tomatoes and other vegetables from the summer garden. They certainly didn't waste any shelf space. Or unused vegetables. Already, she had plans to begin canning tomatoes in the next few days.

At the foot of the stairs, she adjusted her flashlight, the holder of potatoes in front of her, and started up, trying to stay as close to the rail as possible. Because the stairs were steep and a bit uneven due to the settling of the earth, she was extra cautious.

Upstairs, she pushed the unlatched door open with her right sturdy shoe and stopped, blinking and adjusting her vision to the vast adjustment from dark to bright sunlight that poured in through the large screened kitchen windows. With great care, she set the heavy container on the floor.

Maemm's soft, concerned voice floated through the air. "Anna, I hope you got a good night's sleep. They say nothing heals a wound faster than rest."

Maemm stepped closer. "Hold still a moment. Let's take a look at that jagged cut."

As she took in *Maemm*'s narrowed brows, Anna closed her eyes to enjoy the reassurance of her mother's affection.

"That was some accident. And I want you to know that I disagreed with your *daed* about stitches. He insisted you didn't need them. And I guess he was right. By the looks of that cut, it seems to be healing just fine without them. How long do you think you were on the ground before Jesse came along?"

Anna thought about the question and shrugged. "I'm not sure."

After Anna picked up the potatoes and carried the container to the tiled countertop, she hugged her *maemm*.

Firmness edged her mother's voice. "What's important is that you're okay."

"God looks after me." Anna leaned forward with her elbows on the countertop to look out of the window. "The storm did quite a bit of damage."

Her mother smiled a little. "*Jah*. To be honest, though,

your *daed* was relieved there's not more to repair." As her mother ran a feather duster over the knob of the silverware drawer, she shook her head and lowered her voice so Anna could barely hear her.

"Material things?" She shrugged before planting her palms affectionately on Anna's shoulders. "They don't matter. But human beings?" She closed her eyes a moment before continuing. "We're God's creation. He designed each and every one of us. In His eyes, we're all masterpieces." She stopped and let out a sigh. "Can you imagine being so special that He counted every hair on our heads? Chose our eye color?"

For a moment, Anna took in the comments that she knew to be true. And the amazement never ceased to take her breath away. Although she'd always known that God had made each and every person unique, the special emphasis her mother put on the hairs and eyes added even more appreciation and awe.

Her *maemm* continued working with her duster as she moved onto the other cabinets. "Just listen to me ramble on. What I've been trying to say is that you're okay. And that's what matters. And Jesse Beiler?"

Anna listened.

"We surely owe him a good dinner."

Chapter Three

Later that afternoon, as Jesse worked in the barn where he and Anna had gotten to know each other quickly, he couldn't get Paul and Naomi King's *tochter* off his mind. Or her plan. *She must really want her dream, to risk so much.* He shook his head and tried to focus on what needed to be done.

And thanks to the storm, there was plenty to do. He welcomed the opportunity to work for the Kings. Especially to farm the acres behind their house.

From childhood, he'd always planned on being a farmer. On owning enough land to put food on the table for the family he would have. Unfortunately, land prices were high.

That was why a lot of his church friends found themselves doing other jobs, like welding. Cabinetry. Still, he had faith that God would help him to one day have his own farm. Just like Anna had faith that God would help her to win that scholarship.

And this job offered him an opportunity to save more money. He'd had a savings account since he was a kid. He smiled a little as he thought of the large family he'd sit down with every night for dinner. *I have a dream, just like Anna. In that way, we're alike. Only our wants couldn't be further apart.*

The humidity from the rain was high. Jesse caught a bead of sweat that rolled down his neck. He pulled in a determined breath and hoisted a bag of oats over his shoulder. Careful steps took him into the barn, where he lined up the bag with those he'd already placed neatly against a wall.

As a gentle breeze moved in through the two large, open doors, he stopped to roll up his shirt sleeves and offered a prayer of thanks for all he had. Life was a blessing. And everything good came from God.

All through the day, his time with Anna floated through his thoughts. He'd heard that with Anna's convincing, Paul had decided a visit to the doctor hadn't been necessary. Jesse lifted a skeptical brow as he recalled the wound.

The smell of oats and other grains filled his nostrils. From his peripheral vision, he glimpsed a rat stealing a morsel before disappearing under the structure. He chased it, but it had slipped away.

His mind drifted back to Anna, and how he'd learned so much about her yesterday in just a short time. He found it amusing that she'd believed her artistic talent had been a secret. Yet, thanks to his seat right behind her in school, he'd been aware of it for years.

As he swatted away a fly, he acknowledged that the bold print above the contest entry had been easy to absorb. He took a quick step back so a goat could get by him. Behind him, two smaller ones played with a rag.

As he proceeded to the barn's side to pull a broom from a hook on the wall, thoughtful steps took him back to the area where he'd started. He began sweeping loose grain into a pile and continued to line up the bags in a neat row.

But as he swept the kernels to his right, to his surprise, his mind lingered on the paper that had escaped Anna's clutches. And the more he considered the entry, the deeper his frown became.

At the same time, he was fairly certain that Anna was fully aware of what winning this particular contest would bring; that was, if she won.

He considered her strong faith and her obvious talent. *Between the two, it doesn't matter how little formal training she's had. She's talented and more determined than anyone I've ever met. Her faith is strong, and she prays for God's help. How can she not win?*

His brows narrowed as he wondered if she'd actually given thought to what she'd do after she won. *If she wins, then what? Will she move to St. Louis? Something like that can't happen without a lot of planning. What will she tell her parents? Her fellow churchgoers? And how will they react to her plans? Especially my* daed?

His heart sank. His pulse picked up to a nervous speed. All the while, he was fully aware that he'd committed to keeping Anna's secret. Because of his promise, it didn't matter that his *daed* was the bishop. A secret was a secret. And a promise was a promise. And he'd been raised to respect both.

The ear-piercing sound of a rake sliding over concrete made him turn. When he opened his eyes, he glimpsed Anna on the opposite side of the large structure, cleaning the horse stalls.

Automatically, the corners of his lips lifted. He was

glad to see her. He reasoned that it was because of her injury, and that he felt a strong need to protect her. To check on how she was feeling.

He propped his broom against the wall, shoved his hands into his pockets with his thumbs looping over the top, and made his way to her. While he traversed to the opposite side, her back was to him, and he took advantage of the opportunity to observe her. The ease at which she seemed to move the rake back and forth.

The Amish women he knew worked extremely hard. Some specialized in baking and other tasks that were more "indoor" things. But from what he knew about Anna, she preferred the "outdoor" chores, and there were plenty of them. She certainly wasn't afraid of getting her hands dirty.

He'd seen her plenty of times cleaning up in the bakery, too. And at church, she helped with small children. He'd really never looked at her as a woman, but now, as he glimpsed her alone in the barn, he took in her fit figure. He was fully aware that raking and spreading straw took stamina.

Again, he contemplated what winning the contest would mean to Anna. He didn't want to borrow trouble, but he was fairly certain she would have to permanently separate from the Amish faith.

Their church didn't really push for higher education unless it was something like local night classes for a GED. For the jobs they did, there was no need to pursue other degrees. They certainly weren't against education, but they discouraged exposure to temptations that might make them leave the faith.

His curious nature made him want to ask Anna more

about it, but his *maemm* had always taught him to mind his own business. And in this case, he didn't want to appear nosy.

With a gentle motion, he took her rake. "I'll do that for you."

She startled, and the wooden handle fell from her hands. With a swift reaction, he caught it.

As he did so, she tried to save it from falling, too, and his hands covered hers. Her jaw dropped as she turned to him.

As their gazes locked, he glimpsed surprise in the large green depths. Long, thick lashes hovered over them, and wisps of jet-black hair had escaped her *kapp* and clung to her flushed cheeks. For a moment, he was so close to her, he paid special attention to the small beauty mark underneath her right eye that he'd noted yesterday.

"How's that cut?"

"Here." She smiled at him and eagerly lifted the hair from her forehead. "Look for yourself."

As he gazed down at her, taking in her innocent face, he wondered how he could have known her for so many years and never recognized her obvious beauty. He silently chastised himself for noticing now; he had been raised to focus on what was inside a person. But at that moment, he found it difficult to look away.

For some strange reason, he touched the area around the wicked-looking wound. When her eyes grew larger, he realized the awkwardness he'd created between them and found his voice. He slowly pulled his hand away and realized the inappropriateness of his touch. But was it really *inappropriate* in this particular case?

"That's still quite a gash."

She smiled and lowered her gaze to the floor before looking back up at him. "I think it looks worse than it feels. At least it stopped bleeding."

A short silence ensued while he tried for the right words. Usually, he didn't have problems knowing what to say. But for some reason, today, when he was so close to her, he was tongue-tied.

"Could you use some help?"

He silently scolded himself. Of course she could, but he had his own jobs to do. Chores he was being paid for by her *daed*. So what was he doing, asking if he could help her when he had a list a mile long of his own?

The light shade of pink in her cheeks darkened a notch when she smiled at him. She propped the rake against the door of the stall and put her hands on her waist.

"It's all right. Thanks for the offer, but I'm sure *Daed* has plenty for you to do. Especially after the storm."

The corners of his lips lifted into an amused grin.

She started to speak, then stopped.

He lifted a curious brow. "What were you going to say?"

She offered a dismissive shrug. "Oh, just that I kind of enjoy being in the barn." Before he could respond, she went on while continuing to rake. "I know some consider these 'dirty' jobs, but I really love being out of the house. There's just something about physical work that makes me feel *gut*." She took a breath. "And . . . you know what?"

"What?"

"It might seem strange, but when I'm out here, ideas come to me. For sketches," she added.

The statement prompted him to realize something he should have taken note of before. This girl in front of him was even more different than other Amish girls he knew than he'd thought. He admired her passion for art.

Her surprising statement prompted him to think for a moment before he responded. "It makes for a *gut* life when you enjoy your work, *jah*?"

She nodded. "But I do like it better when the humidity isn't so high."

"I know what you mean. But you can't have rain without it, and rain is *gut* for the crops, *jah*?"

After a brief pause, she spoke. "I guess it's like a sponge cake. When you eat one, you get the calories that go with it. They're a pair, and you can't have one without the other."

A long silence ensued between them while he tried to think of something clever to say, fully aware that he had more than a day's work ahead of him and that there were only so many hours of light. "I was just about ready to go outside to enjoy the breeze for a few moments."

The corners of her lips dropped a notch, and she tensed. "Could we talk a little bit more?"

Her question surprised him. "*Jah.*"

She motioned outside. "It will be nice to sit on the bench for a few moments." She grinned. "I think we did enough chitchatting in here yesterday."

He didn't want her to be nervous, and it was important to him that she feel free to converse with him. He frowned, uncertain why he would care, but continued by taking her rake from her, propping it against the metal part of the stall, and offering a friendly motion with his hand. "After you."

Outside, the bright sun made him blink. A green oak leaf floated down from the tall tree and landed on his shoulder. With one swift motion, he brushed it off. As they approached the wooden bench, he motioned her to sit.

She did so, and he claimed the spot next to her, leaving adequate space between them to make sure it was proper. He took a swig from his water bottle and turned to her.

"Something you wanted to talk about?"

He noticed how she straightened until, finally, she turned to better face him and smiled a little. "Jesse, I want so very much to win that contest."

He smiled a little at her honesty. "I figured."

After a slight pause, she went on. "But there's more to it."

He lifted a curious brow as he took another swig.

"You don't know me that well, but . . ." She paused to draw her palms to her chest and breathe in and close her eyes. The moment she opened them, he was quick to note moisture on her pupils that sparkled like dew on a morning leaf. His heart warmed.

She turned closer to him and lowered the pitch of her voice to a more emotional tone. As she spoke, compassion edged her voice. The white flecks on her pupils danced with a sense of energy. He listened, but what intrigued him most was the most genuine, heartwarming expression he'd ever seen on a human face.

"First of all, I want to thank you for so many things. For getting me in to the barn, safe and sound. For helping to stop the bleeding from my forehead. And . . ." She paused, and her breath hitched. "Especially for keeping my secret. I'm truly grateful. And I owe you."

"You don't owe me a thing."

"*Jah.* I do. And sometime, when you can think of some way for me to repay you, let me know. Like you, I keep my word. You can trust me."

He grinned. "I think I know how much you want your dream to come true." He shrugged his shoulders and moved closer to the edge of the seat. Knowing he couldn't sit here all day with this beautiful, interesting girl, he strummed his fingers against the bench and put his right foot forward as he prepared to stand up.

She cleared her throat and looked down at the space between them before darting him a wide, appreciative smile. "I know your word is *gut.*"

For long moments, he stared at her. It wasn't the desperation in her tone that pulled at his heartstrings; rather, it was the way her large eyes begged him with such sincerity and strength.

He offered her a nod. "You've got my word, Anna. Again, no need to worry."

A newfound excitement edged her voice. "Thank you again, Jesse. I was a little bit nervous asking so much of you. I mean, it wasn't your fault you saw the contest entry. And I know that your *daed*'s the bishop . . ." She hesitated. "I don't want to get you in trouble."

He lifted a hand to stop her. "You won't. Besides, who my *daed* is doesn't matter when it comes to keeping my commitment to you. I prayed about it last night. And you know what?"

She looked at him to continue.

"I can tell how much you want to win that contest.

And if you decide to go for a four-year degree, who am I to stop you? You don't have to thank me. Whether or not you enter that contest really isn't any of my business."

He moved both hands to the sides of his thighs and slapped his palms against the boards. After he stood, he smiled down at her. "And *gut* luck."

As they started walking back into the barn together, questions flitted through his mind about this sweet, ambitious girl and why he cared so much that she won.

"I've never really discussed this with anyone . . ."

He lifted his chin a notch. "I feel special." Then he recalled the circumstances, and he grimaced. "'Course, I s'ppose you felt you had to tell me. I mean, after I saw the entry."

"I did. But now that I look back, talking about it wasn't such a bad thing." She looked up at him and pressed her hands against her hips. "When I actually hear the words, they give me hope. I don't know what my chances are, Jesse. I mean, I've sketched for years; it just comes naturally to me, and I've learned a good share from books at the library, too, but like I told you yesterday, I've never had formal instruction." She shrugged.

When he didn't respond, she went on. "I know this sounds silly, but it's kind of fun having a confidant. I've never talked about this to anyone." She hushed her voice. He wasn't sure why. There wasn't anyone else around. "It's fun sharing my secret with you."

Her honesty touched him. To his surprise, he didn't want their talk to end. It wasn't the actual subject that compelled him to keep up the conversation. On the contrary, it was her honesty about the subject. The excitement and emotion in her voice. The light dancing in her eyes.

As a monarch butterfly floated above them, Anna went on. "Jesse, I've always sort of looked up to you."

"You have?"

She nodded.

"Even though we've never been close, somehow I always knew I could trust you. And that's why I'm comfortable sharing something else with you."

He narrowed his brows. "Sharing what?"

"That my strongest weapon to win this contest is prayer. I believe that the more prayers God hears, the more He listens. So there's something I need to ask you."

"What?"

"Will you pray that I do the right thing?"

"Of course. Earlier, I was thinking about what you're about to undertake, and I was wondering if you had a plan for after the win."

The expression on her face took on a more serious look.

"I have, a little."

Surely she wasn't so naïve that she hadn't considered the church's reaction. He didn't like to be nosy. At the same time, he wanted to help this girl who was such an odd combination of savviness and vulnerability. And his protective nature wanted to ensure she understood exactly what she might be getting herself in to.

"Anna, if you win, what about the Amish faith?" He held up a hand to let her know that his intention was to help her, not hurt her. "I'm sure you're aware that our faith doesn't believe in a need for higher education."

He paused to lift his shoulders. "I know that some

within our community have taken night classes for their GED. But I'm sure you're aware that going to school in the city would expose you to things our church would disapprove of. And I can say with a large amount of certainty that there are many who won't support what you plan to do. I want to make sure you know what you're up against."

A long silence ensued, while the leaves of the tall oaks rustled with the breeze. A redbird perched on one of the branches. From where they were, farmland stretched on and on. Which reminded Jesse why Paul King had hired him. It certainly hadn't been to talk to his daughter about higher education.

Finally, she responded. "I know. And, you see, I love Amish life. But Jesse, do you really believe that our faith is the only one God recognizes?"

The question stopped him. He wasn't sure why. Perhaps it was the directness in which she posed it. Or maybe it was because he'd never really considered the validity of other faiths.

When he didn't reply, she offered a helpless lift of her palms. "I'm sorry if I'm out of line, asking you that."

Several heartbeats later, he responded with a shake of his head. "No. You're not out of line at all, Anna. To be honest, I've never really given much thought to other churches."

He frowned. "I've heard people mention that they like to think outside the box. And of course, I'm sure our Lord and Savior loves everyone who believes in Him. John 3:16."

She nodded in agreement.

"I can't imagine living any other way than Amish. At

the same time, God is loving and kind. He created us all. And I think we just have to pray and use our best judgment about how we believe He wants us to serve Him. We're all different."

"*Jah.* We are. Jesse, I've prayed about studying art for years. Like I said, it's the only bond I have with my real mamma. At the end of the day, there's a reason God blessed me with the ability to sketch." She offered a dismissive shrug and locked gazes with Jesse. "I don't know what the future holds, but I'm praying for God to help me take the right path. And to be completely honest, that could very well be not joining the Amish church."

That afternoon, the earthy smell of freshly cut alfalfa filled Jesse's nostrils as he took in Paul King's garden from the field. Only a portion of Paul's farmland was used for this crop, which would feed the cattle this winter. The scent was far from sweet and flowery.

The fresh alfalfa fragrance was what Jesse considered to be a country ambience. And the plant's aroma produced a sense of familiar comfort throughout his entire body.

As the bright sun caressed his face, he considered how his life had changed within the past twenty-four hours. Since getting to know Anna, a girl he'd been acquainted with most of his life, he was wondering things that had never piqued his curiosity before.

He contemplated the unusual conversation he'd had with Paul King's *tochter* that very morning. As a breeze gently caressed his moist brow, he realized how thirsty he was. It was time to stop to give the horses an apple, too. He realized that many of his Amish friends looked at animals as merely a means to getting things done. Maybe some of Dr. Zimmerman, the local veterinarian, had rubbed off on Jesse because to him, animals meant much more. He considered them a blessing and offered them the best care he could. He figured that God would protect him if he looked after the least of God's creatures. In fact, the book of Revelations even mentioned horses in heaven.

"Whoa! Whoa!"

He tightened the reins and moved his feet farther apart to better balance himself while he came to a bumpy stop. The horses snorted. He smiled a little.

Because he was new at working for Paul King, this particular team didn't know him. But from experience, he guessed they would catch on to his routine quickly. A stop meant a treat. And this morning, *Maemm* had stuffed a Baggie of sliced apples in both pockets of his work pants.

He focused on balance because it was more difficult to stand on the platform while moving at a slower speed. Finally, they stopped, and he stepped off, careful to keep away from the sharp blade behind him.

There was only room for necessities, and of course, sliced apples. It would be impossible to give the horses water because each animal could drink up to five gallons a day.

He plopped down on the field and stretched his legs. As he downed a bottle of water, Anna floated through his thoughts. He wasn't sure why she was encompassing so much of his time, but he finally figured out there were many reasons.

He lifted an inquisitive brow. On one hand, he wasn't used to conversing with Amish girls who were as driven to accomplish their dreams. At least, if they were, they didn't tell him. And when he considered what would follow if Anna won the contest, he let out a low whistle.

Secondly, the more he got to know her, the more she intrigued him. The way she viewed things prompted him to take a closer look at his faith and to appreciate how he'd been raised. When he considered her moving to St. Louis to an entirely different way of life, he narrowed his brows in concern.

He certainly wasn't a biblical scholar. But in his heart, Jesse was sure God didn't care if he rode in a horse-pulled buggy or drove a car. *Knowing our Lord and Savior is the key to getting to heaven.*

He flattened his palms against his thighs and narrowed his brows while he took in what was around him. Horses. Cut alfalfa. White fluffy clouds that were scattered throughout the deep blue sky. The Kings' yard. Other houses miles away.

Even though the land was still moist from the rain, the hot sun had done a good job of drying the earth enough for him to work the field. The rain had been a much-needed blessing.

But unfortunately, with rain came mosquitos. Like he'd said to Anna yesterday, sometimes bad accompanied good, and vice versa.

Still, Anna's mention of a four-year degree and leaving the Amish faith whirled in his head until he shook it to rid it of the chaos. When he'd first glimpsed the contest entry, he'd merely taken it at face value. He hadn't begun to consider the repercussions if she won.

But their last conversation had left him with a lot to think about.

Focus on what's gut. *That's what* Maemm *always says. Worrying about things that haven't happened is a waste of time. And what Anna's about to undertake? It's not really terrible, is it?*

He wasn't sure. As they turned at the end of the field, Jesse had a bird's-eye view of the Kings' typical Amish yard.

He glimpsed their garden with neat, even rows of vegetables. The storm had damaged some of the plants. Different colors of towels and linens hung from the clothesline, moving up and down with the breeze.

A propane tank sat next to the house. Cattle grazed in the pasture. The large backyard was littered with goats and chickens.

A spare buggy parked near the house by the long dirt lane led out to the blacktop road. The humble, familiar scene in the distance prompted the corners of his lips to lift a notch.

As he took in the fields of corn, beans, and alfalfa, a sense of calmness and security swept up his arms and landed at the tops of his shoulders.

And he let out a satisfied breath. *There's nothing like this. It's God's country. And I'm blessed.*

Chapter Four

Later that day, Anna breathed in the scent of freshly cut alfalfa as quick steps took her to her special sketching place: Pebble Creek. That wasn't its official name, but it was common knowledge that Annie and Levi Miller had coined it years ago. She'd never told her parents she sketched. She considered it a private blessing.

The actual creek went on for miles, and fortunately for Anna, it touched the edge of her family's property. From where she was, she could glimpse the out-of-place hill where the late Old Sam Beachy had asked his beloved Esther for her hand in marriage. The very place that Levi Miller had asked Annie Mast to spend the rest of her life with him.

That very realization made her draw in a wistful breath, and she stopped for a moment. She had gotten out of bed an hour earlier this morning in hopes of finding time to draw.

As she walked, she considered the contest and her longtime plan for a four-year degree. The whinny of a horse interrupted her thoughts, and she turned to her left.

In the distance, she glimpsed four horses and Jesse.

She recognized him immediately. And within the few moments she'd seen her *daed* last night, she recalled hearing him mention that the alfalfa was ready to cut.

Trying to get Jesse's attention, she waved. She wasn't sure why, but the thought of him prompted the corners of her lips to lift into a wide smile.

In her other hand, she carried her mini hope chest, which had been made especially for her by Old Sam. Jesse returned her wave. She let out a sigh of contentment and continued her walk to her preferred spot.

But her thoughts stayed with her confidant. *That's what he is, really. I confided in him. I trust him. And for some reason, I enjoy sharing my dream with him. That makes Jesse Beiler a very special person in my book.*

As she continued walking in the fresh air, her worry about the contest repercussions seemed lighter. In fact, after seeing Jesse, and knowing he was close, her outlook had, amazingly, taken on a much more positive tone. And when she considered the life-changing blessings that had happened at Pebble Creek, her pulse picked up to a more confidant pace.

She considered the well-known story of Levi and Annie Miller. About what they had been up against before they married. *If God helped Levi join the Amish church after his father had been shunned, surely He can help me pave the road for my dream to come true.*

In fact, the more she contemplated what the former Annie Mast had been up against when she'd fallen in love with an *Englischer*, the more she was sure she could handle what followed the contest.

She recalled a verse from the book of Matthew and

whispered the passage: *And Jesus answered and said to them, Truly I say to you, if you have faith and do not doubt, you will not only do what was done to the fig tree, even if you say to this mountain, Be taken up and cast into the sea, it will happen.*

She lifted her chin, straightened her shoulders, sucked in a deep breath, and smiled. *Inspiration. Pebble Creek is my inspiration. And Jesse . . . he's my sounding board. I can't wait to talk to him again.*

As she stared out at the postcardlike view, she considered what she was about to do. To even begin such an endeavor was daunting. Because even if she didn't win the contest, huge challenges needed to be met. First and foremost was to perfect her sketch to fit its theme.

All the while, she would need to pay for round-trip transportation to St. Louis. All entrants were required to be present at the judging to explain the story behind each sketch and answer questions.

The mere thought of being there with her project forced a deep breath. She closed her eyes and smiled a little.

This weekend, she would see Jesse at the church cookout at William and Rebecca Conrad's place. Hopefully, she would have an opportunity to talk to him. Most of the congregation would be there, and that was close to two hundred people.

Even though Jesse worked for her *daed*, it would be unlikely she'd get a lot of time to spend with him. Especially because he had so much work in the field.

With a new-filled spirit, she said a quick prayer out loud. "Dear Lord, the contest is August 25. Less than a month away. I know You have given me my talent for a reason. And I pray that You will help me to use everything I have to serve You and only You. Amen."

The day was perfect for a church cookout. Anna drew in a grateful sigh for two reasons. One was that she loved picnics. The smell of grilled meat floating through the air. And it was fun to get together with her friends outside of church, especially Mary Conrad.

The second reason was that this was another opportunity to see Jesse. She'd make their interaction brief. She didn't want others to believe he'd been privy to her plan. Especially because he was the bishop's son.

In the house, a mélange of conversations morphed into one solid sound. Because there were so many bodies inside the two-story Conrad home, and the two large battery fans appeared to struggle to keep the place cool, Anna quickly stepped outside to enjoy the light breeze.

Holding a glass of lemonade, she blinked at the brightness of the late July sun. Amazingly, the ground had already dried from the recent downpour. In the distance, the Conrad fishing pond loomed. Anna could glimpse it in the far backyard. Green leaves of tall oak trees wrestled with light summer breezes. A honey bee hovered over a clover.

In the large front yard, tall evergreens scented the air with their fresh, woodsy aroma. Trees. The mouthwatering smell of grilled chicken.

She looked on as some children tried to befriend a

goat, while others petted the new pony William Conrad
had just adopted from Dr. Zimmerman's horse shelter.

A friendly touch on Anna's shoulder made her turn.
"It's so *gut* to see you!"

She hugged Mary before holding her at arm's length.
"You too! Isn't this fun?"

Someone hollered for Mary, and she offered a reluc-
tant hand in farewell. "I'm kitchen help, and it's nearly
time to eat. I'll save you a seat next to me at the picnic
table nearest the grill!"

"*Gut!*"

Quick steps took Mary down the dirt trail to the side
of the house, while Anna moved aside to avoid two boys
chasing each other in a game of tag. Laughter filled the
air, and the bright sun created a nice, warm day. The
pleasant, simple picture represented everything good in
life as people she knew well said their hellos.

While Anna talked to churchgoers, loud, drawn-out
whinnies from the horses tied to posts along the long
Conrad drive chorused through the air. As she took in
the queue of buggies, it reminded her of weddings. Only
this was more fun, because it was informal.

For a moment, she took advantage of the calm and
the love that emanated throughout the place and finally
beamed a smile while she drew an affectionate hand to
her chest and kept it there.

As she expelled a sigh of satisfaction, Mary rejoined
her. In a breathless tone, she exclaimed, "I wish your
parents could have come."

Anna nodded. "Me too." She lifted a concerned brow.
"I really miss them. To be honest, with the expansion of

the bakery, I don't see them much. I've been doing the chores while they've worked at the family business."

Mary raised the pitch of her voice as she caught one of the Glick nieces and ordered her to stay in the group she had obviously taken charge of.

"And I've got my hands full, too!" She motioned to a dozen youngsters who played around her. "These children need to get into the house to wash up for lunch." She lifted a set of helpless palms to the sky. "You wanna help?"

"Of course!" One girl tugged at Anna's dress before giving her a hug. Anna released her and smiled down at her. "Hannah, you must have grown six inches since church last Sunday!"

The petite child beamed before running to catch up with another girl. As Anna counted heads, she acknowledged all the children. And one especially: Reuben Schmucker. Despite his strict Amish upbringing, trouble always seemed to find him. And vice versa. His uncle, Israel, had gone to school with Anna and had been the one who had stolen her homework. He had recently passed from a heart attack, but she remembered him all too clearly. Unfortunately, Reuben's *daed* was gone, too.

Mary held a hand over her mouth so only Anna could hear her. "Anna, as you know, Reuben's *maemm* is going through chemo. So even though he's a handful, don't ya think he deserves a free pass?"

Anna offered a quick nod as Israel's nephew sprinted to get ahead of everyone else. Mary cupped her hands around her mouth like a megaphone and hollered for everyone to stay in the front.

While kids laughed and played, Mary talked more to

Anna about the boy who was living up to being as ornery as his uncle had been. She spoke in a lowered tone. "I guess you could say he's really reacting to his *maemm*'s health issues. Poor kid."

Anna looked at Mary and used a very soft voice so as not to be heard. "I know. Cancer. Thank goodness our church is helping with food and support. I signed up."

"Me too." Mary gave a sad shake of her head. "To be honest, Anna, there's only so much everyone can do."

The joyful expression on Mary's face changed to a combination of disappointment and frustration. "I can't imagine being a single *maemm*, Anna, and going through chemo. Or going through chemo under perfect conditions, for that matter. From what I hear, she's having a rough go with the treatments and is bedridden. Thankfully, in a couple more weeks, she should finish her last round."

Anna observed Reuben and lifted a brow. From church, she already knew that he was difficult to corral. He looked just like the other kids. Suspenders, short sleeves, and slacks that came up above his ankles. Some were barefoot.

But it was Reuben's interaction with others that made him stand out. His behavior appeared to be more aggressive. When he tagged another friend, he pushed so hard, he nearly shoved them to the ground.

He was extremely quick on his feet. It was obvious that God had blessed him with the ability to run fast. As a result, the others had to do the chasing, and Reuben usually got away. For the most part, Amish kids in their church were well behaved. Of course, they weren't perfect.

As Anna and Mary helped two girls who had tripped over each other, Reuben and a couple of boys ventured out of the front yard, heading toward the back, and Mary held her fingers around her mouth and hollered, "Hey, come back! Reuben! Amos! Get back here! Right now!"

What came next happened quickly. As a jet left a trail of white in the sky, Anna realized the two had ventured behind the house. Mary turned and motioned urgently with her hands. As she did so, Anna doubted that she and Mary, in long dresses and sturdy shoes, could catch the boys if they didn't stop.

Mary ordered the rest of the group to stay put while Anna took quick steps to reach Reuben and Amos, who'd gone out-of-bounds. She shouted, "Boys! Come back! Don't go near the pond!" Mary turned in the other direction and hollered as loudly as she could, "Someone, help us get the boys!"

But as Anna also shouted for help and quickened her pace, her lungs pumped hard while she fully realized the danger the boys were in. It was common knowledge that the Conrad pond was quite deep and only used for fishing.

Instinctively, she went after the kids, hiking up her dress to keep from tripping. Behind her, Mary followed. Anna knew because she could hear her holler. But the low sound of her voice told Anna that her friend was now quite a distance away. Anna shouted, "Reuben! Amos! Come back right now!"

She nearly lost her balance while avoiding a rut. By now, they were far ahead of her. Hopefully, an adult had heard the pleas for help. They were far from the church party in the large backyard that eventually met farmland. As Anna ordered her lungs to keep pumping, she watched in horror as the nightmare she'd anticipated unfolded in front of her.

Running with his back to the pond, Reuben hit the water. Anna watched the large splash that was immediately followed by a second one as Amos also fell into the pond.

Panic swept through her chest as she finally got to where the boys had fallen in, ripped off her apron, yanked off her shoes, and jumped into the large body of dark water to save them.

Fortunately, as she landed, her feet touched bottom. As soon as her head bobbed above the water, she coughed. Automatically, she made a circular motion with her arms to move toward the boys.

To her right was another big splash. From Anna's peripheral view, she glimpsed Mary jump in and grab onto tree roots that stuck up out of the pond. Fortunately, it didn't take long for Mary to grab Amos with her free hand.

Reuben's head bobbed above the water and went back under. Anna couldn't swim, but she was tall enough that the water stayed below her mouth.

Without wasting time, she grabbed his arm, kicked her feet to stay afloat, and pushed off the muddy bottom when her feet touched it.

Reuben coughed. While Anna walked on the pond's bottom, her mouth barely above water, clutching the boy's arm and holding up his neck.

I'll save you. If it's the last thing I do. Dear Lord, please help me. And please let him live.

Just when she couldn't go on, a welcome arm came around her waist and pulled them the rest of the way to the shore.

Jesse's voice was firm but reassuring. "I've got you, Anna. You and the boys will be okay."

She recognized the soft, low timbre with full clarity. She tried to talk. She couldn't. She coughed. But she would be okay. The boys, too. Jesse had said so.

Thank you, Lord. "Hang in there. Help's on the way."

Commotion stirred all around her. She felt two hands laying her on the ground.

When she opened her eyes, she was on her side. Someone was hitting her back, and she expelled a little water. Afterwards, she enjoyed the warmth of the blanket someone threw over her shoulders.

An odd combination of reassurance and fear edged Jesse's voice as he scolded her. "What am I going to do with you, Anna King?"

"She's okay," someone hollered.

She could hear children sobbing. A male voice she didn't recognize ordered everyone to step back.

Finally, she got a clear vision of the crowd watching her as she lay on the ground. A paramedic was beside her. He shouted, "No one needs CPR."

Annie Miller came to her and squeezed her hand. "God put you here today to save Reuben. You and Mary are heroes! Heroines," Annie corrected with a laugh.

She could hear Amos screaming as his *maemm* tugged at his arm. A rescue worker asked Anna how she felt. Surprisingly, she felt okay, considering what she'd gone through.

"I think we can say there are lessons to be learned here," one of the rescue workers said to the boys and to the adults, as well. "I'm aware that this was an accident, but never go near water where there's no life guard. This time we were lucky. But next time, we might not be. And take swimming lessons. You never know when you might need them."

A long silence ensued while Anna enjoyed the warmth of the blanket around her. Then the rescue worker continued. "I think we should take the boys to the hospital just as a precautionary measure. If water's still in their lungs, there's a risk of secondary drowning."

Hearing that warning made Anna yearn to hear Jesse's soothing voice and to know that he was here with her. Her heart fluttered as she realized what that yearning meant. That her feelings for Jesse Beiler were definitely stronger than those of mere friendship.

She'd come to know him better so quickly, she considered him a new friend. She'd never been courted by anyone, but common sense told her that her reaction to him was more of the reaction a woman would have to a man she liked that way.

As the paramedics wrapped blankets around the boys, Anna sat up and took in the crowd from left to right. She glimpsed different expressions. Most were looks of approval. But she quickly caught the expression of disapproval on Mrs. Graber's face.

Her left eye twitched, like it always had when she'd looked at Anna in class. The corners of her lips turned down. Automatically, a sense of shame swept over Anna until tuned into Annie Miller's voice as she thanked her over and over for her courage. Anna nodded her head in acknowledgment.

In the background, adults argued. "The kid's bad news. Just like his father. And his uncle."

Anna started regaining her strength. Automatically, she wondered why Jesse had been the only one who'd jumped in to help. Perhaps it was because he had been the first on the scene. She would find out.

According to facial expressions, there were numerous reactions to what had just taken place. And by the glances coming her way, what she'd just done hadn't won her universal approval.

Automatically, her gaze drifted back to her former teacher. The woman's obvious disgust sent a shiver up Anna's spine. She was the woman that Anna had once overheard call her "only Amish because she'd been adopted." Anna tried to forgive her. As she always had.

Mary Conrad joined Anna. She was drenched from head to toe. Anna tried to stifle a laugh and realized she must look as soaked as her friend.

Mary's voice shook as she spoke. "The boys are safe. Anna, if it hadn't been for you . . ." After a slight pause, she went on. "Are you okay?"

Anna stood. The moment she did so, the paramedics stopped her. "Should we take you to the hospital?"

Anna shook her head. "No, thank you. I'm fine. What I need is a hot shower. I'm freezing." Her entire body shook. Mary was shaking, too. To her relief, she saw that both boys seemed all right.

Mary took Anna's hand and, together, they started toward the house. Anna immediately forgot about the crowd until others quickly joined the two women, offering to help. Mary's mother, Rebecca, and Annie Miller insisted on taking care of her until she was fully recovered.

Annie's tone had been an odd combination of concern and relief. "My, my, Anna, what you did . . . It was so brave." Rebecca's voice cracked with emotion. "Do you even know how to swim?"

The realization of what had truly happened finally sank in and Anna smiled a little. "No." After a brief hesitation, she went on. "Just so the boys are all right." She shuddered. "I was afraid they would . . ." Her voice broke.

Mary's voice was edged with optimism. "They're okay, Anna. That's all that counts. God was with us today."

Annie and Rebecca, off to the side, offered firm nods at the same time. Rebecca stepped closer to pull Anna's wet hair back over her shoulder, out of her face.

Annie spoke next. "They'll be fine. Reuben's *maemm* will be most grateful to you, Anna. She's going through so much, and poor little Reuben is expressing his insecurities in ways that challenge us all. And that's why we're trying to help." She gave a sad shake of her head.

"Pray for Reuben, Anna. Because what we're offering . . ." She offered a helpless shrug. "I'm just not sure God has given us that special tool to help him. We can offer him love and make sure he's fed and clothed, but pray for his *maemm* to recover. As hard as we try, all of us girls in church can't replace the one person he loves and needs most. Of course, his *daed*'s with the Lord."

Anna absorbed the seriousness of their words and nodded in agreement. No one in the world could replace a kid's mother. As they walked down the dirt path and got closer to the Conrad home, Anna considered her own *maemm*. Not her biological mother, but the woman who'd raised her.

Without a doubt, Anna loved her *eltern* with all her heart. Sometimes, she wondered what would have happened to her had they not adopted her. Immediately, she knew she loved little Reuben.

She guessed that, in many ways, he was a lot like her. His birth mother was still alive, but she was sure the boy was afraid of losing her. She closed her eyes and said a silent prayer. *Dear Lord, please heal Reuben's* maemm. *Amen.*

Inside the house, Rebecca walked with Anna and Mary upstairs to Mary's room. Inside, Mary pulled her spare dress from the hook on the wall while Rebecca went for towels. She returned with a neat pile, which she set on the end of Mary's bed.

Rebecca started walking toward the door and offered a goodbye wave before stepping outside. "Anna, is there anything else I can get you?" She glanced at her *tochter*. "Mary?"

Anna smiled a little. "No. *Denki*, Rebecca." Mary shook her head.

"Then I'll let you two have your privacy, and please, girls, holler if you need anything else."

After she exited the room, Anna could hear creaks as Rebecca descended the tall flight of wooden stairs. She and Mary regarded each other with affection before

Mary pressed her lips together and put her hands on her hips.

All of a sudden, they burst into laughter. "We are soaking wet! With our clothes on!"

They continued to laugh until Mary waved a hand. "You shower first, Anna. But make it fast! I can't wait to feel heat on my cold skin!"

Anna didn't argue. Quick steps took her into the bathroom that was attached to Mary's bedroom and removed her wet clothes. When the door clicked shut, she peeled off her garments. As she did so, her gaze wandered the room and, without thinking, she took in the plants.

A peace lily sat on a stool in front of one of the windows. In front of the other window was a small round table, and on the top, a vase of freshly cut red and white roses bloomed.

As Anna stood under the spray of hot water, relief swept through her veins. She hadn't realized how very cold her skin was until the water caressed away her chills.

She considered what had happened at the pond before acknowledging Mary Conrad's love for plants. Anna knew for a fact that whenever anything green was pronounced unsalvageable, Mary took it as her personal challenge to save it.

As water soothed her shoulders, an idea came to Anna's mind, and she pressed her lips together thoughtfully. As she continued thinking, the corners of her mouth gently lifted into a satisfied grin.

Both rooms were lacking a sketch of a plant. While Anna closed her eyes to enjoy the warmth, she had another item to add to her list.

Several minutes later, she dried and pulled Mary's dress over her head, hung her wet clothes on the nearest peg, and cracked the door. Anna would find out her friend's favorite flower.

Next, Mary showered. While Anna listened to the spray of water hitting the side of the wall, she considered everything that had happened in such a short time, including the art contest. And her feelings for Jesse. Chaos cluttered her mind until she closed her eyes and took a deep breath.

Finally, she opened her eyes and began combing her hair. The moment she hit a knot, she let out a loud moan. Getting the tangles out wouldn't be easy. She narrowed her brows.

When Mary finally appeared in dry clothing, she wrapped a white towel around her head and offered to comb Anna's hair. Anna got comfortable on the edge of the beautiful quilt of blue- and cream-colored hues.

Mary held out her hand to display the turquoise comb. "I'll try real hard to be gentle, but let's face it: Your hair looks like one solid knot. I'm sure mine is, too."

Anna sat very still while Mary started running the comb through the ends.

"You okay?"

"*Jah.*"

Mary stopped. "You don't say that with a lot of confidence." After a slight pause, Mary went on. "If you need reassurance, I can say that I've had some practice . . . when I babysit. Sometimes, before the *kinder* go to bed, I comb their hair and French braid it for fun."

Anna took in the interesting statement and smiled a

little, careful not to move for fear of her friend combing a knot. "I didn't know you had a thing for fixing hair."

"I don't, really." After a slight hesitation, she corrected herself. "Okay, maybe I do. A little."

"Where did you learn how?"

A small laugh came out of Mary's throat. "I've never told anyone this, but you know those hair magazines next to the checkout at Walmart?"

"*Jah.*"

"While I wait in line, I browse through them. Of course, I'd prefer plant magazines, but they put those at the back of the store."

Mary's hand brushed Anna's shoulder, and she stopped what she was doing. "You're still as cold as ice."

Anna agreed. "I'm really chilled."

As Anna sat very still on the bed, Mary combed.

"Ouch."

"Sorry. But my best friend here has the thickest head of hair I've ever combed."

"I do have a lot to work with."

"But that's a good thing. I mean, it's better than having no hair at all."

"True."

After shifting on her hips for a more comfortable position and considering Mary's comment, Anna finally replied, "It's what God gave me."

"I've wondered what your hair looked like without a *kapp.* I've always wanted long hair."

"Really?"

Mary nodded. "But for some reason, mine just won't make it past my shoulders." After a short pause, she went on. "You're still shivering." Without saying anything else, Mary jumped up and stepped out of the room. When she returned, she wrapped a shawl around Anna's shoulders.

"Here. This will help. What you've got is a good case of chills. Thankfully, I just finished knitting this scarf for the winter. But I figure this is a good excuse to use it."

Anna closed her eyes as she touched the soft fabric of beautiful pastel hues. Her chills eased. "It feels *gut*."

"But I'm afraid I won't be able to comb around your neck as long as the scarf's there."

Anna pulled the fabric from her neck and plopped it on her lap, where she wrapped her hands inside the yarn. "This is beautiful. When did you find time to make it?"

As Mary went on to talk about her interest in knitting, Anna closed her eyes, enjoying the feel of the comb against her scalp. Her shoulders relaxed, and she began to think of what she was doing here. In the Conrad home. With her dear friend. And suddenly, what had happened at the pond rushed back into her thoughts and made her sit up a little straighter.

Uncertainty edged Mary's voice. "You want to know something?"

Anna turned a little. "What?"

After a slight hitch in her voice, Mary went on. "You really had me scared when you jumped into the pond." Before Anna could say anything, Mary continued. "It's deep, you know. In some places anyway."

A long, thoughtful silence ensued before Mary softened her pitch to a confidential tone. "I didn't even know you could swim!"

Anna cleared her throat. "I can't."

"Me neither! But I made my grand entrance by those big tree roots because I knew I could grab on to them."

Anna smiled. "It's all *gut*."

"Can I ask you something else?"

"*Jah.*"

Mary softened the pitch of her voice to a more inquisitive tone. "Why did you jump into the pond if you can't swim?"

"What I did . . ." Anna considered her words as she wondered the same thing. "I guess you could just say it was an automatic reaction. In fact, I didn't even think. I just reacted." After a short hesitation, Anna went on. "But Mary, there wasn't an option, really. I had to try to save the boys. I couldn't just stand by and watch them . . ." Her voice cracked. "And if I hadn't jumped in . . ."

Anna squeezed her eyes closed as she realized the severity of the situation and the worst that could have happened. A long silence ensued before Mary spoke. This time, emotion filled her voice. "I really admire you for what you did, Anna. You risked your life for the boys. God protected all of us."

Anna waved a dismissive hand. "If I hadn't jumped in to save him, someone else would have." As she contemplated what she'd said, she immediately realized that might not have been the case. Because the rest of the group hadn't made it there in time. "But you did, too."

Mary's reply was delayed. "Sort of. What I did wasn't as brave as you. I mean, I went in where I could hold on to the tree roots. You, my friend, went in without a life vest!"

They laughed together.

Anna lowered her pitch to a more uncertain tone. She

tried to conceal her emotion as she thought of the little boy she'd rescued from the pond. "What are you hearing about Reuben's *maemm?* Do the doctors think she'll be okay?"

Before Mary could respond, Anna continued in her thoughtful, concerned tone. "It's no secret that cancer's a tricky thing to fix."

Mary let out a breath. "To be honest, I haven't heard one way or the other. But I can tell you this: We're all praying for her. And for Reuben. What I am sure of is that God answers prayers."

Mary's voice took on a more hopeful, positive tone. "Anna, sometimes I just take a moment to say a prayer to God to thank Him I was raised by two parents. Christian parents. I know there are always issues to deal with. And sometimes they can be overwhelming. But when you really think about it, next to being a Christian, nothing else matters, really."

The comment prompted Anna to think a moment about the woman who'd given her up for adoption. About Anna's dream of getting an art degree and sharing her artwork.

After several moments of consideration, Anna agreed with her friend. In the entire scheme of things, knowing Christ was all that mattered. In the end, she'd meet her birth mamma and find out everything. As Mary ran her comb through Anna's long hair, a knock on the door made them turn.

They both faced a smiling Rebecca and Annie. The two women stepped just inside the door. Relief edged Rebecca's voice. "Reuben and Amos are just fine." There was a slight pause. "Except they're a little bent out of shape. They're getting lots of scoldings. And they're inside for the rest of the afternoon. But now . . . things have finally calmed down."

Annie piped in with her soft, compassionate tone. "But everyone's asking about you girls. Anna, Mary, how are you holding up?"

Anna turned to face the two women, laying an affectionate hand on Mary's shoulder. "I will be fine as soon as our plant guru gets the knots out of my hair."

After the women left and the door clicked shut, Mary cleared her throat. "There's something we haven't talked about."

Anna narrowed her brows. "What?"

Mary paused and lowered her voice. "You tell me."

Trying to decide what her friend was getting at, Anna's interest had been piqued. Now she had to know what was going through her friend's mind.

"I noticed a certain man at the pond who couldn't take his eyes off you after he pulled you out of the water."

Anna's heart picked up speed to a pace that was a strong combination of excitement and uneasiness.

Anna knew that Mary already had her answer. But Anna had to know more.

"Jesse Beiler."

"Uh-huh."

Mary stopped for a moment and let out a sound of impatience from her throat. And Anna laughed. Because she knew her friend so well, and whenever Mary wanted to know something but pretended she was only casually interested, she made that particular sound.

"Anna, what's up?"

Anna feigned ignorance. "Thank goodness he got to the pond fast. Otherwise, I might not be here patiently waiting for you to untangle my hair."

Mary stopped what she was doing and made a quick move to sit opposite Anna. As they faced each other, the expression on Mary's face gave her curiosity away. The light in her eyes hinted that she knew something was going on and that she couldn't wait another minute to find out what it was.

Not saying a word, Anna lifted her palms to the ceiling in a helpless gesture. The last thing she wanted was to give away her true feelings. There was too much at stake. First of all, if she won the contest and went to St. Louis, she didn't want Jesse's name connected with her because he might very well be blamed for conspiring with her. Secondly, she didn't want to talk to anyone about Jesse. Not right now. Because her feelings for him were so strong, she was afraid to verbalize them.

"Anna, you don't have to say a word. Your face gives away everything."

"What?"

"There's something between you and Jesse. It's written all over you. It was in his eyes, too."

Not able to let the comment go, Anna leaned forward and whispered, "What was?"

Mary harrumphed. "I don't know what it's like to be in love, but I can imagine. And while the paramedics got water out of your lungs and made everyone stay away, I could tell by the way he looked at you with great affection that he was worried to death."

Mary let out a sigh. "I've always heard my *Englisch*

friends say that a picture's worth a thousand words. Now, I'm Amish, so I don't have a photo. But that look of his is etched into my mind like DNA. I'll never forget it. It reminded me of a picture book showing a lioness guarding her cubs. Only I don't think that what he feels is maternal. No, not at all."

Chapter Five

Monday morning, Jesse balanced himself on his platform while his team of four horses pulled him through the remainder of the alfalfa behind the Kings' property. This afternoon, he would finish the cutting.

As he breathed in the earthy scent of freshly cut plant, a sense of comfort filled him, caressing his soul like nothing else in the world could.

A satisfied grin tugged at the corners of his lips as the bright sun slipped behind a cloud. If God offered him the opportunity to be in any other place in the world right now, Jesse knew he'd decline. Because there was nowhere else he would rather be than here in this field, cutting alfalfa to feed the cattle during the winter months. He enjoyed the entire process that would ultimately end in storing the bales of hay in the upper loft of the Kings' large barn.

Automatically, his thoughts floated to only a couple of days before and the church gathering at the Conrad home. A deep, uncertain breath escaped him as he straightened to keep his balance, bump after bump.

What had happened at William and Rebecca's was

the talk of the small town. And since pulling Anna and Reuben from the pond, he'd thought of little else.

He ached for the little boy. The poor kid's *maemm* was very ill. And sometimes in life, he was sure, there wasn't a perfect solution, despite anyone's best intentions.

As he worked, he glimpsed a figure in the distance. Sitting by Pebble Creek. He guessed it was Anna, because he didn't know of anyone else it could be. And as he got closer, he confirmed that it was she. He noted the outline of her visage. And he saw the sketch pad that was propped on a small easel in front of her.

The corners of his lips drooped. Automatically, he contemplated the upcoming contest and wondered if she'd win. He'd started praying to God to do His will. The more he considered her winning, the more he wondered what would become of her *eltern* and their church if she decided to leave the faith.

An ache pinched his stomach. He wasn't sure why, but whenever someone departed their tight-knit community, a sense of sadness filled his heart. Because even one individual's absence affected the entire area.

As four horses moved him forward, he balanced himself on the small platform. As they veered to the right, Anna looked up, and he lifted a hand in greeting. She responded with a friendly wave before returning her attention to what she was doing.

As Jesse bounced up and down, he knew he had a huge responsibility to help Anna make the decision that God would want her to make. He believed that it was not a coincidence that her contest entry had fallen out of her satchel in front of him. That it was God's hand at work, which meant that the Creator of the universe intended for Jesse to play a role in Anna's future. The bright sun slipped behind a large, fluffy cloud that looked like an oversize helping of *Maemm*'s mashed potatoes.

Jesse frowned, aware that because he was privy to her plan, it was his responsibility to convey to her why she should or should not enter. And if she won, what to do. But what should he tell her?

Jesse hadn't said that he really couldn't understand why anyone would even think of life outside of their Amish community. By the same token, he acknowledged that not everyone appreciated the same things. As he recalled Anna sketching during class, he smiled a little. For as long as he'd known her, she'd been different from the other Amish girls he knew. Growing up, while most of them had expressed interest in making pies and sponge cakes, Anna had been sketching on her pad. And now he also knew that she'd been dreaming of studying art. But she differed in other ways, too.

Years ago, he'd overheard her being teased about her tanned skin. It was common knowledge that she was the only one around who'd been adopted.

Jesse frowned. He disapproved of gossip. It was hurtful. And minor stories could turn into major ones. And he'd never felt good that, to some, Anna had been considered different, even though she was. In a good way.

Most were accepting of her; however, to his disappointment, he had overheard unkind remarks. In his heart, he knew that everyone, no matter what color his or her skin, was a child of God.

When he nearly lost his balance, he focused his attention back on the task at hand. Paul King's *tochter* was definitely made of different stuff. What she'd done at the picnic only two days ago . . . that had confirmed that nothing about her was cowardly. Jesse smiled, and his heart warmed. Because he liked everything about her.

That evening, at the Kings' dining-room table, Jesse nodded in great appreciation as he took a bite of roast.

"Mrs. King, when I smelled pork baking, I was hoping you'd ask me for dinner. I've tasted some good meat, but this has got to be the best!" He swallowed and looked across the table to Anna's *maemm*, who glowed.

After helping herself to carrots and potatoes, Naomi glanced at Jesse and then to Anna. "I'd love to claim credit, but the truth is, it goes to Anna."

Jesse took in the dark-haired daughter and smiled a little. "And we've known each other way too long for you to be so formal. Naomi," she added.

Naomi's voice softened while she offered an affectionate smile. "As you're aware, Paul and I have been spending so much time at the bakery, Anna's been holding down the fort here. And she's doing a remarkable job."

Anna looked up from her plate just long enough to respond. "*Denki*."

Naomi smiled a little.

"Honey, we need to tell you more often how much we appreciate you."

Jesse checked Anna's reaction. To his surprise, he didn't see one. Even so, he was certain that inside that head of hers, a lot was going on. He guessed that she must be losing sleep over the contest and what to tell her *eltern* if she won.

And even though he was sure there would be many entries, he believed in his heart that Anna would win. She was talented, and he couldn't imagine that any entrants could be more faithful.

Jesse acknowledged that it was family time. Yet he needed to let Paul know that he was on schedule. "The alfalfa's cut. By tomorrow afternoon, it should be dry enough to rake."

"*Gut.* Perfect weather for drying. The forecast shows eighty-five by midday."

"Jesse, we want to thank you again for everything you've done for us. For Anna, too. We're so glad you could join us. I regret that we didn't invite you sooner. But now that we're all together, we want to express our great appreciation for what you did for Anna during the storm."

Naomi took a drink of water. "And now, there's another thanks in order." After letting out a breath, Naomi gave a shake of her head. "I still can't believe what happened at the Conrads'. It's fortunate no one drowned."

Jesse considered her comment and nodded in agreement. "Thanks to Anna and Mary." He turned his attention to Anna.

Paul King's voice was gruff, as usual. "That pond has always worried me, I mean, when William and Rebecca have company. I suppose we're fortunate this was the first time something's happened. You can never be too careful around water."

A long silence ensued before he went on. Concern

edged the pitch of his voice as he dragged his hand over his face and chin. "I'm surprised the *kinder* weren't supervised. Word has it that there were plenty of adults there. How did the boys manage to make it all the way out to the pond?"

Jesse took in the uncertain expression on Anna's face. "*Daed*, it just happened. I was helping Mary watch the kids. We were close to the house, and the children were playing tag. Mary told them to stay in the front yard, but before we knew it, Reuben and Amos were in the back and headed for the water."

Paul and Naomi exchanged a look before shaking their heads in disbelief.

Paul pressed the subject. "But where were the other adults?"

Anna cut in. "Everywhere. Mostly the front yard, which, as you know, is huge. In the house. Out by the pasture. I understand how it would seem irresponsible."

She lifted her palms to the ceiling. "Mary and I were with the children. We've managed groups like this numerous times at picnics and weddings. But . . ."

She paused to take a drink. After she swallowed, she went on. "To be honest, everything happened unbelievably fast."

Naomi chimed in with interest. "But didn't you shout for help?"

"*Jah.* And it came." She bobbed her head at Jesse. "Just not as fast as we needed it."

Anna regarded her parents and softened the pitch of her voice. "I wish you could have been there."

Paul nodded in agreement. "Me too. Soon, things are

gonna get back to the way they were. Hopefully, the bakery won't need us every second of the day."

Naomi added, "Thank goodness, we can see the end." She smiled sympathetically at her *tochter*. "Then we'll spend more time as a family. Like we used to."

As Jesse contemplated Naomi's words, he narrowed his brows, pretending to pay special attention to the food on his plate. Paul and Naomi might think that most of their work was behind them, but they had no idea of the storm that would hit when the Amish community found out that Anna would be moving away and going for a four-year degree. If she won, of course.

The only sound was the clinking of silverware against plates. Ice cubes against glasses. The blades of the large battery fan whipping in circles and the air coming from it.

"I guess what's done is done." Paul King looked at his wife before leaning forward for the casserole dish. His acceptance was evidenced by a long exhale.

"That's probably why they call 'em accidents." To Jesse's surprise, the man at the head of the table threw a warm smile to Anna. "Anna, what you did . . . God will surely bless you for it."

Anna beamed.

Naomi spoke next. "Not to change the subject, but we want you to know that we consider you part of our family, Jesse."

The comment prompted an emotional knot to form in his throat. He swallowed it.

"That's kind of you to say, Naomi."

Naomi smiled widely. "My, my, Jesse. Why, we've

known you and your family for years. We've been through births together. Deaths, too." She shook her head. "To us, you're *familie.*"

For some reason, the statement prompted a strong rush of emotion to sweep through Jesse. Her unexpected revelation pulled at his heartstrings. And the expression on Naomi's face was so sincere, he didn't doubt for one moment that what she said had come from the heart.

"*Denki.*" He smiled a little and tried for the right words, not sure he would find them. "You don't know how much it means to hear those words." After a lengthy pause, he lowered the pitch of his voice. "*Ich bin dankbar.*"

The man at the head of the table raised his voice to a level of newfound enthusiasm while he grinned from ear to ear. "There's no finer family 'round here than the Beiler clan."

He took a drink of black coffee, returned his mug to the coaster, and looked around the table before focusing on Jesse. "God has given us a tremendous blessing. Not only did He provide us our families, but He also gave us our church members in the name of Christ."

His eyes glistened while he lowered the tone of his voice. "Through Christ, we're all one big family."

After the statement, Jesse happened to catch the corners of Anna's lips droop. *There's obviously a lot I don't know.* When she caught him looking at her, their gazes locked.

Then he realized that Paul was waiting for him to respond, so Jesse tried for the right words. "I agree."

At the same time, he wondered if Anna's folks would

still consider Anna a part of their Christian family if she became *Englisch*.

The following day, Jesse balanced himself on his small platform while his team of horses pulled him and the rakes through the alfalfa. In the distance, he glimpsed a figure by Pebble Creek. *It has to be Anna.*

Careful to keep his focus, his eyes followed her as she moved forward. She carried something in her right hand as she stepped near the back of the property to the place where Pebble Creek met their land. Whatever was in her hand appeared to be some sort of chest.

In some ways, he felt a bit sorry for her being an only child. During dinner, their house had been so quiet. A sharp contrast to his own. Not only that, but since he'd begun working for Paul King, he'd noted that Anna spent most of her time alone. He frowned.

He wasn't sure if things had always been as such, but if they had, he completely understood why her passion for sketching fit with her life. No brothers or sisters. And parents who had little time for her.

He thought of his own family of five older brothers and smiled a little. Now they were all married and out of the house, but growing up, their household had been chaotic. *My upbringing was nothing like Anna's. We're both Amish, but we've lived totally different lives.*

When he'd finished what he'd begun a couple of hours ago, he'd stopped to take a break. The sun slipped under a cloud cover, and he enjoyed the short breeze that followed. From where he stood, he could see for miles.

He glimpsed the home that Old Sam Beachy had left

to his great-niece, Jessica, who would be going through classes this fall to join the Amish church and marry Eli Miller.

While he considered his and Anna's different upbringings, he acknowledged that their pasts hadn't differed nearly as much as Jessica and Eli's. After all, Eli had been raised Amish. Not only that, but he loved the faith and had always yearned to marry within the church and continue the life he'd always had.

Word had it that before inheriting the Beachy property, Jessica hadn't even believed in the Lord. While Jesse thought of the huge change she must be going through with her newfound faith, he let out a low whistle. He didn't doubt that it had been the hand of God that had brought her to Arthur to meet the man who would help her to know God.

As a light breeze caressed the back of his neck, he ran his forearm over his brow and finally laid down the rake. He stepped to his water bottle and took a few swigs, standing very still in appreciation of the thirst relief.

As much as he tried to focus on work, he found himself watching Anna. She pulled something from the chest, and he could see her draw. He recalled how he'd rescued her during the storm. Their private time together inside the large barn. And he'd never forget the shocking moment when he'd glimpsed her in the pond.

Fear of her drowning had prompted him to jump in and save her. But he was fully aware that the strong feelings he was starting to have for Anna bordered something he'd never experienced before.

He watched for her. He liked talking with her. *I want to spend more time with her.* At that realization, he frowned. Because he knew he was beginning to fall in love with someone who might very well leave the community. And the Amish faith.

Still, after tying the horses and feeding them apples, he eventually found himself making his way toward where she was. The speed of his pulse picked up to an excited pace, and he silently chastised himself for his reaction. *But how can I control what my pulse does? And my heart?*

He proceeded, and she didn't look up. Apparently, she was immersed in whatever was on the sketch pad in front of her.

Sometime later, he spoke in a soft, appreciative voice. "That's interesting."

She was startled.

"Sorry. I didn't mean to scare you."

"Jesse." She straightened and looked up at him with a surprised smile. "It's *gut* to see you." She motioned. "Have a seat."

He folded his legs underneath him and wondered what to say. His instinct had been to join her. *Now what?*

"What do you think?" She turned her pad for him to glimpse the picture. "It's for the contest."

His heart sank. *But you knew her plans.*

"I have to come up with a theme, so this is what I thought of. It will be me now, in the center, and me in the background, if I'd been raised by my birth mother," she explained. "In both sketches, I'll be the same woman physically, but inside, I am different. Because of how I've been brought up."

He contemplated the deepness of the subject and looked at her. "I can't wait to see it finished."

She beamed. "I want you to see it."

Not sure what to say next, he thought of the obvious. "Beautiful day, isn't it?"

She smiled a little and continued to sketch while they talked.

She lifted her palms to the sky. "It's wonderful. And nothing makes me happier than coming here."

"So you like this spot?"

She nodded. "It's where I've always been inspired. When I sit here, ideas . . . they come to me so easily."

He considered her revelation and suddenly, *he* was inspired. "I can understand why you chose this place." He looked around. "It's inspiring."

When she smiled at him, he found it impossible to look away.

"You know what the true beauty is around here?"

He eyed her to continue.

"Pebble Creek."

He offered a nod of agreement. "Aw. I can't argue with that."

"Even though the land was Old Sam's, we get to look at it and admire it. I love this place where the creek brushes up against our property. And the hill . . ."

She looked to her right. "It's a miracle, really. The Midwest is flat; I suppose that's why I love the hill." After a thoughtful pause, she crossed her legs at the ankles and laughed. "It's like it was pulled out of some other state and planted here."

He lifted his palms in the air in a hopeless gesture. "There's nothing like it."

He realized that he'd spoken absently. Of course, she must agree. He looked at her to respond.

A few moments later, she spoke. To his surprise, the tone of her voice wasn't as convincing as he'd expected it to be.

She lifted a brow. "Nothing like what?"

"All of this. It's amazing. I think of it as God's country."

From his peripheral vision, he caught the uncertain expression on her face. He lowered the tone of his voice to a more skeptical pitch and turned to better face her. "You don't think this is awesome?"

Finally, she nodded. "*Jah.* I love the summertime."

Without thinking, he asked, "What do you like about it?"

A dreamy expression crossed her face, and she glanced at him before directing her attention to her family's land.

She breathed in, leaned back, pressed her palms against the green earth, and gazed up at the sky. When she turned toward him, he took in the expression on her face. It was a combination of satisfaction and happiness.

"I love the sun's warmth on my face. The feel of the gentle breeze against my eyelashes. It feels . . . *gut.*" She started to go on, then stopped.

"What? What were you going to say?"

The corners of her lips drooped a notch, and her eyes took on a more serious, uncertain look.

After a short pause, she looked down at the ground and went on in a soft voice. "Sometimes I wish there were only good things in life. That nothing bothered me."

He frowned. "You mean like winning the contest?"

She shrugged. "Maybe. But it's so much more than that, Jesse."

"But life is the *gut*. And it's the bad. Life is both of those thrown together. Of course, it would be impossible to live in a world where one hundred percent of things go the way you want them to. But Anna, when I look at you, I . . ."

She glanced at him to go on.

While she waited, he decided on an honest, straight-forward approach. For some reason, he sensed that this conversation was important. That the Amish girl he'd grown up with must have other issues, and this was his opportunity to help. And that's exactly what he intended to do.

"Jesse, you're already keeping my secret. And I'm grateful." She swallowed, and her voice cracked with emotion. "Really, I am." There was a slight pause while she swatted away a fly.

"When Old Sam was alive, he used to say that God creates the entire plan for your life. That you can't have good without bad."

"Really?"

"*Jah.* And when you think about it, it makes a lot of sense."

She looked at him to go on. "Give me an example."

"The strongest one that comes to mind is eternal life. Look at what had to happen in order for us to have it." After a pause, he softened his tone to an emotional pitch. "A brutal death."

She lowered her lashes and nodded.

"I like that analogy."

"To me, the creek is like a picture that winds its way through the property."

Finally, he relaxed. Her words were so thoughtful. And their appreciation of the beauty around them was something they shared.

He looked up at the sky. "When I sit back and take in this land, I always dream."

She eyed him. "What do you dream of?"

Her question prompted a myriad of thoughts. Whenever he considered his future, emotion claimed him. "Of having my own farm. To me . . ."

He extended his arms and lifted his chin. "Nothing's more beautiful than this. I love everything about it. And when I have a farm of my own, I want to come home every evening to a loving wife and a dinner table filled with children. I dream of providing for my family."

He looked down at his boots before turning to lock gazes with her, quick to note the long, thoughtful pause that lapsed until she finally said something. When she did, her voice was soft and understanding.

"I hope your dream comes true, Jesse. It's totally unselfish."

He raised an inquisitive brow. "It's funny that beauty is different things to different people. What's it to you, Anna? What's your dream? Besides getting a four-year degree and being an artist?"

She cleared her throat. He was quick to notice that she had tensed. That she clasped her hands together on her lap so tightly that her knuckles turned white. Obviously, she was hesitant to share her dream with him. To make her feel more at ease, he added in an apologetic tone, "Sorry. I don't mean to pry."

She smiled a little. "You're not prying. And there's nothing to be sorry about, Jesse. It's just that . . . You seem very sure of your dream. But mine?" She shrugged. "I don't really know what mine is. I mean, besides pursuing art."

She drew in a hopeful breath. "And . . . to meet my mamma. After the contest is over, and I know my plans, I'm going to try to find out who she is." She shrugged. "I need to feel complete."

Her words stopped him for a moment. Finally, he softened his voice. "I understand. And I truly hope that happens."

A long silence passed. "Do you have other plans?"

She shook her head.

"No?"

When she turned to better face him, he noted an odd combination of sincerity and uncertainty in her eyes. To his surprise, it was as if she was searching for words to convey her thoughts.

"I know this might sound like I'm trying to figure out my purpose. What God wants me to do with my life. In fact, that's exactly what's going on here. Jesse, you seem to know exactly what you want, and you don't long for something that may not exist. Maybe I don't know myself as well as I'd like to. I mean, I have a dream . . . but there must be something to go along with it. I'm just not sure what it is."

"Really?" Trying to ascertain the crux of what she'd just said, his response just came out. "When I think of everything I have, I long for nothing more. I've been raised in a good Christian family. Where we live . . . well, we don't have to worry about crime. And we've got plenty of food on the table. I feel like I'm living a dream. But I understand how you feel about knowing where you really came from. Truly, I do."

As he studied the uncertainty in her eyes, he realized that, without a doubt, the Amish girl next to him was much, much different from him. Uncertainty about herself and her life prompted him to furrow his brows in doubt. They'd gone to church with the same people and had schooled together; yet it had suddenly become obvious to him that they didn't think alike.

One by one, she ticked off things they had on her fingers. "We've got great families. Loving parents. The best support any person could ever have within our church. We both live in the country, where there's plenty of space and fresh air."

"And God blessed you with an extra bonus, Anna."

At that last statement, she sat up straighter, and the white flecks on her pupils danced with excitement.

"You're a very talented artist."

"That's the nicest thing anyone's ever said to me, Jesse."

"That you're talented?"

She nodded. "Everything that you've just said. Maybe I needed to hear that. Especially now. For reassurance."

He lowered the pitch of his voice to a tone that was barely audible. "Especially now that you're setting out to win a contest so you can nail your dream?"

"Maybe. I've done lots of thinking over the years. And dreaming." She hesitated and adjusted her hips as if deciding what to tell him. He sat very still, listening with interest.

"You're right about our upbringings. We've been raised with everything anyone could ask for. Yet we're different. I know this might sound ungrateful to you, and that's certainly not my intention. Of course I'm appreciative of the blessings God has given me. We're surrounded by wonderful people, Amish and *Englisch*. But having been raised Amish . . ."

She lifted the palms of her hands to the sky in a helpless gesture before resting them on her thighs. She cleared her throat, and her voice cracked when she finally spoke in an uncertain, sad tone. "I feel like I've never really been accepted for who I am. For my interests. For what I have to offer."

As he took in her statement, he studied her with curiosity. "Really?"

She pressed her lips together in a straight line before responding. "It's hard to explain."

"Try me."

He noted the hesitation on her face.

Finally, she spoke. "It just that I've grown into the woman my parents want me to be. The person my church expects me to be." She pressed her lips together in a straight line and fidgeted with her fingers. "I'm having trouble explaining."

"Keep trying. I want to help, Anna. That is, if you'll let me."

When her eyes widened in a combination of relief and surprise, he went on in his most reassuring tone. "And I'll keep what you say confidential."

A sigh of relief escaped her. "I've never talked to anyone about this."

He smiled a little. "That's exactly why you should

tell me what's bothering you. Obviously, I don't have a degree in higher education, but sometimes I can figure things out and make good decisions."

She turned to better face him. "That's just it. There's so much I want to learn."

"Like what?"

She pressed her palms flat over her knees just below her white apron and shrugged. "Jesse, I long to become a better artist. To learn another language. To explore other cultures. Arthur is such a small part of the world."

She pointed to her face. "Obviously, my birth family is Latino. Unfortunately, I know nothing about my heritage. There are so many people in the world. We can't all be the same, and I'm wondering who God really intended me to be."

"What's wrong with who you are?"

She shrugged. "Nothing. Like I said, the last thing I want to seem is ungrateful. My *eltern* adopted me, provided a good home, and, most importantly, taught me about God, and I'm forever indebted to them. I know this sounds complicated, but it's true. I'm who I am because of how my parents have raised me. But Jesse, what if I had been raised by my birth mamma?"

A long silence ensued. "I'm fairly sure I wouldn't have been Amish. Because of that, I probably wouldn't have had the same thoughts and beliefs. And the truth is that even though I've been raised here, I've always felt different than the girls I went to school with."

"How so?"

The corners of her lips turned downward. She let out a sigh, and uncertainty edged her voice. "I don't think you'd understand. And to be honest . . ." She shrugged. "I shouldn't complain."

"Please tell me what you mean. Anna . . ." Their gazes locked in some sort of mutual understanding.

"It frustrates me that my birth mother gave me up. Didn't she love me?" Anna shrugged, and the distress in her eyes was visible. "Maybe her circumstances were bad, and she did what she believed was best?"

After a short pause, she went on. "Growing up, I was different from the girls in our church. Even my *gut* friend, Mary. Not only because my hair's darker than anyone else's around, and my face, too, but growing up I heard comments that made me feel I was less of a person than everyone else. Hurtful things that made me feel I didn't fit in."

He knew. Because he'd heard some of the comments.

"I heard the phrase *not really Amish.* More than once. And, of course, the word *adopted.*" Her voice cracked with emotion. "Mrs. Graber said it. And Saturday, after you pulled me out of the pond, I caught her looking at me. And the expression on her face was like I'd done something wrong. But she's always looked at me like that. I think that, this time, she probably disapproved because my clothes were stuck to me. I'm not sure."

Her confession nearly stopped his thoughts. He couldn't believe he'd heard correctly. As he contemplated what this girl had gone through, anger brewed inside him. But he definitely needed to show his support. Because there was so much turmoil going on inside Anna. And, unfortunately, some of it had to do with what was out of her control.

"Anna, you're a child of God. And Mrs. Graber had no right to say that. I'm sorry."

She smiled a little and offered an appreciative nod. "Thank you, Jesse. But don't you see?"

When he lifted a brow, her eyes reflected a sudden sadness. Disappointment edged her pitch. "Part of me, inside, is missing. Because I know nothing about my real background. So I always figured I was a backup."

His jaw dropped. He'd never realized there was so much chaos inside this beautiful, brave, talented girl. He had to pick up her spirits. Finally, he found the right words. He forced a confident smile, made a fist, and pressed it against his chin. "I'm guessing that your birth *maemm* loved you very much, Anna."

A surprised expression crossed her face. "Why do you say that?"

"Because she had you." He paused, not wanting to make the situation worse than it was. "I'm not worldly at all, but I do know that the world isn't always protective and kind. Or Christian. And it's a known fact that some pregnant women elect not to bring their babies into this world."

Her mouth parted in surprise. "*Jah*. I know."

"But your *maemm* . . . Anna, she had you. She gave birth to you. Women in this world don't always do that. And because she kept you, to me, that alone says to me that she loved you." He softened his voice. "It must have been extremely difficult for her to have let you go. I'm sure she made the very best decision she could. For you. And now you're here."

He saw her face light up. He let out a breath of relief.

Anna softened her voice. "I wish I could talk to her. It would ease my pain if only I knew her story. Why she gave me up. If it was because she couldn't afford me . . ." She shrugged helplessly. "I don't know. I wonder if she'd kept me, what my name would be. What kinds of friends I'd have." She lifted her palms and shrugged. "I have no way of finding out. And you must understand now why I wonder where I really belong."

Jesse swallowed. "This, I'm sure of. I don't ever want anyone to hurt you again. Or for you to think that you don't belong."

He lowered his lashes and leaned closer to her, looking her directly in the eyes to make sure she knew he meant what he said. "For what it's worth, Anna King, you're a blessing. The most special person I've ever met."

Chapter Six

The contest was coming closer. August was passing quickly. Anna sat in her room on the navy rug next to her hope chest. While she considered her recent conversation with Jesse, the mouthwatering aroma of chicken broth filled the air.

The roaster she'd put in the oven would be done by the time she went to sleep. She would hear the timer go off.

Her parents were still at the bakery. *I can't wait for things to get back to normal. I'm lonely.* Automatically, the thought of her birth mother came into her head. Her mamma. That's what she called her.

Mamma, did you know I was a girl? Did you get to hold me? I don't know why you gave me up, but I forgive you. There's so much I'd like to find out, but even more I'd like to tell you. Unfortunately, I don't even know your name.

A lone tear slid down Anna's cheek, but she didn't try to catch it. She looked around her room. There wasn't much in it, really. Two pegs on the wall. A twin bed with a beautiful handmade quilt of blues and creams that she'd made herself.

Beside her bed was a simple oak desk and a chair her *daed* had bought from Conrad's Cabinets. The light scent of lemon Pledge hovered in the air. Light blue curtains attached to holders to allow a grand view of the backyard and their farm during daylight.

She opened her hope chest and pulled out the sketch she'd started for the contest. As she held it in front of her and studied it, she frowned. Because the scene she wanted to capture on paper didn't pull her in as she wanted it to.

Perhaps it's because I don't know what's going on inside the mind of the Anna who wasn't adopted. The expression on her face . . . it doesn't reflect anything. How would I feel if I had been raised Englisch? She shrugged.

As she studied her work in progress, the cookout at Mary Conrad's house floated in and out of her thoughts, and amusement lifted the corners of her lips as she recalled her and her dear friend in the pond's murky waters. When they'd been drenched from head to foot.

At the time, the scene had been anything but funny. But now that it was over, and she, Mary, and the boys were safe and sound, Anna grinned at the recollection of the two girls, soaking wet, muddy, and still wearing their long dresses. Anna laughed out loud.

Mary's favorite flower is a rose. Peach-colored, and I'll sketch one for her wall. Automatically, Anna stood and stepped to the window to take in the family farm as the sun slipped into the horizon. As she did so, she recalled Jesse's dream.

She arched a curious brow. It sounded like a simple goal. But was it? Anna was fully aware of how difficult it was these days to get farmland. When it did go up for sale, it was expensive.

And that was exactly why many Amish in her church did jobs outside of farming. Most of the land in their area had been passed down through families. But she yearned with all her heart for Jesse's dream to happen. As much as she prayed for her own to materialize.

As she recalled their most recent conversation, she thought of her hope chest and the special sketches inside it. While she considered Jesse Beiler, his reassuring words from the afternoon resonated with her until a newfound sense of hope and relief filled her chest, and her tears stopped. "You're the most special person I know."

As evening sounds floated through her window screen, she tried to absorb the significance of his words. Of course, she couldn't read too much into what he'd said. After all, he was kind, and she sensed that his aim was always to make her feel better.

She pressed her lips together thoughtfully and dared to imagine that he felt something for her. Other than friendship. *Don't go there.*

But she couldn't get him out of her mind. Finally, she returned to the rug next to her hope chest. She held her contest drawing with both hands in front of her. Until a compelling idea struck her.

Setting that sketch to her right, she began drawing what was inside her heart. A couple of hours later, she looked at her work. And smiled.

Without a doubt, she was in love with the art in front of her. It was Jesse. As she took in his face, what was inside him was obvious. Kindness, gentleness, and something so rare that wasn't tangible.

She'd taken note of every small detail of his face when he'd rescued her from the storm. And she'd been able to capture those very details on paper so that the visage looked real.

But Jesse is *real. He's the most special person I've ever met. And I will tell him so.*

Days later, laughter filled the Beiler home when Jesse stepped inside.

"Hello!"

Three of his brothers, Gabriel, Isaiah, and Jonah, stood in front of him with their wives while their *kinder* played in the background. The large battery fan made a light noise as the blades whipped round and round in a circle. The mouthwatering aroma of chicken and dumplings filled the room. Jesse's stomach growled.

"Uncle Jess!"

The moment he was inside, the youngsters rushed to him, nearly knocking him down, and he gave each one an affectionate hug.

While they embraced, Gabriel spoke. "How's everything at the Kings' place?"

Maemm waved a dismissive hand in the air. "We'll find out after the prayer. Time to eat!"

At that time, everyone made their way to the large table and two card tables that had been put up. "I'll be in after I wash up!" Jesse told them.

"Don't take long!"

Quick steps took him to the hall bathroom. He rubbed his palms together and breathed in the cherry-scented soap that lathered between his fingers. An amused grin curved his lips. When *Maemm* said it was time to eat, she meant it. No one argued.

As he dried his hands on the navy towel, without warning, this afternoon's conversation with Anna floated through his mind. Closing his eyes for a moment, he let out a deep breath and furrowed his brows.

So much had happened since he'd begun working for her father. He let out a low whistle. He'd never guessed how deep Anna's feelings went about her identity and what she'd gone through her entire life.

I can't imagine hearing such hurtful things. No wonder Anna isn't exactly sure of who she is. What she overheard about herself as a child set her back. Made her doubt her self-worth.

Maemm's order made him rush. "Jesse! Hurry up, now!"

He quickly took his seat opposite Jonah and bowed his head while his *daed* said the prayer. "Amen."

When Jesse lifted his head, his *eltern* conversed with one another wearing serious expressions. As always, his *daed*'s voice was stern. "Did you hear that the farm a couple of miles north is going up for sale?"

His mother nodded. "*Jah.* Word has it that Judith and Howard Norris are relocating to Arizona. And from what I hear, their move is long overdo because Howard has severe health issues. His doctor recommended a dry climate."

Jesse's father spoke in a low tone while he passed the

casserole to his wife. "This mornin', I heard in town that they've already got their eyes on a place in Scottsdale and plan to put their farm up for sale within the next few weeks."

Jesse swallowed a bite of mashed potatoes and froze in his seat as he absorbed the significance of what he'd just heard. The particular parcel would be just large enough for him to farm and to make a good living. A little over a hundred acres.

At the small tables, there wasn't a peep from the children. After some comments by his brothers, Jesse turned to his *daed*. "Is it really true?" he asked.

Maemm looked at him and smiled a little with a nod.

Jesse piped in, "Their farm's really going up for sale?" He tapped the toe of his boot against the wooden floor to a fast, nervous beat.

As usual, his father's tone lacked enthusiasm. He was the antithesis of Jesse's mother, who loved to smile and laugh. But people respected David Beiler for his calm, steady leadership in the church.

"From what we've heard. And you know, Howard has permanent lung damage from pneumonia." His mother lifted her chin and glanced around the table. "Hopefully, they'll both be healthier out west."

Jesse lowered the pitch of his voice to a combination of hopefulness and anxiousness. "Any idea what they'll ask?"

His *daed* furrowed his brows. "Not yet, but it's no secret that those acres are prime. And nowadays, farmland's hard to come by 'round here. And when it becomes available, it goes fast."

Jesse tapped the toe of his boot again and leaned forward as the news floated through his head. "Sure hope I'll be able to afford it."

His mother smiled a little and regarded him with affection. "It's no secret you've always wanted a farm."

Gabriel cut in. "But the cost . . ."

Daed eyed him a few moments before speaking in a thoughtful tone. "You know, between your *maemm*, me, aunts and uncles, we just might be able to come up with enough for a serious offer."

"Offer?" Before anyone could respond, Jesse went on. "Won't there be an auction?"

"This time, I don't think so. Word has it that a real estate company will be listing it."

Jesse no longer tasted the dumplings. While he swallowed, his imagination worked in high gear. He could already envision horses pulling him in his field. A dinner table full of children and dumplings in the middle. He longed with all his heart to have a wife to kiss him when he came home from the field.

He furrowed his brows and pressed his palms against his hips. A large part of his dream was having a family. For his clan to grow together in Christ. But at twenty-two, he'd never been interested in any of the women who attended his church.

Now there was an opportunity to buy a farm. And for certain, that wouldn't be easy. But his other dream might prove to be even more difficult. If not Anna, who would he share it with?

* * *

That evening, the only sound was the light brushing of the branches of a large oak tree against Anna's bedroom window as she sat on the round, handwoven rug threaded with shades of blue on the hardwood floor. She leaned forward to close her hope chest lid. As she did so, she stared in amazement at the cross Old Sam had etched into the beautiful wood.

As she took in the lid's details, she blinked at the sting of salty tears. With great awe, she moved closer to the art and traced a blade of grass in the oak.

As she did so, Jesse entered her thoughts, and she parted her lips in awe of everything she'd experienced with him within such a short time. So many details flitted through her thoughts as the sun took another dip into the west.

The storm . . . their time together in the barn . . . the unexplainable expression on his face as he'd pulled her out of the Conrads' pond . . . and, most especially, their delicate, touching conversations. What they'd shared with each other.

She closed her eyes and drew in a slow, thoughtful breath. His words stirred an odd combination of peace and havoc within her. Peace because of the calmness that had filled her heart and soul as his kind, reassuring words had taken root. Havoc because every time she prospered from his goodness, she wanted more of his attention.

Finally, she acknowledged what she'd realized at the picnic. The fact that she'd tried to nix from her mind. She was falling in love with Jesse Beiler. She opened her lids and frowned.

This can't be happening. Because nothing can come from my feelings.

She sensed that he liked her, too. Definitely, he trusted her and respected her enough to keep her secret. His unexpected friendship had been a welcome blessing. Even so, she considered where her heart's path would eventually take her.

She straightened. Her shoulders tensed, and she rolled them once to relax. The more she liked him, the more difficult it would be for her to leave if she won the art contest.

At the same time, in her heart, her desire to come through with her life's dream tugged at her heartstrings. It was more than that, though. She would never rest until she was free to explore who she was. To taste other cultures. Meet people from different backgrounds.

Yet the last thing she wanted was to hurt or to disappoint Jesse. A soft sigh escaped her throat. She closed her eyes a moment. When she opened them, she tried to make sense of everything.

He hadn't said that he wanted to court her; at the same time, he'd told her she was the most special person he'd ever met. She'd also noted that his chest sometimes rose and fell too quickly when they were close.

She hadn't missed the vulnerable expression in his eyes. Most definitely, thinking this way was self-destructive. *Jesse's goals are very simple and clear. So are mine.*

He wants everything good in life. To buy a farm, marry, and to raise an Amish family in Christ's name. Nothing out of the ordinary. But he knows who he is. I feel divided inside. Part of me is Amish, but my other half is unknown.

God has a purpose for my talent. To use it for Him. I believe He wants me to share what gets my heart beating. My passion. So others can experience such joy.

As she traced her finger over the cross, his soft voice filled her thoughts. *Anna, you're the most special person I've ever met.* Jesse's words warmed her heart like a soft, cotton blanket on a winter's night. That he believed this and felt this about her was so overwhelming, she shivered.

The familiar scent of freshly mowed grass floated in through her screens. Even though people in her church were loving and kind, she'd never felt as if she were one of them. The main reason stemmed from hearing her teacher's hurtful comment about Anna not being a true Amish.

Of course, she'd never moped about it or let it anger her; it was just a fact, and such remarks about her skin color over the years had produced that sentiment. When she got down to it, she'd only heard the painful gossip from two women: Mrs. Graber and her teacher's Aunt Sarah.

Secondly, she'd always guessed that since her parents couldn't bear their own children, she was their backup plan. Of course she loved them, and they loved her. But if they'd produced their own, would she be a King? She shook her head.

She'd give anything to find out why her mamma had given her away. A lone tear slipped down her cheek. And an all-too-familiar loneliness swept up her arms and landed in her shoulders.

Do I have sisters and brothers? If mamma didn't want me, why didn't my biological father raise me? He didn't want me either?

She stopped a tear and lifted her chin with newfound confidence. Because now, Jesse thought of her as extremely unique and special. *His words mean everything to me.*

Again, her gaze landed on her hope chest lid, and her thoughts automatically drifted to the late Sam Beachy. Automatically, the corners of her lips pulled upward.

She knew quite a bit about the old hope chest maker who had gone to the Lord at over one hundred years of age. But her stronger sense of curiosity prompted her to wonder what thoughts had passed through his mind as he'd sketched beautiful lids.

Anna firmly believed that her sketches conveyed her own interpretation of life. That when people observe art, each individual views it in a different way, depending on how they were raised and how they looked at the world.

As she took in the detail of the rugged cross in Old Sam's hope chest lid, she couldn't help but note the great detail. The different dimensions.

And apparently, when Sam Beachy imagined, he'd had the keen ability to capture every small detail. *If each person could glimpse that much detail in small things that happened every day, we'd have more appreciation of God's blessings to us.*

She took her pencil between her fingers and added to the sketch she'd done of Jesse's visage. With great concentration, she added a more serious expression to his eyes. With thoughtful care, she detailed the flecks on his pupils as she remembered them when he'd told her how special she was. The gentle curve of his mouth.

She stopped to adjust her hips to a more comfortable

position and balanced the pad on her lap. Studying what she'd started, she added long, dark lashes and thick brows that rested above a set of serious dark eyes. She added to his thick head of hair that covered part of his forehead.

As she touched up her work, she pressed her lips together in a straight line and recalled their most recent conversation about the contest she would soon enter. To her surprise, he hadn't tried to sway her against doing it. On the contrary, he said he prayed for her to win.

She stretched her legs, leaned back, and closed her eyes. In front of her, she pressed her palms together and spoke in a quiet, pensive tone. "Dear Lord, please hear my prayer. You know how much I respect and admire my family and this community. At the same time, You must understand my desire to be loved and accepted as the unique person I am. When You created me, I believe You saw me as a masterpiece. Unfortunately, not everyone appreciates that I'm different. But in my heart, I don't want to be like everyone else. I wish so much to be accepted for who I am, not who others believe I should be. Please continue to give me the courage to pursue my dream. Dear God, I know You brought me here for a purpose. Please guide and direct me down the path You created just for me, and please protect my parents from unfair talk that will inadvertently come about if You bless me with a contest win. Amen."

She swallowed. And smiled with relief. As long as she communicated with her Lord and Savior, He would protect her. For years, she'd thought about a departure from the Amish community. If she followed through with her plan, she'd definitely need a cell phone. She wasn't sure how to go about getting one under her name. But she'd cross that bridge when and if she came to it.

She wished she could speak openly about this to Mary Conrad. Anna could trust her. But she was afraid to involve her for fear that her friend would eventually suffer. She trusted Jesse more than anyone. But he'd become involved by accident, and getting him more involved than he already was . . .

She gave a decisive shake of her head, then stood and pulled her Bible from the shelf behind her bed. In times of need, she could always find a scripture to encourage her. To help her to realize her self-worth.

She turned to Psalms 107:1 and read out loud, "'Oh give thanks to the Lord, for He is good, for His steadfast love endures forever.'"

Her shoulders relaxed as she held the Bible on her lap. She swallowed an emotional knot. Joyful tears blurred her vision. As she gazed at the cross on her hope chest, she'd never felt as loved as she did at that very moment. At peace. Because her Savior's love for her would last forever.

Jesse couldn't stop thinking about the farmland that would soon be up for sale. The pulse on his wrist danced to an excited beat at the Kings' the following morning.

Jesse spotted Anna in the garden. Quick steps took him from the barn to where she was, while waving a friendly hand in greeting. As he made his way toward her, the image of her in William Conrad's pond flickered in his mind. He grinned, sure it was a sight he'd never forget.

Anna didn't look his way. That was all right, because he could take advantage of the opportunity to watch her. He'd always been taught to focus on a person's heart rather than how they looked. But he couldn't help liking the way Anna looked. He knew how long her jet-black hair was, thanks to her accident in the storm. And the incident at the Conrads'.

Her straight white teeth were pretty when she smiled. She wore no mascara, yet her long, black lashes were thick. Her lips had color, even though she didn't use lipstick.

And her strong determination . . . he smiled a little before the corners of his lips fell a notch. He found it ironic that what he loved most about her could be the very reason he'd soon have to let her go. But did he have her? *No. So I guess I wouldn't really be letting her go.*

He watched as she bent to drop something into her wicker basket before straightening. As he continued to the garden, he took in the pleasant scene in front of him, which was all too familiar. Chickens plucked at the ground. One goat chased another, and they butted heads in play. The empty buggy. Farms all around.

The rich green grass prompted a streak of happiness inside his chest. To him, everything about the country epitomized beauty. The smells. The plants, the crops, the livestock grazing. There was nothing like it. And it was something humans didn't have the ability to create. These gifts were God-given.

Finally, she noticed him and offered a wave. Closer, he could hear the softness of her voice. "Jesse, what a lovely day it is."

At the garden, he stopped, taking in the plant-filled plot of land. He was sure that Paul had planted straight rows with plenty of room in between vegetables, but the plants were so full that it was difficult to see the spaces between them.

Anna picked up her wicker basket and happily displayed it in front of her. "*Daed*'s plants are doing so well, I'm going to have to get another basket."

When she stepped toward him, he waved a hand to stop her. "That's where I can help," he responded with a smile. "Where do you keep them?"

She gave a quick shake of her head. In a polite tone, she replied, "That's not necessary, Jesse. You do so much for us. Without you, *Daed* wouldn't have had time to raise alfalfa this year."

He lifted a hand. "I insist." He winked.

She grinned. "Okay, then. They're on the back porch." Then she quickly added, "On top of the cabinet." Uncertainty edged her voice as she went on. "There's no need for you to get another one, Jesse. I should have known I'd need more room."

"I'm happy to help." He turned, and as he did so, he motioned to her basket, which was filled to the top. "Hand it to me and I'll leave it on the porch."

"Thanks." She did as instructed, and he took the basket with both hands, kept it close to his chest, and finally lowered it to his waist while exiting the garden. The house was a good distance away.

He enjoyed helping others. But while he considered Anna, he acknowledged that he especially liked helping *her*. Since his first day of working for Paul and Naomi . . . the very day he'd carried Anna into the barn, he'd known how much he enjoyed making her happy.

Perhaps it was because she was his boss's daughter. He wasn't just working for Paul; in the entire scheme of things, he was employed by the King family, which included Anna.

He frowned and stepped to the side to avoid a dip in the earth. As he approached the small back porch, he arched a skeptical brow. *That's logical. But is that all there is to it? Is that the only reason I enjoy making Anna happy?*

He took in two large terra-cotta holders that held eye-catching hot-pink geraniums on both sides of the two steps at the back porch.

On the narrow dirt path, a light scent floated through the air, and he breathed in the pleasant aroma of flowers. A bed of deep red geraniums occupied a small area to the right.

He laid the vegetables on the bottom step while he opened the screened door. It creaked. He held it open with his foot while he bent to retrieve the basket.

Inside, he was careful to place the vegetables on top of the cabinet and gently pushed it back far enough from the edge. It didn't take long to select the right empty basket, and swift steps took him back to the garden where Anna continued to pick produce. He eyed the pile of red at the edge of the garden and nodded his approval.

"Those are mighty fine-lookin' tomatoes."

Anna reached for the basket he handed to her. She proceeded to place it next to the pile on the ground. As she began filling the new container, Jesse knelt beside her and did the same.

Squatting, Anna turned and reached for a tomato close to Jesse's knee. As she tried for it, she lost her balance and began to fall forward. Quick to react, Jesse leaned toward her just in time to prevent her hands from meeting the dirt.

He caught her and pulled her closer. He realized, of course, that their accidental embrace wasn't proper; he was a single Amish male and she a single Amish female. Yet, for some reason, he didn't let her go.

Several moments later, with great reluctance, he found his voice and gently released his hold on her. The moment he'd held her hadn't lasted long; still, he recognized that something about it had felt comfortable. Right.

Maybe it was the way her navy dress and white apron smelled of tomato vines. Or perhaps it was her soft hands that had wrapped around his shoulders when he'd saved her from the fall.

The scent of her hair smelled of fresh peaches. Even though most of it was tucked under her covering, several unruly strands had escaped. But to his dismay, there was something nice about the way they helped to frame her flushed cheeks.

Embarrassed at their physical closeness and especially his thoughts, he struggled for the right words. As their gazes continued to lock, he finally found his voice. In a soft pitch that was barely more than a whisper, he started. "Anna, I'm sorry I touched you . . . Please forgive me. All I meant to do was to stop you from landing facedown in the dirt."

A short silence ensued until, to his surprise, she laughed. The sound was so innocent. But as she spoke, he glimpsed her fingers and noted that they were shaking as she plucked each tomato from the pile on the soil, one at a time, and placed them in the basket. And when she talked, her voice sounded out of breath. Her cheeks were flushed, taking on a rosy appearance.

"There's absolutely nothing to be sorry about, Jesse. No need for an apology. What you did was common courtesy. In fact, thank you for saving me from what could have been an embarrassing situation."

After getting her breath, she went on. "It's ridiculous to think you did something wrong." She lifted a challenging brow. "I'm sure you wouldn't enjoy seeing me with dirt all over my face." She smiled widely. "And dirt has never been on my food list."

Together, they laughed. Letting out a satisfied breath, she lifted her palms to the sky in a helpless gesture. "And I'm even more certain I wouldn't want you to see me fall face-first into the ground."

As she talked, a breeze caressed the back of Jesse's neck. While it did so, more jet-black strands broke free from her *kapp*. To his dismay, he found it impossible to look away from the beautiful flush in her cheeks and the wavy black hair that matched her dark brows.

To his surprise, Anna lowered the pitch of her voice to a serious tone. "Jesse, if you want the truth, I feel special when you're around." She smiled shyly. "And I love being with you."

He absorbed her words, unsure of how to respond. So he jumped to his feet and stepped to the plant nearest him to retrieve the bright red vegetable that was ready to be picked. While his back was to Anna, he took in the horses and cattle grazing in the pasture.

A welcome sense of calm came over him as he decided to move to a different subject. The contest entered his mind. "I meant to ask you, how's your entry coming along?"

The question seemed to ease her. The flecks on her pupils stopped dancing. Her shoulders relaxed.

"I guess you could say I'm getting closer." She crossed her hands over her chest and closed her eyes in what appeared to be a wistful moment. "But it will get there. I have faith."

She expelled a frustrated breath and offered a shake of her head. "Jesse, it's hard to have a dream and not be able to share it with anyone. You don't know how happy I am that you've become a part of it."

He lifted his chin a notch. "Really?"

A surprised expression flickered across her face, and she responded in a soft, unsure voice. "Of course."

Why did I ask that?

"I want to reciprocate. Really, I do. You've done so much for me in such a short time." She looked away a moment while she started a running list. "Getting me inside the barn during the storm, pulling me out of Conrads' pond, listening to me ramble on about my art and my uncertain future."

"Your future doesn't have to be uncertain," he corrected. As their gazes locked, she parted her lips. At that moment, he knew he was in love with her.

"How can you say that?"

He swallowed, realizing that he wanted her to know just how strongly he felt about her. And how losing her would break his heart.

"Anna, you know what you said a while ago? That you love to be with me?"

Her eyes widened as she offered an eager nod.

"Well, I feel the same around you. But if you want the truth, I'm hesitant at living here . . ." He gestured with his hands. "Without you." His voice cracked with emotion. "Because you've become so special to me."

He went on as their gazes locked. He told her about the farm that would soon be going up for sale.

"I really hope I can buy it."

"Oh, Jesse, that would be wonderful! I will say special prayers that you get it!"

After a pause, he lowered his voice. "No matter what you do, Anna, I'm certain about the two things I want."

"To buy a farm." She hesitated before narrowing her brows. "But what's the other?"

"A future with you."

The following morning, small, gurgling sounds came from Pebble Creek as Anna sat on the small, dark blue blanket she'd knit from beautiful balls of yarn given to her last Christmas. Birds chirped, and a fly buzzed behind her.

She crossed her legs beneath her and eyed the partly finished canvas work in front of her. But as she did so, visions of Jesse floated through her head until she closed her eyes.

He was making it more difficult for her to focus on her dream. Everything about him . . . his warm touch, the beautiful color of his eyes, his soft voice, his reassurances . . . He stopped her thoughts.

And he wanted to be with her. At the same time, she had been quick to note that there had been no mention of love. And she did love him. But she knew from experience that she couldn't have everything in life that she wanted. This was one of those times. Because Jesse conflicted with her dream.

I've got to do this. She swallowed and focused on the canvas. *Here I am again. Trying to get into the head of the woman who isn't Amish. It's starting to be frustrating.*

As she assessed the drawing, she lifted a curious, uncertain brow. In the near distance, wildflowers on both sides of Pebble Creek bent with the light summer breeze.

Where the creek was most shallow, pebbles peeked up out of the water. The water was so clear, it was easy to see them. From where she sat, she had a bird's-eye view of the well-known hill. For years, it had been talked about because it was the only hill in the area. And pretty much everyone knew the story of Levi and Annie Miller carrying stones all the way to the top to sit on.

Anna smiled a little as she envisioned a young girl and a young boy falling in love at Pebble Creek. But they weren't the only ones connected with the hill. Rumor had it that something had happened between Old Sam's great-niece, Jessica, and Annie and Levi's son, Eli, too. They were courting and planned to marry soon.

Drawing in a determined breath, she focused on her

contest entry. As she studied it, she arched a brow. One woman torn between two lifestyles.

The images mirrored her. Because of that, Anna figured it should be easy to make the differences clear. After all, it was Anna King, and who could better capture that person than her?

She pressed her lips together and tried to envision the real differences. While she sat very still, she took in spread-out two-story country homes and fields of tall corn, beans, and alfalfa.

She breathed in the familiar scent of manure, acknowledging that many would wrinkle their noses at it. However, Anna would much prefer using nature on crops over man-made fragrances.

That was one of the things she loved about her Amish community. For the most part, they were for going the natural route with what God had given them. There were many other things about the faith that she appreciated, too.

She'd always been a horse and buggy fan. For some reason, she'd never been drawn to automobiles. And as far as the air-conditioning that the *Englisch* used? She lifted a skeptical brow. She didn't like cold air on her skin and much preferred the outdoor air that came in through the window screens.

At the same time, there were things she didn't care for. Like the way Mrs. Graber had treated her growing up. Of course, that was just one person. Two, really. Mrs. Graber and her aunt. To be fair, they certainly didn't represent everyone in their community.

There had been many times when Anna had yearned to voice her thoughts, but inside, she'd known that some within her church wouldn't have approved. If she had grown up in the *Englisch* community, would things have been different?

She wasn't certain, but she knew plenty of *Englischers* in town, and it seemed as though they were more outspoken than the Amish. Except for Mary Conrad. And Annie Miller. The thought of two of her favorite women pulled the corners of her lips up.

What Anna was sure of was that there was no perfect faith. Of course, she didn't expect perfection in every area from the Amish. But it was difficult to compare the Amish to the *Englisch* because she had no actual experience as an *Englischer*.

While she stared at the pencil sketches of both faces, she whispered, "Which one is Anna King?" For a moment, she paused and pressed her lips together thoughtfully and pondered the serious question.

Right now, the answer was unknown. But she believed that finding the truth was within her power. Of course, it wouldn't be easy. Unfortunately, the only way was to step outside the tightly knit Amish community and find out. *Rumspringa* hadn't offered her enough opportunity or enough time.

Swallowing an emotional knot, she tucked a strand of hair back under her *kapp* and frowned. While the gentle breeze loosened more hair from her covering, she didn't bother to restrain them. She enjoyed the light caress on the back of her neck.

Moments later, she acknowledged that her real concern wasn't about where her life would take her after the contest. Or if she won or if she lost. She would leave that to the Lord. What did bother her was the fear of disappointing her parents.

Still, even that couldn't stop her from yearning for a broader view of life. A world without rules for what you could do and what you could wear. A feeling of guilt washed over her, and she acknowledged that despite the strictness, Anna's mind was still free to think independently. And she did. Fortunately, her mind was out-of-bounds for rules. It was a place that no one could see or control.

She focused her attention on the unfinished art and narrowed her brows. *Okay, I'm not* Englisch, *so right now, I must use my imagination to get to know the person I'd be today had I not been raised Amish.*

For several heartbeats, she squeezed her eyes shut and tried with everything she had to see herself in that manner. Finally, she opened her lids and began moving her pencil back and forth. She smiled a little while the speed of her heart picked up to an excited pace.

As she sketched, she pondered the limitless opportunities. She'd definitely wear her hair down. She drew strands that fell over her shoulders. Suddenly, an idea struck her, and she began moving her pencil quickly for fear of losing her thought.

She'd been to an *Englisch* wedding and had been captivated by a black dress worn by one of the women. It was sleeveless. As she drew herself, showing her uncovered neck and above her breasts, she quickly shook her head and began erasing what she'd put on paper. Even if she became *Englisch*, her strict Amish upbringing wouldn't allow her to wear something so revealing.

How about blue jeans and a casual top? She pictured herself in jeans and sketched. As she did so, she relaxed.

She began making light strokes to create a comfortable top that seemed to say that she enjoyed the outdoors. Before long, she had fully clothed the woman on the sketch pad.

As she eyed her work, she thought of her birth mother and wondered how she'd dressed. If she'd liked being outside. What she'd eaten. If she'd traveled.

The more Anna considered everything she didn't know, she longed desperately to meet her biological mamma. *What did you do in your spare time? How old were you when you delivered me? Were you married? Divorced?*

A sadness swept over Anna, and she quickly forced herself to stay positive. As she lifted her chin a notch, the most potent question of all swept into her head and stayed there. *Why did you give me away?*

Anna studied her contest entry and pressed her lips together in a frown. *I'm closer. But to win, my entry has to be the best.*

She sat up straighter and forced a hopeful smile while she looked at her hope chest from the corner of her eye.

The thought of Old Sam and his beautiful work immediately inspired an excited tingle that swept up her arms. Her shoulders relaxed. So did the speed of the pulse in her wrist.

Even though Old Sam Beachy was no longer with them, she could recall the lines of his weathered face. He'd once joked that every wrinkle represented something significant. The births and deaths of his sons.

Good times. Bad times. That those lines had been earned and that he wouldn't give them up for the world.

Even though he'd never complained, his life hadn't been easy, having lost his sons and his beloved wife. Still, he'd offered tremendous hope and wisdom to everyone with whom he'd come into contact.

As the bright sun caressed the back of her neck, Anna touched the miniature hope chest that contained her most special drawings. She'd much rather place them on the walls of her bedroom, where she could see them day and night, but for now, her sketches remained her secret passion. With one exception, of course. Jesse.

In the distance, two horse-pulled buggies headed south on the blacktop. Houses dotted the spread-out landscape. As she smiled a little, a monarch butterfly floated gracefully near her. A bumblebee hovered over white clover. The air was scented with the familiar aroma of livestock and manure.

An idea sparked inside her, and she leaned forward to capture what she could while the image was fresh in her mind. She continued detailing herself on paper, as people within her church knew her.

In her *kapp*, long dress, and apron. With thick, jet-black hair pulled back and tucked neatly under her covering. The expression on her face was of a combination of humility and kindness. Of secrets.

She pressed her lips together thoughtfully as she moved the pencil back and forth with swift, light motions. A fly buzzed in front of her nose, and she shooed it away with her hand.

It left, but returned quickly, so she repeated her action. The brightness disappeared while the sun

Chapter Seven

That evening, in the Kings' barn, Jesse glimpsed the setting sun in the west through the large, open doors. Dusk was setting in, and the cicadas made their nightly sounds.

Nearby, a goat played with a white rag. On appearance, it seemed that all was normal and calm. Jesse pulled the tab on the bag of oats and carefully slid it across the top to open the seams.

He lifted the grain bag and carefully dumped its contents into the feed containers. The troughs were full.

He considered the docile ambience in which he worked and the turmoil that cluttered his head. He and Anna had ended their last conversation with both wanting to fulfill God's plan for them.

While he worked, he considered the deep conversation they'd shared that very afternoon. While he breathed in the familiar, calming smells around him, to his dismay, he couldn't rid her from his mind.

He knew it was better, safer, for him not to become involved with Anna and what she had planned. After all, her uncertain path might very well lead her right out of the Amish world. A place where he would never go.

He closed his eyes and prayed. "Dear God, Anna needs You. Please guide her to make the right choices and make Your plan clear to her. Amen."

While he emptied more feed into the large tanks, dust whirled and lingered in a fog a few seconds before evaporating like steam from a teakettle.

Automatically, he compared his life's goals with Anna's. Although they seemed drastically different, in the end, really, they yearned for the same things. And that was to lead the lives God had intended for them. But when would God convey which road He wanted her to take?

Naomi King's soft voice prompted him to turn toward the open doors where she stood, waving a hand in greeting. She smiled. "Supper's 'bout ready, Jesse. Won't you stay and join us?"

Before he could answer, she cut in. "I've got a delicious pot roast. With potatoes and carrots. Sure does smell good."

Jesse's stomach growled. Lunch had been several hours ago. The offer tempted him until he answered with an eager nod. He dipped his head and raised the pitch of his voice to make sure she heard him. "Now that's an offer I surely can't say no to. Thank you, Naomi."

She waved an inviting hand. "Come on in."

"*Ich komme*. Just give me a few moments to clean this up."

Jesse finished his task, stepped inside, and, after greeting Paul and Anna, Naomi motioned to the hall bathroom where Jesse proceeded to wash up. When he joined them at the table, Paul pulled out a chair for him. While Jesse thanked him, he darted a smile at Anna from the opposite side.

Paul blessed the food. "Amen." Utensils clinked as they helped themselves to the roast and vegetables that were passed around the table. Jesse watched Anna dish a large helping of potatoes onto her plate.

He noticed that Paul and Naomi were regarding him with curiosity.

"Thanks for having me to dinner." He grinned. "This is the best perk of working here."

Ice clinked against glasses and utensils met plates. In the background, the fan put out a low whistle. After a drink of water, Jesse directed his attention to Anna's mother. "Are things about to wrap up at the bakery?"

Paul sipped black coffee and offered a nod while he returned his cup to the coaster. He glanced at his plate before cutting a chunk of roast into pieces, appearing only half-interested in what he was saying. "We can see the end. Jesse, we're so glad you're helpin' us out."

Jesse could feel the corners of his lips lift. "It's a win-win for all of us."

Naomi chimed in. "Jesse you don't know what a huge relief it is to have your help this summer. We're so thankful." She paused to cut a carrot. "You're a godsend."

After Jesse cut his carrot into bites, too, he looked up. "I'm the one who should thank you." He swallowed before continuing. "From the time I was little, I've dreamed of owning a farm." He glanced across the table at Anna. "In fact, I've been talking to Anna about it. And also about the Norris farm coming up for sale." He smiled. "I hope to buy it."

When the Kings looked at their daughter, Anna

quickly nodded in agreement. Paul ran his hand over his chin and offered an encouraging nod. "I understand where you're comin' from, *sohn*. That sure would be a nice farm for you. When I was young, I wanted the same thing. Ain't nothin' like growing your own food and bringin' it to the table. But sometimes . . ." He cleared his throat. "Our calling ain't what we dreamed of."

He offered a dismissive shrug. "I'm not complainin' by any means. As you know, the bakery is a family business, and that's where God needs me." After a slight pause, he added, "Even if my brother's family runs it."

Jesse set his drink down on a coaster. "I wish the price of farmland wasn't so steep." Ice cubes clinked against his glass.

Naomi nodded in agreement. She met Jesse's gaze across the table. "Over the years, big changes have affected we Amish folk." Several heartbeats later, she went on. "Forty, fifty years ago, most of us farmed. We're thankful for our small farm. But unfortunately, land prices have made it almost impossible for many of us to do that now. So, a number of us have learned other trades."

She paused to scoop potatoes onto her spoon. "When you think about it, half of our church is out doing regular jobs like the *Englisch*. Welding. Machine work."

"It's true. Fortunately," Paul cut in, "the bakery provides for our large family."

"That's because of those delicious cinnamon rolls you bake," Jesse said with a wry grin. After a slight pause, Jesse lowered the pitch of his voice and edged it with curiosity. "I never was convinced that what I heard . . ."

Everyone looked at him to go on.

"About the recipe not being in writing." His fork clinked against the glass plate as he bit into mashed potatoes. "Is that really true?"

Paul offered a nod. "*Jah*. The recipe's strictly by memory. Great-Grandma believed that was the only way to ensure the secret didn't get out. And amazingly, it hasn't." After a short pause, he added, "As far as we know anyway."

"It's a miracle it stayed a secret." Jesse winked at Anna. "You must have a clan of good secret keepers."

As they ate, Jesse considered a different secret. Anna's. He would continue to pray about her and what to advise her to do. As he chatted with her parents, he became even more convinced that what she had planned would send her wonderful, kind parents into shock, at best.

She was their only child. There would be no spares to stay home and help with chores. Still, Jesse wasn't sure if Anna should or shouldn't pursue her dream; that was something that only the Heavenly Father would know. Jesse wasn't about to try to make a call that was God's and God's alone.

The bad thing was, Anna and God weren't the only people involved in her plan. He eyed Paul King. Then Naomi. Two wonderful church members.

Automatically, he wondered how Anna's folks would react if they became privy to their daughter's plan. Of course, he'd given Anna his word that he wouldn't say anything. *Maemm* had always stressed minding one's own business. And although Jesse had concerns about Anna, and that she might leave the community, he would keep it to himself.

But when he glanced across the table and took in the strained expression on Anna's face, he couldn't help but wonder how Naomi and Paul would react if they knew. An ache pinched his chest at the realization that if Anna did win the contest, the month of August would bring huge challenges. Not only for her, but for her family. For the entire church.

So much is at stake because of one contest. Surely God has a role for me. Is it to make sure she stays?

Later that evening, steam rose from two pressure cookers in Anna's kitchen. A permanent fog hovered above the stove top, and she couldn't see past the window. She stepped back a moment to enjoy the air from the battery fan behind her, bending so it hit her face. A small sigh of satisfaction escaped her throat as she enjoyed the light breeze. Satisfaction for what she was doing. As she listened to the water boil, she considered her own special process of canning. Out of all of the chores she accomplished on the farm, this was her very favorite.

Daed had planted two extra rows of the red tomatoes just for Anna. Continuing to enjoy the fan's caress, she smiled a little while contemplating the delicious soup and chili she'd make with them during the winter months.

While the thin fan blades whistled, she arched her

brow. She'd canned so many years, she knew what tricks worked best. In fact, she had it down so every glass jar popped.

First, she washed each tomato, cut out their stems, boiled them just enough to easily remove the skins, and placed the cored vegetables into the pressure cookers with water so that the pot was three quarters full.

Next, she utilized a large metal colander to drain them while the juice dripped into a large white container. After that, she ran a clean, hot dish cloth over the rims of the glass quart containers, stuck them in neat rows inside a baking pan, and added an inch of boiling hot water, which she kept on the two free burners.

As soon as the juice-filled quarts were boiling hot, she ran a clean towel over the rims and carefully added a metal lid to each. One by one, she transferred each filled jar to the corner of the kitchen and waited for the lids to pop.

She stood, made her way back to the countertop that was cluttered with lids and cloths, and proceeded with her task. As she did so, this evening's dinner conversation floated in and out of her thoughts.

In the background, lids popped to an uneven beat. Each time one sounded, she recorded it on a pad of paper. *Maemm* stepped into the room and laid an affectionate hand on Anna's shoulder. "I love you, Anna."

Anna took a moment to face the kind, loving woman who'd so unselfishly taken her in years ago. "Love you, too, *Maemm*." For a moment, Anna wasn't sure what else to say.

Of course she knew her mother loved her; it was

something she'd never doubted. At the same time, Anna wasn't used to hearing those precious words. Her heart warmed, and she put down the tomato she was holding and hugged her mother tightly.

"*Denki.*"

For long moments, Anna relished the rush of warmth that penetrated her body. A happy, satisfied shiver swept up Anna's arms and settled comfortably in her shoulders. "*Maemm*, you don't know how much I needed to hear that."

Her mother held her at arm's length and locked gazes with her. Anna was quick to note the expression of surprise that flickered in her eyes.

"You surely don't doubt it, do you?"

Anna answered with a soft "No." She continued staring at her mother in a desperate need to talk. As if reading her mind, *Maemm* motioned to the table, and Anna gave the stove a quick check before lifting her chin with newfound confidence. "I'm at a good spot to take a break."

In the dining room, she sat opposite her *maemm*, who leaned forward to gently take her fingers and give them an affectionate squeeze.

Anna swallowed the emotional knot in her throat, which had become uncomfortable.

"Honey, sometimes we Amish work so hard . . . and such long hours . . ." She closed her eyes while a sigh escaped her. "I'm afraid we forget to share our love with those who mean the most to us."

Anna looked down at her sturdy black shoes while

she considered the statement, made with such honesty and sincerity.

Naomi drew in a sigh before folding her arms over her lap. Several heartbeats later, she said, "Anna, your *daed* and I have been busier than we'd like." She raised a dismissive hand and softened her voice. "I certainly don't mean to sound ungrateful. I'd never do that when God has blessed us with all this." With a warm smile, she extended her arms and motioned. "There's so much to be grateful for. But don't doubt that even though we don't spend much time with you, we don't love you any less."

Anna met her gaze while the softly said words warmed her heart. Anna leaned forward and pressed her palms against her thighs.

"I've got a lot on my mind. And I've never told you this, but I'm so appreciative that you and *Daed* took me in. I can't imagine being in a more loving family."

The sound of juice coming to a boil reminded Anna of her task. She jumped up to remove the tall cooker from the burner. But her mother's words would forever stay in Anna's heart. She ached to talk to her mother about the contest. She frowned because she couldn't.

As she rescued the juice before it boiled over the top of the cooker, steam filled the area in front of her. But Anna was more focused on her mother's admission than the empty quart jars waiting to be filled. Because the timing of her admission couldn't have been better.

The following noon, the mid-August sun caressed Anna's neck as she sat on the ground near Pebble Creek and lifted a scrutinizing brow at the work on her easel. As she tried to hone the facial features of the Amish woman, she recalled her *maemm*'s unexpected revelation and smiled a little. Hearing that much-needed reassurance had prompted Anna's chin to lift with just enough confidence to capture a certain glow in the woman's cheeks.

To Anna's pleasant surprise, that very glow sparked a new connection with the woman on the paper. Anna pressed her lips together, yearning to imagine what was inside the *Englisch* Anna on the sketch pad.

There were many things, artistically, that Anna could do to reveal what went on inside that person's heart and mind. Usually, these pencil strokes came naturally to her. But this particular project was proving to be her greatest challenge. In order to know what was inside this particular person, it was necessary for Anna to find out who she was, personally, if she had been raised outside the Amish faith. And she wasn't sure that was possible.

As much as she tried, she could only create what she knew on the paper. And because of the circumstances of her birth, there was a lot Anna hadn't learned about herself.

I long to be more. But I only know half of me. I'm fully aware of the woman Anna King. But that's because of the way I've been raised. But if my birth mamma had raised me, I would surely look at the world with a different pair of eyes. Because I would have had a different upbringing. Other circumstances. So how can I ever know the other woman in the picture without having walked in her shoes?

What do I feel? Who am I, really, and what do I stand for? Part of me is Amish. At the same time, my other half's a mystery. If my birth mamma had raised me, would I even believe in God? What would I want out of life if my last name had been Rodriguez or Garcia instead of King?

As she tried to read more into her sketched woman, the sound of light footsteps made Anna turn. Jesse smiled a little and lifted his hand in greeting. In front of him, he held a brown paper bag. "Is it okay if I join you?" he asked as he made himself comfortable on the ground.

She was quick to nod. She looked up at him and smiled. "*Jah.* I'm glad you're here." She acknowledged how much she had to do and how little time there was to accomplish it. Still, she savored every moment she had with Jesse.

"Any word on the farm?"

"Not yet. We're still waiting for it to go up for sale."

As she took in his appearance, she acknowledged that the Anna on paper wasn't the only person she wanted to know. She yearned to learn more about Jesse, too. Since he'd become a part of her life, she'd come to realize just how very special he was. And she cherished his advice. Even though he was steadfast in his goals, uncertainty loomed in front of him, too.

When the bright sunlight landed on his irises, his eyes took on a different color. Perplexed by the beauty of those soft blue hues, she continued to study him with interest. For some reason, she couldn't look away.

And neither did he. As their gazes locked, his facial muscles relaxed. So did his shoulders. And, amazingly, his visage provided her a certain reassurance she'd never experienced before. She took a small breath and let it out.

He finally smiled a little and offered a satisfied nod. "I'm glad to be with you, too."

With one swift motion, she took her pad with both hands and turned it so he could view her work. "What do you think?"

As he observed the sketch, she continued to regard him, noting every detail about him, from the tiny creases that outlined his eyes to the way he tilted his head and narrowed his dark brows.

She leaned forward to turn her sketch pad so he could better glimpse it. A long silence ensued while she watched him. Finally, when he didn't say anything, her pulse picked up to a nervous speed, and she sat up a little straighter.

It was at that point that she acknowledged how very important his opinion was. When she lowered the pitch of her voice, her words barely made it out of her mouth. "Jesse?"

As he continued eyeing the paper in front of him, she went on. "The contest requires a theme, and to sketch a picture that depicts that theme."

Finally, he looked at her, and the corners of his lips lifted into an approving smile. He nodded. "I'm no expert at this and I won't pretend to be, but if you want my honest opinion?"

She offered a quick, eager nod.

"The one woman is definitely Amish." He paused and narrowed his brows. "And the *Englisch* . . ." He shrugged. "I don't want to discourage you, but there's really nothing that makes her different from the Amish girl."

His comment stopped her. As she contemplated his honesty, she finally admitted that she agreed. "One more question."

Before giving him a chance to respond, she went on. "When you look at this . . ." She waved her right hand to the sketch. "Can you guess the theme?"

He leaned closer and furrowed his brows. As he did so, the sun slipped underneath a cloud, and Anna enjoyed the light, comforting breeze that caressed the back of her neck. When the sun reappeared, she blinked to adjust to the sudden bright light.

Finally, Jesse softened the pitch of his voice. "It's just a guess, but I'd say you're trying to depict Amish life versus English? And the conflict is inside the woman?"

The corners of Anna's lips lifted into a huge grin. "*Jah.*" A new excitement floated through her chest. "I'm relieved that at least that part's obvious."

The expression on his visage turned serious. So did the pitch of his voice as he lowered it. "The woman is you, Anna. And this is your conflict, isn't it?"

His words hit her with such a ferocity, she stayed very still while she considered what he'd said. She swallowed an uncomfortable knot in her throat. When she realized he awaited confirmation, she offered a small nod.

"*Jah.* This picture . . ." She nodded to the pencil drawing. "It's much more than a contest entry." She paused. "It's me. In real life, it's me, trying to find myself." Finally, emotion took her over, and her voice shook. "Jesse, I'm torn. Because I'm sure that if my birth mother had raised me, I wouldn't be who I am today."

When he didn't respond, she went on. "I want to be who God intended me to be." She gave a gentle shrug of her shoulders, and her voice softened. "But how can I if I don't know her?"

Offering the picture another glance, he got comfortable on the ground next to her and pulled a sandwich from his paper bag. As he removed the cellophane wrapping, he looked at her. "Would you like half?"

She lifted a hand. "No, thanks, but that's sweet of you to offer."

She changed the subject. "Jesse, I'm getting anxious about this contest, but what I'm afraid of even more is word getting out that I'm entering it. The last thing I want is for talk to start that I'm leaving our tightly knit community. Or my *eltern* suffering because of me."

He put his right hand over his heart and straightened his broad shoulders. "Like I said, Anna, my word's *gut*. I'm a secret keeper." An amused grin curved the corners of his lips. "Remember . . ." He gave a lazy smile.

"What?"

He lowered his lashes and his voice. "I never told on you in school. When you were drawing during math."

The statement prompted her to laugh. "I don't know what I would've done if I couldn't have drawn during that class. It was hard to focus when all I wanted to do was to sketch."

He lifted a challenging brow. "You really don't like math, do you?"

She shook her head. "Jesse, how will math benefit me?"

Before he could respond, she continued. "I understand why I need to know how to add, subtract, and multiply. I mean, when you go to the grocery store that comes in handy. But as far as the more complicated stuff . . ." She shrugged and leaned back to rest on her palms. "Unless I'm going to be an engineer, I don't think it will help." She pressed her lips together. "It would be much more beneficial for students to focus on English."

When he raised a skeptical brow, she went on, her tone taking on a more enthusiastic pitch. "Just think, Jesse. The English language is how you express your thoughts. If you're articulate, people will obviously better understand where you're coming from."

He looked at her to continue.

"When you interview for a job, you've got to convey why they should hire you."

"I see the point." He swallowed. A strange, unexplainable expression crossed his face before he looked down and pulled a bag of potato chips from his brown sack. She could hear them crunch in his mouth. "I want you to win, Anna."

"You do?"

He nodded. "But more importantly?"

She looked at him before locking gazes with the Amish woman on the paper.

"I will pray for you to learn who you really are.

And I'll be completely honest . . ." He swallowed an emotional knot. "I hope that, in the end, it will be the Amish woman."

She watched him drink from his water bottle.

"I think you're making this harder than it needs to be."

She shrugged. "If it were easy, I would know."

He shrugged. "Maybe. Maybe not."

"You've never had to deal with anything like this, have you?"

He was quick to respond with a certain shake of his head. "From a young age, I learned to appreciate the life I have." He smiled a little. "All I need to add, really, is a wife, a family, and a farm."

As she watched Jesse wad the cellophane into a ball and return it to the paper bag, she absorbed what he'd just told her. To Anna, his wants seemed so simple.

He raised a challenging brow. "Sounds easy, doesn't it?"

Her lips parted while she considered his unexpected question. She didn't intend to undermine the difficulty of achieving his life's goals; that was the last thing she wanted. At the same time, she was fully aware that he expected an honest response from her.

"It does."

"But is it really?"

She locked gazes with him, noticing the curious lines that edged his eyes.

"When you think about it, finding the spouse that God created just for you isn't easy." He hesitated while swatting away a fly. "And having a family?" He shrugged. "Again, that's all dependent on God. When you think about it, He creates the embryo. And develops it as it grows. When you get right down to it, a woman can do everything in her power to make a baby. Yet the health of the child and everything else are all up to Him."

She pressed her lips together thoughtfully and contemplated his words.

"And then . . ." he went on with a wave of his hand, "buying a farm. Nowadays, it's almost impossible."

She considered his statement before finally offering a nod of agreement. "*Jah*. Because none's for sale. Land usually stays in the family. But soon, you're going to be the new owner of the Norris farm."

Anna listened while he told her more about the farm and the house that went with it. As he spoke, she took quick note of the enthusiastic, hopeful lift of his voice. White flecks on his irises danced with joy. And as he went on about the couple who planned to move to Arizona, he pulled a dandelion from the ground and began playing with it.

As she watched and listened to him, Anna's spirit filled with a newfound joy. Here she was, hearing someone's dream that was about to come true. But that person wasn't just anyone. It was the man who'd rescued her in a storm. The man who knew about her own dream. And . . .

She swallowed an emotional knot as she realized something so significant, the truth nearly pulled it out of her breath. Her *daed*'s farmhand wasn't just another worker who'd suddenly entered her life. She let out a sigh.

Jesse Beiler was the one soul to whom Anna had confided her deepest, darkest secret. And, more importantly, he rooted for her to succeed. Even if it resulted in her becoming *Englisch*. Even though what she might want out of life was on a totally different path than his own.

"Jesse, there's something I want you to know."

He looked at her to continue.

Automatically, she leaned toward him and laid a gentle hand on his fingers. She was fully aware that touching him wasn't appropriate by her church's standards; at the same time, her need to do it was so strong, she couldn't pull away.

She could feel the strong pulse at his wrist. It beat to a fast pace. "Jesse, I want you to know that you're truly special to me."

Surprise flickered in his eyes. His pulse jumped against her finger. But as their eyes locked, she realized how very much she'd meant what she'd said. When she removed her fingers from his hand, she watched him. The expression on his face was unreadable.

Anna was still taking in the strength of her realization and her admission when he spoke in a low tone. "Anna, as you already know, you're very special to me, too."

He fidgeted with his hands. "In fact, ever since I carried you into the barn during the storm, my life has changed." A nervous laugh escaped him. "I've been trying to figure things out."

"And?"

"I'm not exactly sure. But . . ."

He looked at her to continue.

"It's important to me that you find what you're looking for. And I'll do whatever I can to help."

When she responded, her voice was so soft and filled with such gratitude, it was barely more than a whisper.

While she considered Jesse's goals and what he was up against, she used her most sympathetic tone. "You're right, Jesse. And what you're trying to do . . ." She lifted her shoulders. "It won't be easy. But there must be a way I can help."

Before he could respond, she considered her statement and the question that followed. "Surely our mutual support of each other will lead to us having our dreams."

Her statement made the corners of his lips lift a little with a combination of happiness and satisfaction.

"It means a lot to hear that, Anna. *Denki*."

"In fact, I pray for your life to be everything you want it to be."

After a thoughtful silence passed, he shifted on his hip, propped himself up on one elbow, and looked directly into her eyes. "I wish I could help you discover who you are."

She considered his statement. "I wonder if I'll really ever know."

"I think you will. But say strong prayers and look for signs."

"Signs?"

"*Jah*. I mean, we Amish pray a lot. In church, we're always praying for things to happen. We pray about births. Deaths. For sick people to recover."

Anna agreed.

"But you know what I think?"

"What?"

"That we're so busy asking for things, we miss the answers."

She considered Jesse's take on prayer and arched a brow. "But don't you think that answers are hard to recognize?" When he didn't reply, she went on to clarify what she meant. "I don't think it's always easy to know."

"I agree. So . . ." He stretched his legs and leaned back on his hands.

She let out a frustrated sigh. "I'll depend on God to help me find out." The sun slipped behind a cloud again. For several moments, the only sound was the soft buzzing of a honey bee on a nearby clover.

As the light breeze nudged several loose strands of hair from Anna's *kapp*, she could smell the scent of earth on Jesse's clothes. It was such a different smell from the clothes her *daed* wore at the bakery.

Suddenly, it mattered to her whether he agreed. She wasn't sure why.

"Jesse, I know I'm a little more independent than other Amish women my age."

The corners of his lips curved in amusement. "Ya think?"

She'd laid her pencil on the ground, and for some reason, she'd totally dropped what she'd been doing and was dead set on convincing Jesse Beiler to see her point of view.

"Okay. But I care that you agree with me."

He lifted a brow.

She offered a gentle lift of her shoulders. "I'm not sure why."

He grinned. "Maybe it's because I'm your confidant."

She shrugged. "Perhaps."

"Even so, why would it matter to you if I agree or disagree with you?"

She stared straight ahead, pressed her lips into a

thoughtful line, and considered the question. The more she contemplated it, the more uncertain she became about why she would care.

Finally, a laugh escaped her throat. She threw up her hands in defeat. "I don't know. But what I'm sure of, Jesse Beiler, is that I'm happy when you agree with me."

He smiled. "I'm glad."

"You are?"

He nodded.

She continued her train of thought. "Why does that make you happy?"

He lifted a pair of palms up at the sky and shrugged. "Undecided. But it doesn't really matter, I guess."

"You're probably right."

The corners of Jesse's lips drooped a notch, leaving an uncertain expression on his face. His jaw was set. "That's just it, Anna. Our lives . . ." He offered a dismissive shrug before continuing. "They should be about what God wants for us. Not about our wants."

As she contemplated his words, something inside her changed. "Jesse, I'm guilty."

Before he could respond, Anna lightened the pitch of her voice. "Jesse, what you've just said . . ." She swallowed. "Thank you for that."

"For what?"

"For reminding me that my life isn't about me. It's about what God wants from me."

She rested on her palms and leaned back to look up at the sky. As warmth caressed her face, she closed her eyes. When she opened them, she parted her lips.

"I read something interesting the other day in a spiritual magazine. I think it will help you, Anna."

"Please share it with me."

"It was just a quote from someone at the top of the page, saying that stress is when we try to handle our problems on our own. That we should hand them over to God. And then we're free."

"Jesse?"

He raised a brow and met her gaze.

"You've just given me the best advice."

She straightened before giving her picture another glance. "I'm handing this over to God. And there's something else I want you to know."

He gestured for her to go on.

"It's why I care so much about your opinion." She smiled and said with great affection, "It's because I really like you."

Chapter Eight

Jesse watched his livestock feed inside the large barn. The thought of having his own farm someday made him smile. He glimpsed his family's long drive lined with buggies. He chuckled.

With five brothers and several nephews, there was never a dull moment at the Beiler home. But that was the way he liked it. Busy and filled with love.

He leaned against the post at the end of the stalls and considered how different Anna's home was from his own. While he acknowledged that the two households were as opposite as night and day, he gave a sad shake of his head. There was a huge difference in the noise level between his house and hers, that was for certain.

Footsteps made him look up. To his surprise, his *daed* stood next to him.

Jesse smiled at his role model before returning his attention to the troughs in front of him. "I didn't hear you come in."

His *daed* dragged his hand over his face and spoke in his usual gruff voice. "*Sohn*, we need to talk about the Norris farm. Because it's going up for sale any day, and once it's listed, I'm afraid it will sell fast." Arms folded, he went on. "And I want you to have it."

The following morning, Anna ducked as she stepped outside the chicken coop. The sky was still half dark as the sun just started to show.

For a moment, she stopped and sighed in relief to be outside. She breathed in fresh air, glad to be away from the stuffy-smelling building. Of all the chores, collecting eggs was her least favorite.

There were several reasons for that. The first was because the house of feathered creatures was quite small, and it was necessary to bend while she collected the eggs. Secondly, she disliked the unpleasant smell and dirty feathers that floated around. And the third reason was because at first sight, the eggs were filthy. She grimaced. At least they were before she washed them. Anna admitted she'd never been a scrambled egg fan, like her parents, or any egg lover, most likely because she glimpsed the white and brown shells before they'd been cleaned. But, amazingly, that didn't bother everyone. She knew for a fact that the sight of dirty eggs didn't faze Mary Conrad at all. Or any other Amish girl she knew. But Anna had never gotten past their unappetizing appearance.

The warm August breeze caressed her face when she looked up at the sky. She closed her eyes for a moment to enjoy the day before it became too hot. When she opened her lids, a jet was leaving a trail of white in the sky. The sun came up another notch just enough to allow her to glimpse four horses pulling Jesse on a small platform behind their house.

Looking down at the basket in her hand, she moved a couple of eggs before they fell out. Without thinking, she turned toward the blacktop, where a horse and a buggy were coming in her direction. She wondered who was inside. From where she stood, she wasn't able to see.

Their kitchen needed some items, and Anna planned to take her buggy into town later that day. For now, she enjoyed the country smells and being anywhere other than inside the coop.

She took advantage of this time to be inspired. She loved this part of the day, just as the sun was rising. Sometimes, when she focused, she could feel God planting artistic ideas inside her head. And today, everything inspired her. The smell of freshly cut alfalfa. The pleasant aroma of yeast bread that floated out through the screened kitchen windows. And the opportunity that lay within days to finally have her dream.

The lone horse and buggy approached their long drive. *What's inside of me and how do You want me to live?* For a moment, she stopped and said a silent prayer. *Dear Lord, please guide my life. I am here to serve You. But please let me know how to do it. Amen.*

She expelled a satisfied breath and continued toward the side porch. *God, I'm celebrating handing my life over to You.* She breathed easier. And the morning got even better.

As she stepped out of the path of a playful brown-and-white goat, she recalled her last dinner with Jesse and pressed her lips together thoughtfully. To her, the time with Jesse and her folks had been much more than merely eating.

It had been comforting to be with her parents. And Jesse. She'd felt a strong sense of family, even though Jesse wasn't a relative. She hadn't realized just how very lonely she'd been since the start of the bakery's remodel. But last night, she'd acknowledged a great relief that she hadn't felt in a long time.

And her earlier conversation with *Maemm* floated through her thoughts, too, sending an easy sensation up her arms that landed in her shoulders. *I need to hear that my parents love me. That they love me as if I were their own.*

When the buggy suddenly turned off the blacktop and onto their drive, Anna's heart bubbled with joy. Today, she wanted to talk. Her parents were at the bakery. And Jesse was working in the field. So who was the visitor?

When Mary Conrad stuck her head out of the opened window and waved, Anna instantly lifted a friendly hand in greeting. She stepped inside the porch long enough to put down the eggs in a compartment in the fridge. She'd wash them later. The hinges on the screen door squeaked until it slammed closed. She quickly stepped back outside while Mary tied her horse.

As the large animal clomped its hooves and snorted, Anna embraced her dear friend. "It's so *gut* to see you!"

Mary's glasses slipped down her nose and she shoved them back up.

"I brought a surprise for you."

"*Jah?*"

Without responding, Mary stepped back to the buggy

and pulled something out. The top was covered. With the lift of a challenging brow, Mary looked as though she was dying to remove the top. "Can you guess what it is?"

Falling into step beside her, Anna nodded. "*Jah!*"

Inside the kitchen, Mary set down her surprise and motioned to the cellophane that tried to hide what was obviously a plant. Green stems stuck out at the sides.

Mary looked at her with excitement. "Go ahead. Open it. I hope you like it."

Anna bent to remove the cellophane. "Oh!" She drew her arms over her chest while glimpsing the beautiful rose. "It's absolutely gorgeous! The color . . . it's the most beautiful shade of peach I've ever seen."

Anna motioned Mary to the dining-room table. "Have a seat while I wash my hands." A few moments later, she returned to the kitchen. "There's fresh lemonade in the fridge; I'll pour you a glass."

Mary placed her gift on the center of the table and nodded. "*Denki*. That's one of many things we have in common."

Anna glanced at her while pouring two glasses and carried them to the table.

Mary added clarification to her statement. "We both make fresh lemonade."

Anna couldn't stop a laugh from escaping her throat. "And we both jump into ponds even though we can't swim!"

Mary joined in the laughter as Anna took a seat on the opposite side of the table from her friend. When Anna set her glass down on the coaster of a horse's face,

Mary carefully adjusted her gift so that the sunlight coming in from the nearest window better hit it.

Anna breathed in and eyed her friend with great appreciation. "It's so beautiful, Mary." Anna bent to take in the deep peach petals and delicately shaped green leaves. She closed her eyes in bliss. When she opened her lids, she smiled. "It smells so *gut.*"

"Anna, this rose will bring you beauty for years."

"I will treasure it. And . . ." She pressed her finger to her lips. Anna locked gazes with her friend. "I have something for you."

Mary lifted her chin. "*Jah?*"

Anna nodded. "When we were recovering from our swim . . ."

They both laughed. "I was checking out your room. It's lovely, but . . ."

"What?"

"It lacked something."

Mary furrowed her brows. "*Jah?*"

Anna winked as she rose from her chair and grinned down at her friend, lifting her pointer finger. "One moment, please . . ."

The stairs creaked as she made her way to her bedroom, where she lifted a large canvas from behind her beloved hope chest. Downstairs, she held it in front of Mary.

A gasp of surprise and awe escaped Mary's throat. "It looks so real! And . . ." She stopped to lock gazes with Anna. "You drew this?"

Anna moved to the other side of the table to hand the colored picture of the single rose to her friend. With one careful motion, Mary laid the picture on the table but continued to study it. "I've always known your love and fascination for roses."

"Did I ever tell you that?"

Anna shook her head. "You didn't have to. All I needed was to look at your garden and I knew. And by the way, the two vases of roses by your bedroom window were dead giveaways, too."

Mary drew her hands to her chest and crossed them. "I didn't realize my addiction was so obvious, but now that you mention it, I guess my passion has never really been a secret."

Anna lifted her arms in a helpless gesture. "And it shouldn't be! Every time you look at this . . ."

Mary jumped in. "You'll remember the day we both jumped into the Conrad pond!"

They both laughed.

The corners of Mary's lips curved upward into a huge grin. "And just think of the fun we had talking about it afterward."

While the fan blades put out a light, pleasant breeze, Anna considered her friend's take on the day at the Conrads' and pressed her lips together thoughtfully. A bird chirped on the kitchen sill. At the same time, a squirrel peeked in the window.

Anna finally offered a shake of her head. "I couldn't forget that afternoon if I wanted to." A sudden chill swept up her spine, and she shivered. "I was so afraid the boys would drown. The fear that went through me . . . Mary, that awful feeling will stay with me forever."

Mary grimaced. "I know what you mean. But our story, fortunately, had a happy ending."

"*Jah*. By the way, any word on Reuben?"

Mary looked down and expelled a frustrated breath. When she lifted her chin to meet Anna's gaze, she shook her head. Her eyes sparkled with moisture. "Reuben . . . he's still struggling. And from what I hear, news has it that his *maemm* may not be around much longer."

Anna let out a sigh of regret and closed her eyes. When she opened them, she said softly, "Oh, no. That poor little boy."

After a slight hesitation, she went on with a sad shake of her head. "I've been praying for him and his *maemm*. My heart breaks for them. For some reason, I felt a connection with him."

"Really?"

Anna nodded. "Probably because he was at the cookout without his *maemm*."

Mary arched a curious brow. "I don't understand. How does that connect you to him?"

Anna contemplated the question and wondered why she'd mentioned how she felt. The subject wasn't one she really wanted to discuss. However, as Mary waited for her to continue, she decided to offer clarification.

"I'm not in any way complaining. But as you know, my birth mamma gave me up for adoption." She bit her lower lip. "I have wonderful parents who love me, but . . ." She offered a gentle lift of her shoulders. "I've always felt a little like an outsider."

The curious expression on Mary's face turned to shock. Her jaw dropped in disbelief.

When she didn't say anything more, Anna explained. "Obviously, something happened for my biological *maemm* to give me away. And my parents?" Anna lifted her palms in helplessness and smiled sadly. "It's no secret they adopted me after trying for their own children."

As Mary regarded her with her mouth open in surprise, Anna cleared an emotional knot from her throat. "So it's obvious I was a second choice. That they would have preferred to have their own *kinder*."

A long, agonizing silence passed. In a softened voice, Anna finished, lifting her palms to the ceiling. "You can surely understand why I bonded with Reuben. At the cookout, he was the only child without a parent there. Besides me, of course." Mary's jaw dropped a notch lower. "I wonder what my life would have been like if my parents could have had their own children, and if my birth mamma had raised me."

Following a heavy silence, Anna tried her most logical voice. "Mary, you can surely understand my curiosity."

Mary spoke in a defensive tone while lifting a hand to stop her. "Whoa. I don't believe what you just said."

Anna regretted this conversation, but, in a way, it felt *gut* to voice her thoughts. This was the first time she'd ever mentioned her adoption to anyone but Jesse, even though she'd thought about it for years.

"Anna, do you know how hurt your parents would be if they knew you felt this way?"

"I know, Mary. But the circumstances of me being here . . . Sometimes, I just wonder." She lifted her shoulders in a gentle shrug. "Wouldn't you?"

As a bright ray of morning swept in through the window, a wave of remorse came over Anna. She should have kept her mouth shut. She hadn't regretted what she'd said, just that she'd voiced it. Some things, although they were true, were better left unsaid. And this was definitely one of them. Besides, the last thing she wanted was to seem ungrateful to *Maemm* and *Daed*.

Finally, Mary smiled sadly. "I never knew you felt this way, Anna. It makes me feel bad." After a slight hesitation, she furrowed her brows in doubt. "But I understand. I guess it's something I've never had to think about."

She fidgeted with her hands in front of her. "I mean, there's no doubt in my mind who I would have been if my parents hadn't raised me because they did."

Anna's voice cracked with emotion. "For a moment, imagine that your mamma had let you go and that you didn't know why. That as a kid, it was brought to your attention that your skin and your hair were darker than anyone else's. That your parents had adopted you. Like you weren't a real Amish person. Like I said, I'm not complaining, but be honest: Don't you think you'd feel kind of like an outsider?"

Mary's glasses slipped down her nose, and she shoved them back up with her pointer finger. "Maybe. But I never realized that you were battling such serious issues, Anna. Did someone really comment about your skin? If so, that's awful."

Anna gave a slow nod, and Mary didn't ask who.

"Then I want to help you move past this. To be honest, this comes as a complete surprise to me. In school, you were always so smart. And independent. I didn't think you had a care in the world."

Anna responded eagerly. "You always offer *gut* advice. Old Sam left the community with a lot of wise sayings." Anna pointed to her face and grinned. "But as far as my tanned complexion?" A laugh escaped her throat. She wasn't sure why. "I don't think you can change it. And I wouldn't want to. What I always yearned for, though, is for others to accept me as I am."

A heavy silence went on until Mary broke it. "I wish you could talk to Old Sam about this, Anna. For some reason, I believe he could put this into perspective for you, so you'd be at ease with what happened. With being adopted, I mean."

"I wonder what he would have told me."

Mary hesitated and pressed her lips together. Finally, she lifted a brow. "I think I know."

"You do?"

Mary nodded. "Once I had a conversation with him, and he said that in God's eyes, I was a masterpiece. That He'd created everything about me to His liking. And that regrets over yesterday and worries about tomorrow are twin thieves that rob us of the moment." Mary smiled. "He said that too many times to count."

Anna considered the wise words.

Mary expelled a breath and scooted back in her chair, resting her hands on her thighs. "I'm not going to pretend to have answers to everything, my friend, but I am sure that Old Sam's wisdom makes sense. I mean, think about it, Anna. In the whole scheme of things, we're here to serve God. And there are a lot of things we wonder about, but we'll just have to wait to meet Him to get the answers. But I'm sure that, even though sometimes we're not sure of who we are, we must be certain what we're here for. And that's to serve our Savior, who died on the cross just for us. And when we're in heaven, He'll answer all our questions."

After letting out a breath, she went on in a softer, more serious voice. "Think of what a hard life Jesus had. Compared to what He went through, our problems seem irrelevant. The disciples had it hard, too."

Anna absorbed what her friend said.

"Old Sam once said that God is there to give us strength for every hill we have to climb. That life is not a problem to be solved but a gift to be enjoyed. Just think, Anna. Both of us were so important to God that He gave His life for us." The corners of her lips raised into a grin.

"Of course, there's a lot we don't know. But compared to God's sacrifice for us, does it really matter?"

That evening, Anna washed dishes while *Maemm* dried. As they chatted about the farm Jesse wanted, Mary's visit, her gift to Anna, and Anna's present to her, Anna's heart was filled with love.

Without thinking, Anna said, "Mary's visit was just what I needed to cheer me up."

Anna was quick to note the surprise in her mother's voice. "You needed cheering up?"

While Anna contemplated the question, she realized that her own *maemm* didn't know her well. Working twelve hours a day at the bakery was taking a toll on their relationship.

However, the reason Anna didn't discuss her own issues with her parents was to spare them the worry. They worked so hard. The last thing she wanted was to cause them concern.

Her mother didn't let the subject drop. "You didn't answer my question."

While Anna turned to her *maemm*, she noted sincerity in her eyes. "You and *Daed* are so *gut* to me."

"Honey, we're your parents. That's what we're here for. And Anna . . ." She took her by her shoulders and moved closer, so Anna could clearly detect concern in her mother's clear blue eyes. Usually they were the color of the sky on a cloudless day. But this evening, Anna noted that they'd taken on a darker, more turbulent shade. The shade reminded her of a storm brewing.

"Oh, it's nothing you and *Daed* have done. It just . . . about me." A frustrated breath escaped her. "I'm afraid I've been going through a sort of identity crisis."

Her *maemm* reached for her hand. "It's time to talk."

Anna didn't argue while they stepped to the living room, where *Maemm* motioned to the soft blue sofa. Without a word, Anna sat down. Her mother claimed the cushion next to her and turned toward her. Their knees lightly touched.

As their gazes locked, her mother spoke in a soft yet firm tone. "I want to hear about your identity crisis." After a short pause. "Not to be nosy, but to help. Please, Anna."

Ashamed of herself, Anna started to lift a dismissive hand. But her mother quickly wrapped her fingers around Anna's and narrowed her brows in concern. "Anna, I'm sorry we've been away so much. And we've left you to hold down the fort all by yourself."

She placed a gentle finger on the cut on Anna's forehead and softened her voice. "If we'd been here during the storm, this might not have happened. And if you're going through anything, I'm responsible for it."

Anna shook her head. "You're not in any way to blame for my insecurities." Anna stopped, thinking about what she'd just said. Insecurities. Was that the crux of her problem?

When her mother continued regarding her in silence, Anna knew the best thing she could do was to be honest, as she'd been taught. Besides, there was no way out. The last thing she wanted to do was to take time away from her mother's busy day to focus on herself, but now that they were here together, she had no choice but to voice her thoughts.

Expelling a deep, thoughtful sigh, Anna tried for the right words. Finally, emotion overcame her, and salty tears stung her eyes. She blinked at the sting. *This is not who you are. You're strong.*

Anna cleared the uncomfortable knot from her throat and breathed in, lifting her chin a notch in forced confidence. "Lately, I've been questioning my role as a person. After all you and *Daed* have done for me, I'm embarrassed to say that I've been feeling like I don't deserve you." She lowered the pitch of her voice.

"This doesn't have to do with being adopted, does it?"

After a slight hesitation, Anna nodded.

Her *maemm* leaned forward and hugged her. As they embraced, Anna allowed herself to enjoy the security and comfort she so desperately needed.

Anna's words came out in a whisper. "It's no secret that you and *Daed* tried to have your own children."

Her mother teared up. For a moment, Anna thought

the woman next to her would cry. The expression, a combination of dismay and shock, made Anna's chest ache.

She had hurt her own *maemm,* even though that hadn't been her intention. This conversation was Anna's fault. *How can I live with myself?*

Anna wanted her words to come out with more logic and less emotion. "If you'd have been able to get pregnant, you and *Daed* wouldn't have taken me in. And I don't know where I would've ended up because my birth mother didn't want me."

Her mother's voice was firm as she came forward on her knees and claimed Anna's arms with her hands and held them tightly. "Anna, none of that's true. Long before we married, we talked many times about having a family. And Anna, your *daed* and I had always planned to adopt." She gave a gentle lift of her shoulders. "Ever since I can remember."

The confession took Anna's breath away. As she studied the sincerity in her mother's eyes, Anna's fingers shook while she absorbed what she'd just heard. Because she'd always believed she'd only been adopted because *Maemm* couldn't give birth to her own child.

Anna experienced an odd combination of great joy and chagrin. Joy because she'd just learned the opposite of what she'd believed for so many years. That her parents had wanted her, regardless of whether they'd had their own offspring. And chagrin that she'd obviously hurt her *maemm*. She hoped she could repair the undeserved sadness in the eyes that faced her.

Anna finally broke down, and her mother embraced her. "Honey, I'm so sorry you felt that way."

Several moments later, Anna forced her tears to stop. A huge force of relief swept through her. With one quick motion, her *maemm* got up, stepped to the kitchen, pulled a tissue from the box on the countertop, and handed the Kleenex to Anna.

As Anna dabbed at her eyes, she smiled. "You don't know what it means to me to hear that."

Her mother reclaimed her seat, scooted toward the edge, and rested her palms on Anna's thighs. "You know what they say? That something good always comes out of something bad?"

Anna continued to blot her eyes and offered a quick nod.

"It just happened. A painful conversation gave you the truth you needed to hear."

Anna leaned forward to hug her mother. As she wrapped her arms around her *maemm*'s neck, Anna closed her eyes and said a silent prayer of thanks for the truth. "I almost feel like a whole person."

Surprise danced on her mother's irises. "Almost?"

"While we're having this conversation, I may as well tell you the whole story. I believed two things that ate away at me for years. The first was that I became a part of your family only because you and *Daed* couldn't have your own family. And . . ."

She hiccupped. Then she laughed. So did *Maemm*. "You were saying?"

"Secondly, that my birth mamma didn't care about me enough to keep me. Obviously, I wasn't worthy of her love and her time."

A long silence followed as Anna tried to read her mother's expression. Finally, the loving woman who'd raised her let out a long, defeated sigh. But the heavy silence between them continued to loom.

"Anna, life is never perfect. And although your *daed* and I did our best, there are definitely things we could have done better. I suppose right now is the time to give you something."

Anna straightened and waited for her to go on.

Tears filled *Maemm*'s eyes, and her voice shook slightly as she took Anna's hands in hers and squeezed them with affection. "Honey, your birth mother loved you very much." Moisture dampened *Maemm*'s eyes. When she spoke, her voice was barely more than an emotional whisper. "In fact, she left you a letter."

Anna's heart nearly stopped. "Why didn't you give it to me?"

"Your *daed* and I . . . we were really never sure when to give it to you. We didn't know if it would be better for you to read it or not to. I'm sorry, Anna, but sometimes, as parents, it's hard to do what's best for your children."

A long silence ensued before *Maemm* went on. "We never opened it. After we took you in, a priest looked us up and mailed it to us. He said he'd made a promise to your *maemm*. I can see that we should have shared it with you years ago." She stood and smiled a little. "I'll get it for you."

While the stairs creaked, Anna's head was spinning. What she'd just found out was a lot to absorb. Her parents hadn't adopted her simply because they couldn't have their own children. They'd always planned it. And her birth mother had loved her and had left her a letter.

Anna's heart jumped with a newfound happiness and excitement. Soon, she'd read her birth mother's own words. She took in a deep breath and pressed her palms on her thighs. She watched with great anticipation while *Maemm* descended the stairs, envelope in hand.

Anna could barely contain her excitement as she took the large envelope. As she retrieved it, her fingers shook so much, she dropped it. She bent to pick it up. And as she did, she stared at the name in beautiful writing. *To My Daughter*. There was a hospital name and a San Diego address in the corner.

Suddenly, so many questions flitted through Anna's mind, she couldn't even think. *Maemm*'s soft voice startled her. "Aren't you going to open it?"

That evening, Jesse filled the troughs in his barn with water. When they were full, he turned off the spigot and returned the long green hose to the wall, where he continued to neatly wind it several times around the holder.

Afterward, he proceeded to the feed bags, where he pulled the strings at the top to open them. With one deep breath, he bent to lift the oats and distributed them as evenly as he could in the long metal feeders.

After emptying the first bag, he proceeded to do the same with the second. The sound of footsteps made him turn to the large front doors.

"Evening, *sohn*."

"Evening, *Daed*."

As Jesse pulled a rake from the wall and began moving dirty bedding into a pile, his father did the same. As they chitchatted, the rakes' metal tips meeting concrete made a light, unpleasant sound.

In the background, the back door of the barn was propped open, and the cattle's moos and horses' neighs could be heard. At Jesse's boots, a rat stole an oat. Jesse chased him away while the family dog, Buddy, joined him with a moan for attention.

Jesse spoke to the needy canine. "I'll give you all the attention you deserve, boy. But first, I've got work to do."

When the mixture of rat terrier and chihuahua whined for some reason, Jesse felt the need to explain. "I make sure you've got a comfy bed. Don't complain."

With a dissatisfied whimper, Buddy made himself comfortable on an empty bag of grain, where he put his head between his front legs and took in Jesse and his *daed*.

His *daed* started the conversation in a low, thoughtful voice, as usual, stopping to run his fingers through his thin head of hair. In his typical stern voice, he started. "I had coffee at King's Bakery this morning, and everyone in there was talkin' 'bout the Norris farm goin' up for sale. Word has it that the listing paperwork is done and it'll be up for sale tomorrow."

While Jesse considered his *daed*'s words, the speed of the pulse on his wrist picked up. At that moment, he began imagining the land as his own. Of four horses pulling him on a platform to plant soybeans. Of coming home to a family and dinner on the table.

When Jesse didn't respond, his father cleared his throat. "For years, I've thought about how to get you a farm. Now, I've talked to other family members, and

Chapter Nine

Anna stepped inside her room and closed the door behind her. As it clicked into the lock, she held the large envelope with great care and took a seat on the edge of her bed. Even though the quilt beneath her was soft, she couldn't get comfortable. Her entire body shook. Her lungs pumped for air. Her heart raced.

She studied the envelope, drew in a deep breath, and let it out. *To my beloved daughter, Luciana.* The words certainly didn't give any indication that her mother hadn't loved her. Quite the opposite.

Now, Anna was more curious than ever about what was inside. While her heart pumped to a fast, nervous, excited beat, an odd combination of anxiety and relief swept up her spine and landed at the back of her neck. *This is the moment I've waited for my entire life. To hear from my birth mamma. What will she say? Maybe I'll get to meet her.*

She opened the envelope, careful not to tear the letter or whatever was inside. *There's only one way to find out.*

With great care, she removed two things. A neatly folded paper and a sketch of a beautiful woman who looked just like her. Only the thick head of hair wasn't hidden underneath a *kapp*; on the contrary, it cascaded gracefully down her shoulders.

Anna sat very still, holding her breath, as she took in the large eyes and long, wavy hair. "It's her." For long, emotional moments, she stared at it before putting the sketch aside. She unfolded the other paper and began reading out loud the neat handwriting.

"To my beloved daughter, Luciana. I am writing this letter in hopes that you will never read it. I have been warned that my pregnancy is risky. However, I will do everything in my power to survive, and that is why I write this with a happy heart. My doctor was clear to me that my pregnancy had serious complications, that my survival chance was small. But I believe that you will be a miracle in the world. That you will be strong, brave, and unafraid to do what you believe is right.

"As I start labor, I imagine what you will look like. I want to hold you. To teach you to speak English, and Spanish, my native language. I have dreamed of braiding the thick black hair I know you will have. Most of all, I want to take you to Mass every Sunday. I'm Catholic, like my parents, who are already with the Lord, and if my Savior takes me, it is my prayer that a loving couple will raise you and teach you about Jesus. I believe God will love and protect you, whether I raise you or someone else does."

Anna swallowed as wet, salty tears stung her eyes. She blinked at the sting. With one quick motion, she ran the back of her hand over her cheek to catch a tear. Anna pressed her lips together in a straight line and continued reading.

"If I don't meet you on earth, I will see you in heaven. I've prayed for God to fill your heart with His love. That you will be strong and brave. That you will welcome challenges, not hide from them.

"Know that your decisions will not please everyone all the time. But if you're anything like your mama, you'll hold your own. Voice your thoughts. When you express yourself, you will most likely have disagreements. But if you're silent, you're not contributing. And your real self is worthy of being heard. You don't have to be like everyone else.

"Last but not least, I pray with all my heart that you will find true love. My daughter, if you do, you will have something so precious. Rare. What I wanted most but never found. If you find a man who loves you the way you are, keep him. But use good judgment. And always look to God for guidance. That way, you can't go wrong. What's most important in our short lives on earth is serving Him. Remember that.

"I am enclosing a picture of me that I sketched. It's always been my dream to have a daughter, Luciana. I have other dreams, too. But none come close to raising you. I love you so much, Rosalinda Sanchez."

Anna let out a breath of relief, surprise, and wonder as she contemplated the strong, unexpected words from the woman responsible for Anna's life. Absorbing the serious letter, Anna stood and stepped quickly to her hope chest.

She sat down in front of it and stared at the cross on the lid. For some reason, the powerful message she'd just read seemed to go hand in hand with the cross that was etched into the lid.

With great care, she laid the letter to the left of the chest and her birth mother's photo to the right. As Anna focused on the woman who looked all too familiar, she teared up. Her chest ached.

So much emotion filled her: happiness, sadness, anger that her mamma hadn't lived, and a great joy at this unexpected communication.

Suddenly, she needed air. She needed to breathe. God had answered something she'd prayed about since a very young age. Her parents had wanted her regardless of whether they'd had their own children. And her brave birth mamma had loved her enough to risk her own life.

Anna closed her eyes as she absorbed that her life had changed. And she needed to talk to Jesse Beiler.

When the sun was starting its show the following morning, Anna knew where to find Jesse. Quick, urgent steps took her to their barn. This was an emergency. As Naomi's and Rosalinda's messages flitted through Anna's mind, her pulse jumped with nervous, excited energy.

My birth mamma loved me. And my parents wanted me, even if they'd had their own children. My life has changed! Where do I go from here? Jesse will help me figure it out.

Inside the barn, Anna looked for Jesse. "Jesse!" When she couldn't find him, she cupped her hands to her mouth and hollered.

"I'm up here, Anna. I'll be down in a while."

Anna expelled an impatient breath and started toward the ladder that was attached to the loft. "This can't wait! I'm coming up!"

Without hesitation, she started up the steps, hiking up her dress so she didn't trip on the uneven rungs, and, at the same time, holding on to one side of the ladder. At the top, she let out a breath and lunged forward to push herself on to the platform.

Jesse's voice startled her. She wasn't sure why. Perhaps because it was edged with irritation.

"What on earth are you doing?"

She caught her breath and pulled her feet up as she fell back against a bale of hay. "I need to talk to you."

He eyed her *kapp*, stepped closer, and pulled some pieces of loose hay from the fabric.

"There." He narrowed his brows in an odd combination of curiosity and disapproval. "Now tell me what is so important that you climbed all the way up here in a dress in eighty degrees." As he motioned to a bale of hay, she hopped to her feet and sat on the bale. Without wasting a moment, he claimed the spot next to her.

As she wiped a bead of sweat from her forehead, he lowered his voice. "Something happened?"

Anna nodded, then did a quick turn to face him as she covered the pertinent details. The only breeze was from the open door in the loft. As she talked, she kept swatting away flies that buzzed in front of her.

She poured out everything, from the conversation with *Maemm* to the handwritten letter written by Rosalinda before she had gone to the Lord.

Afterward, Jesse let out a low whistle. "Anna, do you see what this means?" Before she could respond, Jesse went on. "This is an answer to a prayer. God let you know the two things you've wondered your entire life." After an emotional pause, he softened his pitch. "Your birth mother . . . She loved you, Anna."

Anna pressed her lips together and nodded. Emotion claimed her and she teared up. But, ironically, the expression in Jesse's eyes were a combination of joy and understanding that pulled at her heartstrings nearly as much as the letter itself.

As they looked at each other, she saw empathy, compassion, regret, sadness, and happiness in Jesse's eyes. The mixture of emotions was what she felt, too.

As they locked gazes, she took on an even deeper understanding of him. And she realized just how bonded she was to him. That very realization forced a shiver up her spine.

After a lengthy silence, he lifted his palms to the air and smiled a little. "Anna, I don't even know what to say. All the times you mentioned her, I never dreamed she had passed away."

He studied her before continuing. "I'm so sorry. At the same time . . ." He paused, clearing a knot from his throat. "You must feel a sense of relief."

He stood and made a circuit of the small area before stopping to hook his thumbs over the tops of his pockets. As she watched him, and as he looked at her, she acknowledged something very important. Her heart nearly stopped as she considered the truth.

She stiffened and clenched her fists at her sides, allowing herself to imagine what would happen if . . . if she married Jesse. She recalled the words in her mother's letter about finding true love.

She was sure she'd found it. That she loved him for real. And she believed he reciprocated. Their relationship was built on mutual trust and respect. She had what her birth mamma had wanted so desperately but had never found.

No. It can't happen.

Inhaling, she immediately nixed marrying him from her thoughts and focused on what she'd just told her best friend. The significance and how to deal with it.

When he didn't say anything, she finally broke the silence. "What should I do?"

In silence, he reclaimed his seat beside her on the hay. "Anna, I'm no professional counselor. What you've told me runs so deep, I'm not really sure I'm the right person to ask."

She smiled with appreciation and softened the pitch of her voice. "You don't have to be a professional counselor."

He glanced at her and lifted a skeptical brow.

"I'm serious. Jesse, I love the way you see things."

The corners of his lips lifted into a half grin. "Ya do?"

She nodded. "In fact . . ." She hesitated before deciding on complete honesty. "I don't know what I'd do without you."

She swallowed, realizing that what she'd said needed clarification. The last thing she intended was to lead him on. "I tell you things and you offer your best advice. And you never pass judgment on me."

"You've really put a lot of trust in me."

She nodded.

"And I'm honored to be your confidant." He pressed a finger to his chin and tapped his boot against the wooden boards beneath him.

"Okay, let me think a moment." He let out a low whistle. "First of all, Anna, I'm elated." Before she could say anything, he went on. "Just think . . . you have two mothers who offered you unconditional love."

Anna blinked at the sting of salty moisture in her eyes and tried not to get too emotional. Right now, Jesse was sharing his thoughts with her. And that meant that she needed to pay close attention and try to understand his view.

He stood, leaned back against the boards that supported the hayloft, and crossed his arms over his midsection. She eyed him from the corner of her eye. As she did so, the thought she'd promised to vanquish returned. *What would life be like married to Jesse?* Again, she forced it out of her mind.

"Anna, Naomi and Paul loved you enough to take you in and raise you. Surely you recognize what a huge commitment that was."

She quickly agreed.

"And now we know that they would have welcomed you into their family even if they'd been able to conceive a child." His tone took on sudden enthusiasm. "When you think about it, you won the lottery with parents."

"The lottery?"

He nodded. "You know."

"Of course. They sell tickets at the gas station where we buy propane."

He nodded. "So . . . if you really want my thoughts, I believe you have more love invested in you than anyone I know."

She narrowed her brows while she considered his opinion.

When he rejoined her on the bale of hay, she listened as he went on. "Think about it, Anna. Naomi and Paul; I don't think you can question their love for you."

"No."

"And now, you know that your birth *maemm* loved you so much, she gave her life for you." He cleared his throat, and his voice shook with emotion. "When you think about it, Anna, you're truly blessed. And special."

Anna looked down at her sturdy black shoes as she absorbed the enormity of what Jesse had just said. She felt like a huge weight was lifted from her shoulders, only to be replaced by a heavier one.

He chuckled.

She lifted a curious brow. "What's so funny?"

"I never met your birth mother, but from the sound of her letter, you're very much like her."

Anna lifted a brow for him to explain.

"Most definitely, she was all for speaking her mind. And what she said about doing the right thing and letting your voice be heard . . ."

He offered a small shrug of his shoulders. "Think about it, Anna. That's you. It's your decision to enter this contest, to win, and to explore a whole new world." He softened his voice to a more confidential tone. "You're a risk-taker."

She couldn't stop a laugh from coming from her throat. "I am not!"

"Yes, you are!"

They laughed together.

"Now I know where you get it."

"Get what?"

"Your strong mind." He raised a hand, so she allowed him to finish. "And I mean that as a compliment."

"*Jah?*"

"In fact, I admire you for it."

"Really?"

He nodded. "You're different from anyone I know. In a good way. And Anna . . ."

She waited for him to go on.

"You know what I really think?" To her surprise, he moved his hand to hers and covered her fingers with his.

She stiffened. Not because she didn't like his gentle touch; she did. His warmth and the way he took her hand in his created a sensation that was an odd combination of comfort and discomfort.

At the same time, she was fully aware that it wasn't proper. *But why isn't it right? Is it really wrong to touch another's hand when you care about them so much?*

She stayed very still and quickly wondered if God would be unhappy with them for holding hands. She didn't see why He would.

Jesse turned to her and lowered the tone of his voice. "You're so very special." He looked away before returning his attention to her.

When he spoke again, emotion edged his voice. At the same time, the reflection in his eyes was of absolute certainty. And his fingers gripped hers a little tighter.

"In fact, Anna King, you're the most unique individual I've ever met." He stopped for a moment and then continued in a passionate tone. "I never really knew what I wanted in a woman." He whispered, "Until I met you."

Her lungs had difficulty pumping air. Her throat became so dry, she was afraid she'd start coughing. But she didn't. She just enjoyed hearing the words. Because she truly liked and respected Jesse.

After a brief silence, he went on after clearing a knot from his throat. "Let's just say, Anna, that I want you to fulfill your dream; but at the same time, I hope you have a change of heart and decide to stay here with us."

She looked at him to go on.

He smiled a little and seemed determined to finish what he'd started. "I know what I'm about to say might surprise you, but just listen and think about it."

She nodded. "Okay."

He cleared his throat. "Now that you've read the message from your birth mother, things are different."

He paused as if thinking about how to continue. Then he squeezed her hand with affection and leaned closer. "In her letter, she clearly told you not to be afraid of people's opinion. To be strong and to have an open mind."

Anna absorbed his thoughtful words while the sun's rays came in through the open window. She blinked at the unexpected brightness while she silently acknowledged that something had changed in Jesse. She tried to ascertain what it was. It wasn't how he looked. Or anything he did really. Yet since she'd shown him the letter, a new confidence had appeared in him. She saw it in the way the flecks in his eyes danced. In the way he had so confidently taken her hand in his. Even the tone of his voice indicated a change in his attitude.

"And don't get me wrong . . ." He pulled his hand away and held it up in self-defense. Immediately, she missed the warmth of his touch. "I'm not saying in any way that you don't have an open mind; you do, and I'm glad you do. But Anna . . ."

He stopped for a moment, as if deciding how to proceed. "An open mind means looking at both sides. It means you could decide against becoming *Englisch*; that is, if you win the contest. And I'm not talking immediately. Decisions of this magnitude take time, and I believe that if you do pursue life outside our community, I'm guessing everything won't be perfect."

She smiled a little. "They say the grass is always greener on the other side."

He offered a nod and lifted a brow. "But we don't believe everything we hear, do we?"

"No. And I don't expect things to be perfect. Not at all." She closed her eyes for a minute. When she opened them, a cool shiver swept up her spine. She shuddered.

He leaned closer. "Are you okay?"

She gave a slow nod. "I've thought about the changes being *Englisch* would mean so many times. But when it comes right down to it . . ." She lifted her palms to the ceiling in a helpless gesture. "I'm a little bit scared." She raised her chin a notch. "But I've got to try it to know if that's who I am."

The expression on his face was that of great surprise. "Anna King? Afraid?"

She laughed. Not that what he'd said was funny. It really wasn't. But the way the words had sounded when they came out. Exaggerated. And the way he'd said the word was endearing.

To her surprise, he leaned closer. He was so close, she could feel his warm breath. Smell his woodsy scent. The flecks on his irises danced differently than she'd ever seen them.

"Anna, I'm not doing very well at getting my point across, am I?"

She didn't respond. Because she wasn't exactly sure what point he was trying to make.

"Being open-minded means that you can stay here or you can come home after you leave. That is, if you do. And Anna . . ."

He looked away a moment, but when he focused his attention back on her, the combination of seriousness and need in his eyes nearly took her breath away. "If you stay here . . ."

She swallowed with emotion while he paused. And when he finally continued, he lowered the pitch of his voice to a tone that was so soft, so serious, it was barely audible.

"Or if you go away and come back, I'll be here. As a friend. And more."

Anna's heart pumped as it had when she'd run to the Conrads' pond to rescue the boys. As his words sunk in, her jaw dropped. Finally, when she got what he was trying to say, she offered a slow nod of understanding.

"Jesse, I don't want to disappoint you. I don't want to disappoint myself." A breath escaped her throat while she tried to find the right words. Finally, she lowered her voice so that it was barely audible. "You see, I feel the same way about you."

To her astonishment, he gave a nod. "I thought so." After a short hesitation, he added, "And I'm glad."

"We like each other and want to be together. Oh, why is this so complicated?"

His voice was firm yet filled with understanding. "It isn't really, Anna."

"Please pray strong prayers for God to guide me in the right direction."

He offered a nod. But a few moments later, he moved closer to her and took her arms. And he told her about the Norris farm.

Excitement filled her until she wanted to burst with joy. Because Jesse was about to have his dream come true.

Then he took her hands in his. "Anna, I need strong prayers from you, too."

"Because you want the Norris farm?"

"*Jah.* It's up for sale as of today, and *Daed* and I are going to make an offer. This morning, in a couple of hours."

"That's wonderful!"

He nodded. "But mostly because I love you, and I want to spend the rest of my life with you. And if you move away, I don't know what I'll do without you."

His admission took her breath away.

He released a sigh. "There's something else I want, but I'm restricted from doing it."

As she looked at him to go on, the expression in his eyes captured her until she didn't know what to say. She was mesmerized. And her chest was pumping way too fast.

"Anna, can I kiss you?"

* * *

Later that morning, Jesse and his father sat opposite Sandy, the real estate agent who'd listed the Norris farm. He couldn't help reflecting on Anna, his deep feelings for her, what she'd learned about her birth mother, and that she'd denied him the kiss he'd so badly wanted. He felt a bit guilty now for asking but reasoned that this was the girl he wanted to marry.

Inside the old two-story structure that had been built nearly eighty years before, the agent dug into her brown-leather satchel and pulled out paperwork.

She looked up and smiled. "I've let the couple know that a cash offer's coming."

As she got out a pen and looked over the typed pages, Jesse took in the dining room from where he sat at the large cherrywood table. The walls definitely could use a fresh coat of paint. The house had electricity, which the *Ordnung* didn't allow, but there was an easy solution for that.

The home was close enough to town that he'd be able to tap into natural gas, which was permitted. Of course, the change would cost money. But according to the church members his *daed* had talked to, it wasn't complicated. He imagined a gas line that ran across the ceiling and reading his farm magazines in front of the fire in an oversize recliner.

The air-conditioning made a loud sound as it shut off. He enjoyed the cool air on his arms, though he knew he could live without it. But today, he certainly enjoyed it. However, to Jesse, nothing could compare to the outdoors. Fresh air on his skin. The climate God had created.

From the corner of his eye, the open door allowed him a glimpse of a brick fireplace in the living room. An oak mantel loomed above it. The simplicity of it reminded him of the mantel in his own home.

His *daed* offered him an affectionate tap on the shoulder. The real estate agent's voice broke the silence. "Everything's in order here. All I need is your signature, Jesse. And your father's, because he's cosigning."

The enormity of what was happening hit Jesse with such a strong ferocity, he had to catch his breath. Soon the farm would belong to him. Hopefully, anyway. More importantly, the hundred and some acres would be his means of earning a modest living. For the rest of his life, he would put food on his table and feed his wife and family by farming the land. He'd prayed for this for years; even so, it was hard to believe that God was already answering his prayer. *Thank you, God.*

"Okay. The first paragraph just states your current address." She leaned forward and pointed to the following numbers. "Here's the amount of your offering." She moved her finger to another line that was highlighted in yellow. "This shows that it's a cash offer." She smiled appreciatively. "Whether it's cash or loan, the money's the same." She paused while she lifted a thoughtful brow. "However, cash makes things easier because there isn't that extra step of working with a financial institution."

She slid the paper to Jesse's *daed* first. "I'll need both of your signatures here and here." She moved her hand and pointed with long, polished nails.

Jesse's pulse jumped with excitement and a bit of uneasiness while he watched his father examine the fine print. Excitement because this was his dream coming true. Uneasiness because with his name on these pages came a huge financial responsibility. It was common for Amish families within his particular community to help their own by pooling money together. Still, the blessing his parents and aunts and uncles were offering him was so large, Jesse wasn't sure it was possible to thank them enough. *Family's everything. And someday, I'll have my own. We'll raise them to be God-fearing and family-centered. A wife and children will complete my dream.*

He returned to reality as his *daed* dragged his hand over his face and chin before sliding the paperwork to him with one hand. Jesse had never signed anything so important. He carefully read the typed print, signed, and leaned forward to slide the paper to Sandy, who turned that page facedown and to her right.

She continued to explain what lines needed signatures, and Jesse and his *daed* continued to read carefully and sign to the very last page.

"When will we know?" Jesse's voice shook with excitement.

Sandy narrowed her brows as she skimmed each signed page, one by one, and straightened them before putting a binder clip at the top. "I don't see any problem. As soon as I have the owners' signatures, the property will be yours. Congratulations!"

She stood, and Jesse and his *daed* followed suit. A phone ringing interrupted their conversation. Sandy glanced at Jesse and the bishop and held up her hand. "Just a moment. Let me take this."

While she talked, Jesse watched the corners of her lips slip a notch. The pitch of her voice changed from enthusiasm to concern. And her dismayed expression nearly stopped his heart. Her tone became less confident than it was just moments ago.

"There are other offers coming in? But I've already spoken with the owners. And there . . ."

Jesse's heart rose and fell much too quickly. And the expression on his father's face was that of great concern. As Sandy clicked Off on her cell phone, she breathed in and looked down before finally lifting her chin and expelling a discouraged sigh.

"Of course, we shouldn't be surprised that there are other offers. But one's coming in that's for more money than the owners have asked."

Jesse's *daed* spoke in a low tone. His words came out with confidence, but Jesse was quick to note that his fingers hooked over his trouser pocket shook.

"I thought we were the first. And we offered full asking price."

"That's true . . . but here's what's going on. Another farmer from out of town really wants the parcel. He's aware of your offer and is topping it."

Jesse and his *daed* looked at Sandy in silence, waiting for her to continue. "In other words, he's upping the ante."

Jesse let out a low whistle while his *daed* shook his head in dismay. "Can he do that?"

Sandy nodded. "I'm afraid so. In my twenty years as an agent, I've had this happen only twice. But I guess it shouldn't come as a surprise because farms in this area come up on the market so seldom."

She reclaimed her seat and strummed her fingers against the table, pressing her lips together thoughtfully. "We've still got a shot. That is, if you're able to come up with a higher offer. And if you can, we'd better act now. There's not much time."

Jesse's heart sank. Everything was happening so quickly. In his mind, he'd already become the owner of the farm. But reality had quickly snatched that from him.

His father turned to him and laid an affectionate hand on his shoulder. "*Sohn*, never forget that God has the final decision on who gets the hundred-some acres. Let's pray."

While Jesse squeezed his eyes closed, he listened to the heartfelt words. And he felt renewed. That someone else might get the land slipped from his worries. And he directed his attention to Sandy.

She pressed her lips together thoughtfully. When she finally spoke, concern edged her voice. "There's something we can try. But it's up to you and your family." After tapping the toe of her shoe against the hardwood floor, she lifted a skeptical brow. She motioned to the table, where the three reclaimed their chairs.

"We've got to act quickly. Because Mr. and Mrs. Norris will soon have the other offer. Before they sign."

That same morning, Anna and her *maemm* pulled dry laundry from the clothesline in the side yard. The light, warm breeze moved the navy-blue dresses and broadfall pants up and down in an uneven motion. Jesse and his *daed* were making an offer on the land.

Still, he was on Anna's mind. She couldn't stop thinking about the way his voice had cracked with emotion when he'd asked to kiss her. She didn't regret her decision not to let him.

Even though she'd wanted very much to feel his lips on hers, she knew she wanted to save that special first kiss for the man she married. And right now, even though she loved Jesse, she couldn't spend the rest of her life with an Amish man if she left the community.

Anna focused on this special time with *Maemm*. Because, since the remodel of the bakery, she'd pretty much adjusted to life without her *eltern*. However, since *Maemm* had told Anna that she loved her, Anna had felt a strong connection to her.

She broached the subject. "I'm so glad the remodel at the bakery is almost done." In a shy voice, Anna added, "I've missed you and *Daed*."

Her role model eyed her with regret. "And I've missed you, too."

"But . . ." Anna cleared her throat and lowered her voice to a more serious tone. At the same time, excitement laced her words. "I feel like a whole new person now."

Wearing a smile, *Maemm* turned to Anna. "*Ich bin froh.*" After a slight hesitation, her mother lowered the pitch of her voice. "I've been wondering, Anna, what did your birth mother say in her letter?"

Anna told her.

When silence followed the explanation, Anna stopped

to regard her *maemm* with curiosity. "You knew, didn't you?" Before allowing her mother a chance to respond, Anna went on. "That my mom died in childbirth."

Her *maemm* offered a regretful nod of her head.

"Why didn't you tell me?"

As a trail of white lined the sky behind an airplane, her *maemm*'s eyes sparkled with moisture. "We didn't know if we should or shouldn't, Anna. You know . . ." She continued plucking garments from the line as she spoke. "Being a parent, it's sometimes hard to make the right decisions. And your *daed* and I . . . Telling you was something that weighed heavily on our minds, but we never did it. And I'm sorry. I can see now that we made a mistake."

"It's okay. And I understand. About being a parent, that is." Anna smiled a little. "I don't think there's a person in this world who makes one-hundred-percent perfect decisions."

A long silence ensued before *Maemm* changed the subject. Finally, she expelled a sigh and smiled a little. "It's a good thing Jesse's been around to keep you company."

Anna agreed with a nod. She had so much on her mind, the last thing she wanted to talk about was him. Especially because she feared giving away their love for each other. She'd best try to keep it to herself, especially with her future so uncertain.

Because of that, she decided on a simple, honest reply. "He's a hard worker."

Her mother turned to Anna and narrowed her brows. "I know that. Your *daed* and I . . . We can't believe all he's accomplished since he started here. But his most important accomplishment was getting you into the barn during that awful storm." After a short hesitation, emotion edged her voice. "I would hate to think what could have happened to you out here on the farm all alone."

The memory of the time she and Jesse had spent together that day prompted the corners of Anna's lips to lift into a wide grin. A laugh escaped her. She wasn't sure why; there'd been nothing funny about the storm or her injury.

Finally, she reasoned that the laugh was a result of the unexpected happiness she'd found in her *daed*'s farmhand. Finally, she glanced at her mother and realized that her role model was awaiting a response.

"I'll never forget that day. But there's no need to worry about it now. God protected me."

"Jesse did, too," *Maemm* chimed in. "The two of you . . . you both work hard, but I'm hoping you've been able to spend some time together?"

As Anna unpinned a large black sock, she accidentally dropped it, and the moment it met the ground, a baby goat grabbed it and ran. In the distance, Anna watched another goat steal it. She and *Maemm* looked at each other and laughed.

"They're pests, *jah*?"

Anna nodded agreement. But in her heart, she truly enjoyed the mischievous creatures, even though she couldn't trust them.

Continuing to fold and place the sun-dried garments into the green plastic laundry basket, Anna's mother went on in a calm voice. "Your *daed* and I have really taken a liking to the Beiler boy. 'Course, we always knew he was from a good family. And he's always been a hard worker. And polite. But now we realize . . ."

She stopped. For a moment, Anna forgot about the apron between her hands and dropped in on the ground. With one quick motion, she bent to pick it up, brushed off a few pieces of grass, and slowly folded it while she considered where this conversation was headed before *Maemm* stopped in midsentence. She was thankful that the goats were already occupied.

As she regarded her mother, she stopped and rested her palms on her hips. "What were you going to say?"

Several moments later, her *maemm* offered a gentle lift of her shoulders and went on in a steady voice, as if she'd never intended not to finish her sentence. While Anna waited to hear the rest, the delicious-smelling aroma of homemade yeast rolls floated out of the kitchen screen and all the way to the clothesline. Anna breathed in the mouthwatering scent and realized that it was nearly lunchtime.

"Oh, I'm sure it's already crossed your mind." Surely *Maemm* wasn't playing matchmaker. Anna hoped not anyway. In a voice edged with skepticism, she narrowed her brows with curiosity.

"What?"

As if on cue, they stepped away from the empty line and began removing clothing from the second line, which was parallel to the first. "Jesse, well, he's an eligible single man. Paul and I were talking about him the other day, and to our knowledge, he's never courted anyone. And, for that matter, neither have you." She lifted her shoulders in a nonchalant shrug. "And both of you are of marrying age."

While the gentle breeze caressed Anna's face, she took in the significance of her mother's words. She knew where this conversation was leading, yet she feigned ignorance. She wasn't sure why. "What are you saying?"

By now, the second line was empty with the exception of one single pin, which Anna quickly removed and added to her container. At the same time, she and *Maemm* each lifted a plastic laundry basket and began slowly stepping in the direction of the back porch. Anna stepped away for a moment to avoid a dip in the earth. When she returned to her mother's side, the conversation picked up again.

In a soft, thoughtful voice, *Maemm* continued, holding her basket in front of her. "Honey, you're just shy of being twenty-one. Most girls your age are married, with children. Your *daed* and I have never pushed you to get married; we just figured it would happen naturally. But Jesse . . ." She hesitated before going on in a serious voice. "We think you're well-matched."

When Anna stayed silent, her *maemm* added, taking a step back so she walked side by side with Anna, who slowed her pace as she acknowledged what her mother was trying to say.

"Jesse's the answer to all of our prayers. There's no better family in our church than the Beilers. As you know, Jesse's *daed* is the bishop, and his mother . . ." She let out a satisfied breath and lifted her chin with new confidence. "No one in our community does more for the needy; that's for sure."

They neared the porch. Anna was still absorbing how very significant and unexpected this conversation was. Anna frowned at the thought of someone choosing her spouse for her. She appreciated that her parents were trying to help, but when it came to finding a husband, that was something Anna would do by herself.

Without a doubt, her mother's words about Jesse were true. He did come from good kin, but to Anna, having good kin played only a small role when choosing a life partner. Anna hadn't given marriage much consideration, but what she did know was that when she decided to settle down, her partner would have to be supportive of her decisions and love her unconditionally.

She knew women in the community who always agreed with their husbands. She wondered, at times, if those couples really agreed, or if they merely pretended to make peace. So many variables entered into finding the man she'd spend her life with and be with in eternity.

Maemm's voice took on a firmer approach. "He'll make a good husband for you, Anna."

Anna nearly choked as they stepped up the concrete steps to the door. While her mother opened the screen for her to go inside, its hinges squeaked. Anna's heart pumped to a dangerous beat. She hadn't realized that her parents had been planning out her life for her. Especially marriage to Jesse Beiler.

In the kitchen, the aroma of the yeast rolls became stronger. Anna licked her lips. But before she thought about lunch, she was forced to deal with a relationship with her *daed*'s handsome hired hand who, unbeknownst to her before today, her parents wanted her to marry.

The more she contemplated the planning that had gone on without her knowledge, the more her pulse picked up to a speed that was a combination of nervousness and excitement. Excitement because marriage to Jesse was something she wanted. Nervousness because it probably could not happen.

While Anna considered what was going on between her *eltern*, she realized how much more serious the outcome of the contest would be—if she won, of course.

She'd never shared her thoughts about her future with *Maemm* or *Daed*. And that they were playing matchmaker between her and Jesse created an even more serious issue than she'd anticipated.

She considered telling them about the contest, her ambition to be an artist, to experience other cultures, and her decision about joining the Amish faith. All of that would be bad enough.

But now that she'd learned that they were planning a wedding between her and Jesse . . . how much more difficult the break with their faith would be if it materialized.

As her heart pumped to an uneasy beat, she realized that *Maemm* was waiting for her to say something. *But what should I tell her? I can't lie. I don't want to disappoint her; at the same time, I can't lead her on to believe that Jesse Beiler might become their son-in-law. Should I be completely honest and share my plans with her?*

Anna realized that she was still holding the clothes.

With one careful motion, she bent to place the basket on the floor. She glanced up at her mother, and the hopeful, excited expression in her eyes saddened Anna.

I need to say something. It's not right to allow her to believe that there's hope for a marriage between me and an Amish man. Or any man, at the moment.

Anna took her basket with both hands as she and her mother went upstairs. In silence, they returned the clothes to their appropriate pegs and their socks to their respective drawers. But as they worked, an uncomfortable feeling filled Anna's chest with an ache she knew had no remedy. At the same time, Anna wondered what was happening between Jesse and the owners of the farm he wanted with all his heart.

Downstairs, in the kitchen, Anna stopped for a moment in front of the large fan to enjoy the welcome air that cooled her face. The screened windows were also open, as usual. Farm scents floated in through the screens. Freshly mowed grass.

The light fragrance of roses was beneath the kitchen window. The bush Mary had recently given her flourished. Anna had never liked air-conditioning and the cold on her arms. But today, she'd welcome it.

She had just opened her mouth to speak when a knock broke the silence. When her mother stepped to the door, Anna sighed with relief. But eventually, she'd have some explaining to do.

And now that she was aware of her parents' plans for her and Jesse, Anna wasn't sure if she could put her parents through her transition should she win the contest.

The open door revealed Jesse. As Anna took in his

tall, rugged-looking body, her heart did a somersault.
Excitement welled inside her. "Did you get the farm?"

He dipped his head and smiled a little.

Naomi offered a quick motion to the dining-room
table that was only several feet away. "Please. Have a
seat. And tell us all about your morning!"

Not trying to hide her excitement that Jesse might
now be the owner of the farm he wanted, she remembered her manners. "Would you like fresh lemonade?"

He nodded with a handsome smile. "*Denki.*"

"I'll have one, too," her mother chimed in. "Jesse,
we've got chicken salad sandwiches for lunch. Will you
have one with us?"

He waved a dismissive hand. "I don't want to cause
you work."

"It's our pleasure."

Anna took in the concern on Jesse's face. The way he
was acting . . . She continued to study him with a frown.
Usually, he was laid-back.

But today, to her surprise, he appeared uneasy. A bit
too formal. He clenched his fingers into his palms over
his pockets. Anna knew him well enough to sense that
something bothered him. And he hadn't mentioned the
Norris farm.

After she helped *Maemm* with three sandwiches, the
two women stepped to the table, set three medium-sized
plates in their respective spots, and took their seats.
"Let's pray."

After a brief prayer of thanks, Anna softened her
voice so that Jesse would be aware of her concern. "Are
you okay?"

He nodded. "But it hasn't been the best morning."
Anna's mother narrowed her brows with concern while
Anna pressed her lips together in a straight line and
lifted an uncertain brow. After taking a drink, he looked
at Anna before turning to her mother.

Anna and her *maemm* listened with great interest
while he explained the offer he and his *daed* had made
with the real estate agent. She and *Maemm* stopped
eating and sat very still while Jesse told them about the
other offer. Concern edged his voice. He offered an
uncertain shrug as he regarded Anna, then her mother.

Maemm was the first to break the silence that followed.
"We're here for you." She motioned with her hand.
"Please. Go on. And don't leave out anything."

"I know things happen for a reason, but I had already
imagined that farm belonging to me. Of hearing children running around the house. Having a wife fixing
dinner in the kitchen. Because naturally, I thought if we
got our offer in first and paid the asking price, it would
be ours. And I think that's what makes the uncertainty
so difficult." He smiled a little. "Maybe it would have
been easier if I hadn't already planned the rest of my life
with that beautiful farm in the picture."

A long silence ensued while the three sat very still.
The only sounds were the fan blades whirling and birds
chirping on the sill outside the kitchen window.

Finally, Anna spoke in her most logical tone. "Jesse,
of course this isn't the easiest situation. But let's see . . ."
She strummed her fingers against the table and narrowed her brows. "Optimistically speaking, sometimes
we have to fight for what we want most. But in the end,

it will all be worth it." Automatically, she recalled a conversation she'd had just recently about something good coming from something bad. That everlasting life had resulted from the brutal death of Christ.

The corners of Jesse's lips curved in amusement. "I'm glad I brought this to you." Smiling broadly, he added, "Already I feel better."

Anna's heart warmed. She yearned to help him even more and concentrated on his predicament. But it wasn't easy to know what to say because the situation was like none she'd ever come across.

But *Maemm* had always told her that you didn't have to be an expert to apply common sense. And that was what she tried to do. She wanted with all her heart for him not to give up, to keep looking at his glass as half full. But if she understood correctly, ownership of this farm wasn't coming easily.

After a sip of lemonade, she returned her drink to the coaster on the oak table. Ice cubes clinked against the glass. At the same time, *Maemm* scooped a couple of pieces of chicken with her fork and returned them to the sandwich on her plate. "What did you do when the other offer came in?"

Jesse let out a breath. "Sandy, the real estate agent, wrote a new one that topped it." After taking a bite, he swallowed. A few moments later, he glanced at Anna before turning his attention to her mother. "It was several thousand dollars over the offer of the couple who was willing to pay more than the asking price. And to be honest . . ." He lifted his palms to the ceiling and gave an uncertain shake of his head. "I don't know what's going to happen. My *familie* stretched their pocketbooks to lend me as much as they could. But I know God will help me with this."

Anna bit her bottom lip while she tried to absorb everything she'd just heard. As she took small bites of her sandwich, she realized how very much she yearned for Jesse to have his dream. Maybe even more than he wanted her to have hers. She swallowed an emotional knot as she acknowledged how very close he was to having what he'd always wanted. And at the same time, so very far away.

It was unfortunate that she had no experience with real estate offers. But what he'd just said was beginning to make sense to her. "So another couple offered more than the asking price, and their offer went to the owners. But then, you and your *daed* wrote an offer that topped their amount? And now both are in the owners' hands?"

He nodded.

Anna's mother chimed in. "I'm not going to pretend I'm an expert at this kind of thing, but let's use common sense here."

She locked gazes with Anna and smiled a little. Anna returned her smile, knowing that she'd been told that very thing so often by the very woman who was now trying to advise her best friend. "For a moment, let's pretend that Paul and I are the sellers."

She followed with a confident shrug and scooted forward on her chaise. "When I look at the situation like that, it's easy to say what we'd do. Without asking my husband, I am sure that he would agree to go for the larger offer." She hesitated and focused on Jesse. "Yours."

Jesse swallowed. Several heartbeats later, he softened his voice to a more appreciative tone. "You make it sound so simple." He offered a grateful nod. "Thank you for that, Naomi."

Anna added to the conversation. "Jesse, I think we're making this more difficult than it really is. First of all, know that you did all that you could. You raised the ante. I think that, for now, you have to be satisfied with that. And, of course, pray." She lowered her voice for emphasis. "Their offer is out of your control. But you do have control over yours. And you changed it."

"*Jah.* Apparently, they want the land as much as I do. And because my offer was already in, their only option was to offer more than the asking price." He took a drink and returned the glass to the coaster. "Which meant that *Daed* and I had to top theirs. And we did."

He lifted a brow and smiled a little. "*Daed* told me not to worry. That things would work out if we kept faith."

While Anna and her mother sat very still, Jesse lifted a set of helpless palms and expelled a satisfied sigh. "Now you know what's going on. That's where we are."

Anna took the last bite of her chicken salad and swallowed. After following with a drink, she returned her glass to the table and looked at Jesse, edging her voice with as much positivity as she could. "So, the way I see it, the most logical thing for the sellers to do is to accept your last offer. And I don't know why they wouldn't. When will you hear?"

This conversation seemed to have encouraged Jesse. His facial muscles relaxed. So did his shoulders. And he lifted his chin a notch higher. "Any time. Sandy will call as soon as she knows something, and *Daed*'s working in the barn right now, so he'll hear the phone if it rings."

He let out a low whistle. "We'll just have to see what happens. But what I came by for was . . ." He smiled a little at Anna. "I wanted to ask you to ride by the farm with me in my buggy."

"I'd love that!"

He directed his attention to Naomi, dipping his head a notch and lowering the pitch of his voice to a tone that was a combination of hopefulness and seriousness. "May I have your permission to take Anna with me?"

Chapter Ten

As Jesse's horse pulled his buggy, he considered the conversation he'd just had with Anna and Naomi King. Their takes on the farm for sale had boosted his excitement.

As the horse swished its brown tail back and forth, Jesse eyed Anna from the corner of his eye and smiled. "Your conversation picked up my spirits. *Denki.*"

She crossed her legs at the ankles and leaned back on the blue velvet that padded the hard bench. "I'm glad. And the more I think of it, Jesse, the more I'm convinced your dream is about to come true. And . . ."

He offered her a quick glance.

"I have saved money for many years. I want you to have it for your farm."

Jesse swallowed as he absorbed her words. "You would give me your savings for the farm?"

When he looked over at her, their gazes locked for a quick second, and she nodded. He'd noted the sparkle of moisture in her eyes. The serious expression on her face.

"Anna, I don't know what to say."

"Tell me you'll use it. I want you to have your farm."

In a soft voice, she added, "Even more than I want my art degree."

It took him some time to find his voice. What she was offering him . . . Of course, he couldn't take it.

"Anna, I don't know what to say. Thank you. But you'll need that money if you move to St. Louis." His heart nearly broke when he said those words.

"Know that it's yours if you need it."

He thanked her again before a long, thoughtful silence ensued. While the clomp-clomping of hooves made an uneven beat, her words pulled at his heartstrings until his chest ached. He realized how very much Anna must love him. And how much he loved her.

He decided to tell her what was on his mind. "I've learned a lot from this experience, Anna."

"Oh?"

He glanced at her briefly as the animal scent filled the small open carriage, and as the late August sun beamed high in the sky. In the distance, soybeans and corn were tall. In the open country, Jesse decided something very important. And as quickly as he'd realized it, he deliberately nixed it from his thoughts.

Anna's soft voice pressed for an answer. "What have you learned?"

He grinned. "That if the farm becomes mine, that's wonderful. But . . ." He straightened for a more comfortable position after the buggy bounced on the uneven blacktop. "Anna King, what's even more important to me than having the farm . . ." He cleared the knot in his throat and lowered the pitch of his voice to a serious tone.

When he glanced at her, he noted the expression on her face, a combination of eagerness and interest.

"Is having your prayers and support throughout this whole ordeal. There will be other farms. I mean, eventually. But there's only one Anna King." After a slight hesitation, he went on in a more uncertain tone. "And by the way, everything I said about wanting to spend my life with you still stands."

When she didn't respond, he eyed her and saw the devastation on her face. He frowned. "Hey, what's wrong? What I said should make you happy. It's not every day I pay a compliment like that."

She turned to better face him. "Jesse, thank you. What we have . . . it's a friendship I'll treasure forever."

Her comment made his heart sink. Because what he wanted from Anna was much more than friendship. He yearned for a life with her. To wake up next to her every morning. To celebrate holidays with her.

Still, her words shouldn't disappoint him. From his first day at work for Paul King, when he and Anna had talked in her barn, she'd been honest about her goal. And he'd been honest about his. But now that he was close to having his dream, he'd added something else to it: Anna King. He didn't want to live in the large, two-story house without her.

He didn't respond. A long silence passed while they continued to the Norris farm. As they approached it, his pulse picked up to a more excited speed. "Here it is."

After he'd tied the horse, he motioned her up the porch stairs. In front of the door, he looked down at Anna. "They've already moved out."

The real estate's lock box required a code, so he

knocked on the door to make sure no one was inside. When no one answered, he automatically turned the handle. To his pleasant surprise, the door opened. He motioned with his hand. "C'mon. I can't wait to show you this."

He led her to the kitchen, the living room, and, finally, the second story. The stairs creaked as they ascended to the upper level, with three bedrooms and two bathrooms.

The last room he showed her was an empty office. It was between two bedrooms. Inside, they looked out of the large window that offered a distant view of Pebble Creek. He caught his breath. "This is my favorite part of the house."

She stood next to him, breathing in with awe. "I see why! What a great view of your farm. And Pebble Creek!"

While Jesse studied her face, something new came over him. And he recognized that it was something he'd never experienced before. Reality became clear. *She belongs here. With me.*

He decided to share his thoughts with her. "You know what I'm thinking?"

She pressed her lips together and touched them with her finger as she lifted a curious brow. "Let me guess. That you can't wait to move into this home and start farming."

Slow steps took them closer to the large window. Jesse knew if he became the owner of the farm, he needed Anna here. *She belongs here. With me. How can I convince her?*

The decision had to come from her. Nothing he could

say or do could make it for her. It had to come from her heart. But someone could help him.

He squeezed his eyes closed and said a silent prayer. *Dear Lord, I might be close to losing her, and I want her to be my wife. Please let her realize she belongs here with me.*

When he opened his eyes, an idea came to him. "This would be a great art room for you," he mentioned. Hopefulness edged his voice. But he didn't try to hide his dream of growing old with Anna.

She lifted her chin. "It's certainly light."

"The large windows allow the sunshine to come right in."

"And the view of Pebble Creek . . ."

He raised an inquisitive brow. "You know what I was thinking?"

"What?"

"That you could work on your art in here. And sketch." He lowered his tone to stress how very serious he was. "Anna, I know you want to study art, but you can do it without getting a four-year degree. And it doesn't have to take place in a large classroom."

He stepped closer, and their gazes locked in mutual understanding. "God was the greatest teacher of all, and He didn't have a classroom."

He watched the surprised expression on her face.

When she responded, uncertainty edged her voice. "*Denki.* But college will help me to learn so much more."

He smiled a little. "Fortunately, you're a natural. Anna, there are people, like me, who could study art for years and never sketch like you do."

Her cheeks flushed. "Thank you for that, Jesse. You'll never know how much I treasure your belief in me."

"But Anna, there's so much more to my feelings for you."

That night, Anna's conversation with Jesse replayed in her mind until she finally stopped sketching and stepped to her bedroom window to gaze out at Pebble Creek. Of course, she couldn't see it in the dark. All she could glimpse was the half-moon. At the same time, the words of her mamma's letter danced through her thoughts like a soft, comfortable blanket.

She pressed her palms against the windowsill and leaned forward. The light blue curtains her mother had sewn on her old Singer sewing machine were attached to hooks on both sides.

As Anna stared out into the darkness, her mind eventually focused on Jesse, and their serious talks, and a happy sigh escaped her throat. *We're opposites really. I want to go out and see the world. Jesse's content to stay right here, where we've been our whole lives. He's happy to farm and watch crops grow. But our differences are even stronger than that. Jesse has had a typical Amish upbringing from two respected parents. There's no way he can understand what it's like to have been adopted, and not know for over two decades why his mamma gave him up. Of course, that's to his advantage.*

Nothing bothers me now. Not even Mrs. Graber looking down on me and whispering that I'm not a real Amish girl. It doesn't hurt me anymore that I've been looked down on by some because I'm adopted. While they might feel that way, I realize I'm blessed to be here, even if I'm not my parents' own flesh and blood.

I respect that Mamma had me. Like Jesse said, she didn't have to. But she was brave to bring me into this world, and I love her so much for that. Life is a miracle. Doesn't that mean I'm a miracle, too?

In the barn the following morning, Anna fully acknowledged that the contest was fast approaching and, in her opinion, she didn't have a winning entry. The issue was the *Englisch* version of Anna. The woman Anna still didn't truly know. Would she ever be happy with the facial expression of the non-Amish woman? She shrugged.

Anna considered the subject while she raked dirty straw. As soon as she finished, she proceeded to shovel the pile into one of their two large wheelbarrows.

A moderately cool breeze floated in through the large, open barn doors. The exit behind the horses' stalls was open, too. A tiny mouse scurried out to the vast pasture where cattle and horses grazed.

After Anna finished her task, she stepped up the ladder that was nailed to the hayloft, being very careful not to catch her dress on the rungs. At the top, she used both hands and all her weight to push the nearest bale of straw over the edge. As it landed on the floor, she dusted her hands together and sat on the edge to catch her breath.

For a moment, she enjoyed the view from the small window in the loft that allowed a pleasant glimpse of

Pebble Creek. Yesterday's conversation at the Norris farm flitted through her mind until she closed her eyes.

Jesse Beiler wanted to marry her. She still couldn't believe it, because with all her heart, she yearned to be his wife. But the dream she'd carried in her heart most of her life couldn't materialize if she wed her best friend. She thought of the list she'd kept for so many years. And what had always remained first on it.

She opened her eyes and pressed her lips together thoughtfully. What he'd said about using the room that overlooked Pebble Creek as an art studio made sense. But her plans were so much larger than that.

She yearned more than ever to explore different cultures. It was difficult to believe that if her mamma had lived, Anna would have been Catholic. She didn't really know much about that faith, but what she was sure of was that she couldn't wait to visit San Diego, the place she'd come into the world.

Still, the warm sensation of Jesse's fingers wrapped around hers prompted a surge of excitement that nothing in the world could replace. *Jesse Beiler. Anna Beiler.*

Pressing her lips firmly together in a line of determination, she gave a firm shake of her head. Automatically, the memory of Old Sam entered her head, and she smiled a little. She'd heard all sorts of stories about the artistic genius and his loving wife, Esther.

When they'd been alive, Old Sam had carried something special that he'd made just for her for their sixtieth wedding anniversary all the way up the hill. He'd buried it in hopes of giving his beloved wife a symbol of their love. Unfortunately, Esther had gone to the Lord before that day. However, years later, blessings had come from it. People associated with Old Sam always seemed to be blessed.

Miraculously, his niece, Jessica, hadn't even believed in God when she'd come to Arthur, Illinois. Now, she did. If God had created a miracle like that, surely He would bless Anna with one, too.

And there were other stories, too. Levi and Annie Miller had met at Pebble Creek when they were kids. Anna had been told that on the top of that very hill, Levi had asked Annie to spend the rest of her life with him.

Closing her eyes with great emotion, Anna crossed her palm over her chest and drew in a deep, helpful breath. She acknowledged her dream of sketching beautiful canvases all day. Of venturing off to places where human beings practiced different cultures. Different faiths.

However, at the same time, she realized an even greater dream. To find true love and to be a good wife to the man she loved with all her heart. Footsteps interrupted her thoughts, and she heard Jesse's voice. "Anna, what are you doing up there?"

Suddenly, she felt silly that she'd allowed her mind to wander to finding a husband when, really, what she needed to do was finish cleaning the animal stalls and freshen the bedding.

She waved a hand in a friendly welcome and tried for her best explanation. "Did you find out anything yet? About the Norris farm?"

"Not yet."

"I'm ready to spread straw in the horse stalls, and I . . ." She smiled, deciding on complete honesty. "I was thinking of some of the wonderful things that happened at Pebble Creek."

Stepping up to the top of the ladder, he joined her. At her side, he nodded. "I understand. There's nothing like it, is there?"

She silently acknowledged that today, while sorting things out, she needed to stay away from Jesse. Doing that with him next to her was difficult. To clear her mind and look at things realistically. She stood and began carefully stepping down the ladder, which was attached to the loft. At the bottom, she looked up at him and answered. "No, there isn't."

Even in this short time with Jesse, she had experienced a sense of calm and satisfaction that she'd never felt before. She wasn't sure why, but she reasoned it was because he listened to her without judging.

And his advice was well-thought-out. *Jah*, Jesse Beiler put her at ease . . . and excited her at the same time. And no matter how much she tried to rid him from her thoughts and focus on her lifelong goal, she couldn't deny that she loved him.

"You gonna finish spreading straw?"

She nodded. "But I'm behind on my chores today."

He quickly made his way down the ladder after her. All of a sudden, he darted her a handsome grin. "Then I came at the right time to lend you a hand."

He grasped his hands around the cords that tied a bale of straw together and hoisted it over his shoulder.

But she didn't protest. Jesse could carry a bale of straw the long distance to the stalls much more quickly than she could load it into the wheelbarrow and push it herself. And while she followed him, she smiled a little.

No matter how much she tried to put Jesse out of her mind, she never could. *And do I really want to?*

The contest deadline was near. The drawing of the two women still wasn't to Anna's satisfaction. Yet her mind focused on Jesse and what he'd confessed to her at the Norris farm.

She also contemplated the words of her mamma's letter. Still, she was sure that pursuing the *Englisch* life via the upcoming contest was the right route to go. How could she change her mind when she'd had it at the top of her list all these years?

Today, the King home was even more quiet than usual. *Maemm* had told her not to fix a big dinner because she and *Daed* would be home late. As Anna ran the feather duster up the stairway banister, she allowed herself to imagine a life with Jesse. As she closed her eyes for one blissful moment, her heart skipped a beat. When she opened them, she let out a sigh of contentment and proceeded to dust where the oak poles met the steps on the way down.

Thunder interrupted her thoughts. As a bolt of lightning crackled, she glimpsed the sudden downpour from the small stair window. Without warning, a different downpour returned to her thoughts. The storm when Jesse had carried her into the barn. Their conversation. The careful way he'd attended to the cut on her forehead. For a moment, she closed her eyes to savor the memory.

Rain beat down on the roof. Usually, she didn't like precipitation because she loved being outside. But today, for some reason, the weather seemed conducive to helping her think things through.

After she imagined a life with Jesse, she switched to the thought of venturing out into the *Englisch* world. To experiencing a California sunset. To wearing her hair down.

She gave a discouraged shake of her head and finished her task. She stepped to the kitchen to return the duster to its place underneath the kitchen sink and to pull out a container of wood polish.

She stepped back to the stairwell, polish in one hand, thin rag in the other. Careful not to disperse too much dark liquid into her rag, she dipped it and used slow strokes to apply it to the rail that ran all the way up to the second floor.

The contest was just around the corner, and she'd been thinking more and more of the talk that would spread if and when her church became aware of her plans. Fortunately, right now it was still a secret. She'd certainly had heard if it wasn't. Amazingly, she felt closer than ever to *Maemm*. Especially since she'd told her that she and Anna's *daed* had always planned to adopt. Even if Anna didn't win first place, the knowledge of her aim to go after a four-year degree outside of their community could harm her parents. Mostly, she was concerned for her folks. They were always very careful to do what was expected of them.

When her thoughts unexpectedly migrated to Jesse, she pressed her lips together in a fine line while she considered the rugged-looking man who'd quickly become the best friend she'd ever had. While she rubbed deep brown polish in to the oak, she smiled a little.

As long as she'd known him, he'd always seemed logical. Reasonable. He'd never been one to pass judgment. Jesse had always appeared to be on the quiet side, but when something happened that required strength, he'd always been there. For instance, she recalled a time in school when he'd stopped a fight. He'd been, without a doubt, the strongest kid in her class, even though he hadn't been the tallest. Her heart picked up speed to an unusually nervous, fast speed.

I want a four-year degree. Independence to express who I am. But I want to be with Jesse, too. Her shoulders tensed. Then she drew in a deep, relaxing breath as she remembered that the Lord was her guide and her Savior.

How could I have such little faith when You are with me? Dear Lord, please hear my prayer. You know my concerns as well as my lifelong dream. Please guide me and protect my family. Amen.

As soon as she opened her eyes, she heard the side door open.

"*Daed!*" She went to hug him. "You're home early!"

He smiled a little as he grabbed a metal container of cabinet stain. He stepped around the hall to the washroom. As he spoke, she could barely hear him over the sound of the water. "The store's out, and we're almost done, so I'm taking what's here to finish up."

When he rejoined her, he regarded her with a hopeful expression. "I was thinking about your fresh-squeezed lemonade."

"Of course! Let me wash my hands and I'll pour you one."

Quick steps took her to the washroom in the hall. When she returned to the kitchen, she stood on her tip-toes to reach a glass, filled it with ice, and poured her *daed* the freshly squeezed lemonade.

At the dining-room table, she sat down across from him. It was nice to have him home, even if it wasn't for long.

"Anna, when the rain stops, would you tell Jesse that there are extra bags of oats? It slipped my mind."

"Aren't they in the barn?"

He nodded. "But they're on the east side. He might not see them."

"Sure, *Daed*. I'll let him know."

Thunder crackled.

Sitting back in his chair, her father grinned. "At least you're inside this time, safe and sound."

She nodded.

"The scar is healing nicely."

She lifted her hand and traced a finger over the faint mark. "I was sure it needed stitches. But you proved me wrong." After a slight hesitation, her father went on. "Looks like we're going to need more staff at the bakery. Thought it would be a nice full-time job for you."

Anna frowned, trying to hide her disapproval. Compared to working on her sketches, working full-time in the bakery didn't appeal to her at all. She wanted control of her life. To make her own choices, even though she knew her *daed* had her best interests at heart.

At the same time, she was fully aware that the man sitting opposite her loved her, and that his intentions were good. She watched him drink from the large glass, fully aware how fortunate she was to be part of such a loving family, even if it was only the three of them.

There was no one more hardworking than Paul King. And no man around was more honest. Which made what she set out to do much, much harder.

Inside, she shook. She loved her father with all her heart. He could give the appearance of being warm and understanding. But she knew him too well. To her *daed,* there was only black and white. No in between. Right was right and wrong was wrong.

I wish Daed *could better understand that not everyone's the same. That we don't all think alike. And if God blesses me with that scholarship, I'm afraid he will be angry and ashamed. If I don't win, maybe it will be a blessing. But the desire to learn and share with others how I've captured things on paper is so strong. Why did God give me the ability to draw if He didn't intend for me to share the gift He gave me?*

Jesse made his way to Anna's sketching place. He couldn't wait to tell her that he now owned the farm. He'd found out last night, before dinner, and at the dining table, his *daed* had said a special prayer to God. And Jesse continued to give his thanks to the Creator of the universe.

But Anna's contest was only two days away. And even though he had his farm, his life wouldn't be complete unless she came with it.

* * *

Light, gurgling sounds from Pebble Creek floated through the warm, late-summer air. On the ground, Anna rested her back against a large rock and held her canvas on her lap.

She'd risen very early again to start her chores so there would be enough time to work on her sketch at the place that most inspired her. Not only that, but she and Jesse had arranged to meet here.

Hopefully, today, the Norris farm would belong to him. She'd said an extra prayer for Jesse before she'd left her house this morning.

Not wanting to waste time, she began moving her pencil over the pad that rested comfortably on her thighs. The shallow water gently rolled over pebbles, prompting a spirit of ease and relaxation through Anna's entire body, starting at her shoulders and flowing all the way down to her toes.

I'm still taking in how Jesse and I have become so close. It's certainly an unusual relationship because of my contest entry. At first, I feared he'd tell the bishop. But I didn't know Jesse then. Now I do, and I like the part of him that respects my ambition, and the soft side of him that wants to help me.

The water cascading over the pebbles lulled her into a state of inspiration, and she took advantage. As she slid her pencil lightly over the visage of the woman who claimed most of the canvas, a soft, familiar voice pulled her from her reverie.

She sat up a little straighter. Not at all because she was on edge but because talking to Jesse about her project made the pulse on her wrist move to an excited, hopeful pace.

She straightened and waved a hand in a friendly greeting when she glimpsed him coming her way. "Over here!"

This part of Pebble Creek was the ideal meeting place because her family's land brushed up against this branch of the creek. The late Sam Beachy had willed the area that had been coined Pebble Creek to Jessica, who'd come from out of state.

The mere thought of creative genius Old Sam prompted a sense of well-being in Anna's chest. For years, she'd coveted this place.

She'd talked to Jessica Beachy a few times, and Anna planned to ask Old Sam's great-niece to continue spending time here. Quickly recalling her purpose, she watched Jesse wade through the tall, wild grass. When he finally stood in front of her, he offered her a wide smile and extended his arms. "I made it."

As he stepped closer, she jumped up and clenched her palms in front of her. "Did you get the farm?"

The corners of his mouth lifted. "*Jah!*"

Automatically, she threw her arms around him. When she released him, her voice cracked with joy. "Praise God! Our prayers worked!"

He nodded. "They did."

She sat back down and motioned to the spot next to hers. "Jesse, we need to celebrate. Do you know what this means?"

He waited for her to go on.

"Your dream came true! What you've yearned for for so many years . . . you've got it!"

"It's your turn next."

She was quick to note his lack of enthusiasm, but she wasn't sure why he wouldn't be ecstatic. But they didn't have long, so she motioned to her contest entry. "It's almost finished. What do you think?"

All of a sudden, her hands shook as they regarded it together. What if he didn't like it?

"May I?" He took the canvas.

"*Jah*." With great care, he positioned it on his thighs as he sat next to her. While he seemed to take it in, she studied him. Today, he looked larger than usual. As he held the canvas, she glimpsed the way his upper-arm muscles pushed against his sleeves.

When he removed his large hat, the sun lightened his hair a notch to a softer brown. When the sunlight hit it, the shade reminded her of beautiful leaves turning in the fall. Several light-blond strands highlighted the browns.

His square jaw was set as he pulled her work closer to him and then held it at a distance. His dark brows narrowed. The bright sun enabled her to see every tiny line around his eyes. She could barely see a small scar that hovered on his forehead, just above his right eye.

But what captured her attention the most was the way his large hands held on to the sides of the canvas with such gentleness. She drew in a small breath as she took advantage of the moment to absorb everything about this man who lifted such heavy bales of hay yet held with such gentleness the picture that Anna hoped would win her a four-year scholarship.

As she watched her *daed*'s farmhand, she pressed her lips together thoughtfully. But as she noted the serious expression on his face, an unfamiliar emotion touched her. She drew in a small, quick breath of surprise and, without thinking, drew her hands to her chest.

Finally, he turned toward her and lifted a brow. "I know you want my honest opinion."

She straightened and waited for him to go on.

He expelled a deep breath. "The *Englisch* woman just doesn't capture me like the Amish one."

While she took in his feedback, he went on. "There's still something missing in this one." He pointed to the image of her in the upper right-hand corner as an *Englisch* girl. "Even though I can't tell you what it is."

They both turned their attention to the shadow picture on her canvas. "There's definitely a difference between these two."

With one careful motion, he held out the canvas, and she retrieved it. When he didn't speak, she turned to him.

He leaned toward her and put his weight on his left forearm to support his body. "I think I know what's wrong."

"*Jah?*"

He nodded. "The Amish girl looks genuine and the *Englisch* woman doesn't."

Anna finally nodded. "I think you hit the nail on the head."

Time with Jesse was precious, and she didn't want to spend any more of it on her work. "Jesse, it's my turn to listen to you. You've got to tell me everything about your farm . . . When did you hear? What did your real estate agent say?"

His eyes lit up. "There's really not much to say 'cept Sandy got word last night that the Norrises accepted our offer. There were so many hours, after we made our last offer, for them to get back to us. And fortunately, no one topped it."

A combination of hopefulness and great anticipation edged his voice as he looked down at her with a determined expression. "It's the start of everything I've ever wanted."

In silence, she took in the sincerity on his face. She didn't say anything, all too aware of the rest of what he yearned for. He longed for her to be with him. And she couldn't commit.

After a short pause, he cleared his throat and jumped up, putting his hands on his hips. "Time to get back to work."

"*Jah.* Me too."

As quick steps took him back to the field, Anna regarded her sketch. Without waiting, she said a quick prayer of thanks that Jesse was going to have his farm.

She carefully opened her hope chest and slipped her work inside. For some strange reason, Jesse's image loomed in the distance. But she felt as if he was still with her.

She pressed her lips together in a straight, thoughtful line and lifted a pensive brow. She could think of Jesse twenty-four/seven, but right now, there was something that needed to be done. Something that couldn't wait another day. *It's time to tell my parents what I'm about to do. They deserve to know. And as far as my entry, I need to nix it. And try a different one.*

* * *

That evening, the late August sun was setting. Beautiful colors blended into the distant sky. *Maemm* had told Anna she and *Daed* would be home for dinner. Outside, Anna watered the plants around the front of the house. For a thankful moment, she stopped to take in Mary's beautiful peach-colored roses.

As Anna bent to touch one soft, velvety petal, she drew in a breath of deep appreciation. She touched her nose to the flower to enjoy its sweet, light, floral fragrance.

She'd decided to enter her portrait of Jesse instead of the one of the two women. She straightened her shoulders with confidence.

As she used the hose to refill the water pitcher, the clomp-clomping of hooves made her turn in the direction of the sound. She watched as their family buggy came down the long drive and approached the house. She quickly watered the hot-pink geraniums, turned off the spigot, and braced herself. "Dear Lord, thank You for answering Jesse's prayer. And please bless him with the life he's always wanted. But I need Your help right now. I'm about to explain my plan to my *eltern*. And please . . . please let them understand."

During dinner, the conversation focused on Jesse and the farm that was now his. After the dishes were washed and dried, Anna turned to her *maemm*. "There's something I need to talk to you and *Daed* about." The surprised expression on her mother's face quickly reminded Anna that what she was about to do wouldn't be easy.

While *Maemm* went to get *Daed*, Anna stepped to the living room and clutched her palms together as she said another silent prayer. *Dear Lord, please help my parents accept this.*

As they entered the room, her father lifted an inquisitive brow. In his usual gruff voice, he asked, "Tell me."

Before Anna said anything, they sat down on the sofa while Anna claimed the wooden rocker opposite them. Mentally coaching herself to carry this out, she looked at them and sat up straight, placing her palms flat against her thighs. And explained.

Afterward, a long silence ensued while Paul and Naomi exchanged glances of disapproval and doubt. The room was so quiet, Anna could have heard a pin drop. Finally, her mother drew a hand over her chest and spoke in a weary voice. "My, my. Anna, you've taken us by surprise."

Her *daed*'s voice was firm. "Anna, I don't think you're fully aware of what you're getting yourself in to." He glanced back at his wife before his gaze returned to Anna. "It's our job to help you make good choices."

A soft voice piped in. "Did you ever wonder how you'd live in the city? How you'd get around? Where you'd go to church? And what you'd do without us?" In a pleading voice, she added, "Without Jesse?"

Anna hesitated. Because their worries were legitimate. "I've been praying for guidance. And I know God will help me to overcome any obstacles that come my way."

Anna's *daed* stood, stepped closer to her, and looked down at her as he crossed his arms over his chest. "He won't have to, Anna."

While she and her father locked gazes, he moved his hands into his pockets and set his jaw. "I forbid you to go."

Tomorrow, she'd be in St. Louis. At the Marriott Grand. For the art contest. In the Kings' barn, Anna closed her eyes and said another prayer, thanking God for Jesse's dream coming true and praying for Him to guide her, especially because she didn't have her parents' blessing to carry out her own plan.

She spread fresh bedding in the animal stalls while Jesse raked dirty straw into piles and loaded what had been used into the two wheelbarrows. While they worked, he listened to Anna recount last night's conversation with her folks. Paul's reaction hadn't surprised him. But, apparently, by the distressed tone of Anna's voice, she hadn't prepared herself for reality.

She stopped, propped her rake to her side, and eyed him. Sensing that she wanted to talk, he asked what she was going to do.

After a slight pause, she shrugged and smiled a little. "I'm going to follow my dream and see where it takes me. I can't believe the contest's tomorrow."

Jesse smiled a little as he sat down on a bale of straw.

She softened her voice. "But I want my parents' support. Jesse, I feel so much closer to *Maemm* and *Daed* since *Maemm* explained they'd always planned to adopt."

He whistled. "I'm happy about that. But as far as

getting their support?" He gave a quick shake of his head. "That might be asking too much." After a slight hesitation, he went on in a serious tone. "Anna, remember, they don't know anything other than how they've lived their entire lives." He shrugged. "For that matter, neither do you. But your attitude . . ." He considered the right words. "It's adventurous."

She laughed. "You make it sound like I'm going to climb a mountain or something."

He contemplated her statement. "Climbing a mountain might be easy compared to what you're doing. Anna, if you win and move to St. Louis, you'll have to learn a whole new lifestyle. Make all new friends. Remember, there won't be anyone who grew up with you there. Your folks are here, and so am I."

"But Jesse, knowing how my parents feel makes this *adventure* more stressful than it should be."

"Anna, we've both known from the get-go what you were up against. But I've been thinking . . . I've supported you all along. I want to go with you."

She took a breath in and drew her hand over her chest in awe. "You mean . . ."

He offered a slow nod.

Her eyes sparkled with moisture. "You would do that for me?"

He nodded while he acknowledged what he'd be risking. That the people he'd loved his entire life, including his *daed*, the bishop, would most likely not approve.

"I was going to work on our roof with *Daed*, but right now, being there to support you is more important." After a slight pause, he softened his voice, and the flecks danced on his irises. "You've changed me, Anna. In a good way."

"*Jah?*"

He grinned.

"How so?"

"Since I've gotten to know you well, I've done a lot of thinking. And something Old Sam once said tells me you should enter this contest, just like you've planned. Once you find out if you won or not, you can decide about the rest of your life."

"But what about my folks? About our church?"

"It might take a while, but they'll be okay." After a slight pause, he smiled with amusement.

She darted him an expression that was a combination of curiosity and hopefulness. "Why that look?"

He laughed. "It's what Old Sam once said."

In silence, she raised a brow.

"If God brings you to it, He'll bring you through it."

Chapter Eleven

It was hard to believe it was August 25, the day of Anna's contest. Jesse smiled a little as he headed toward her home to accompany her to St. Louis. It would feel good to offer his support.

Anna filled his thoughts as he enjoyed the gentle ups and downs in his buggy on the blacktop from his house to the Kings'. As the cool breeze floated in through the open windows, he found himself excited about Anna's contest and praying that she'd win.

"Dear Lord, Please guide Anna's life. And mine. Please help this to work out the way You want it to, and if it be Your will, bless us with a life together."

As the horse swished its tail back and forth, the sun brightened a notch. Immediately, Jesse's tense shoulders relaxed. The corners of his lips lifted into a curve. He blew out a deep breath.

How could he forget that the One who'd suffered on the cross for his sins had control of his life? As one of the church's ministers had said in a sermon, "Christ is not the victim; He is the victor."

An oncoming car came his way, and Jesse coaxed Serene over to the side of the narrow blacktop. *Letting go of earthly possessions enables us to take hold of heavenly treasures.* Jesse lifted an uncertain brow.

Another of Old Sam's proverbs came to mind. Jesse wasn't sure why; it didn't really apply to his relationship with Anna. But the recollection prompted a silent prayer. *Dear God, I live for You. Please fill my heart and my soul with Your great love. Amen.*

As the car came closer, the peaceful moment quickly turned horrific. Because, to Jesse's shock and dismay, a vehicle behind the car started to pass.

There wasn't time to react. And if there had been, there still wasn't much he could do. As the fast car hit his buggy head on, steel pounded his chest. The loud sound of a continuous horn filled the air as he was thrown from his simple means of transportation and into the air. He screamed in pain. Anna was on his mind as his world went black.

At the Marriott St. Louis Grand, optimism filled Anna as she made her way through the concourse underneath the street level that connected the main hotel to the ballrooms.

At the Majestic Ballroom on the second floor, she took in the light gray walls. She'd learned that the ballrooms had just undergone renovation. She could smell fresh carpet.

She stood very still inside of the foyer outside of the Majestic Ballroom. The area was all windows and overlooked Washington Avenue. As she took in the vehicles on the street, she mentally noted how vastly different St. Louis was from Arthur, Illinois.

The city was far grander and even busier than she'd imagined. Still, everything about today was perfect. Except that Jesse hadn't shown up to go with her. She guessed he'd decided to do his roof.

Her parents had offered their blessing as she'd waved goodbye to them, although they'd done so with a lack of enthusiasm. Even so, her father had kissed her goodbye when she'd climbed into the back seat of her driver's car.

Before stepping inside the women's washroom, she stopped for a moment and mentally ticked off her to-do list. *Get here.* Fertig. *Check in, provide my entry, wear my name badge.* Fertig.

Letting out a satisfied breath, she made her way to the exhibit-style crowded ballroom, where tables of art work were displayed.

As she looked around in awe, voices morphed into one solid sound. She noticed a few curious glances and acknowledged that she must look out of place in her long blue dress and white *kapp*.

But she didn't care. In fact, as she stood in her Amish attire, an unexpected love for her faith swept over her. Words inside a frame on the wall claimed her attention. *Don't try to find your path. Create your own.*

Anna considered that message as she searched among the numerous tables for her entry. That Jesse hadn't shown up nagged at her thoughts. She'd been certain he'd come with her.

However, she was aware that he'd originally planned to work on his roof before tomorrow's rainstorm hit.

Plus, she knew he had big decisions to make regarding his farm. That had to be why he wasn't with her.

Still, she missed him and wished he were there. As she found her table, the words in bold black print claimed her thoughts again. *Don't try to find your path. Create your own.*

As she took in the empty space behind her name on a card, she smiled with satisfaction. She had no doubt that she'd made the right choice by scrapping her original idea of the Amish versus the English woman for the image of Jesse's honest, humble face, representing being true to one's self.

There was now another goal in Anna's life besides being an artist. And that was to spend happily ever after with her one true love.

But it's Jesse. He's what Mamma could never find. I know he's the one. I'm sure because of everything he's said. I could see his love for me in his eyes. The tongue can lie, but the eyes can't.

She startled when her name was called over the loud speaker. Straightening her shoulders, she headed toward the judges' booth. Inside the enclosed area, Anna smiled a little as she shook hands with a middle-aged lady.

"I'm Jane Walker."

"Anna King."

Jane quickly introduced Anna to the other judges and motioned to Anna's sketch of Jesse, which was displayed on a table in a private room where they all could view it.

Being true to one's self. Questions started over the

entry that Anna had decided to title *Friendship*. After saying a silent prayer, Anna folded her hands over her lap and answered the interrogations about her sketch and how she'd captured his character and revealed his emotions so they appeared so lifelike.

She thought back to her time with Jesse while she'd taken in that honest, trustworthy face she'd captured on canvas. She knew every crease around his eyes. Where his hair was thickest. The curve of his mouth when he was about to crack a smile. But the most important aspect of her entry, in her mind, was his eyes. She felt as though she'd captured his heart and soul. When she studied his penciled visage, something tugged at her heart until she swallowed an emotional knot.

As Anna spoke, she discussed the lines of emotion as well as why she'd chosen him, in particular, as her entry. Anna relaxed while she told about her friend and what he meant to her. Twenty minutes later, one of the women smiled. "He sounds like someone I'd want to know. And you're certainly a talented artist, Anna."

Anna beamed. "Thank you."

In silence, the judges began writing notes. As Anna studied them, she wondered how her entry compared to others. Of course, it wasn't just the art that was judged. What was equally important, Anna guessed, was the story behind each entry. And Anna's was genuine.

"This is simple. Yet brilliant. When I look at this picture, I feel as if I'm seeing an actual human being. His eyes look so real. Trusting." She pressed her lips together and took Anna's application in her hand.

"I would trust Jesse with my life."

Jane turned her attention back to the picture. "Anna, you're very talented. Until we compile the scores, I can't promise anything. But I'm extremely impressed with your work."

Anna beamed. "Thank you. And thank you for considering my entry."

Jane lifted a brow and locked gazes with Anna until she spoke again. "There are lots of exceptionally talented artists here. Many great entries. But this one is extraordinary. The winner will be whoever accumulates the highest combination of points. And Anna King, I want you to know that so far, this entry is my favorite."

Anna was the winner. As the crowd in the Marriott Majestic Ballroom applauded, she made her way forward to accept the coveted scholarship she'd prayed for. But as she reached the front, for some strange reason her glory was replaced with a strange sense of uncertainty.

Don't try to find your own path. Create it.

The strong message filled her head as she shook Jane's hand and listened to a statement of congratulations. God had answered her prayer. And she finally knew where she belonged.

An hour later, inside the Honda CR-V, Anna relaxed into the black leather of the back seat. A mélange of emotions stirred within her as Randy, the driver, who lived three miles from Anna's house, cruised through another green traffic light.

Anna looked out of the window to take in the surroundings. Because this would likely be her last visit to the city. The Arch was lit up and appeared as tall and as magnificent as it did in magazines.

As they continued in bumper-to-bumper traffic, the constant blaring of horns and occasional screeching of brakes made it impossible for Anna to relax. Tall buildings were everywhere. Billboards advertising hospitals and car dealerships.

When they stopped at a red light, Claire, Randy's wife, turned back to glance at Anna. "Congratulations, Anna. Winning that contest; it's a big deal."

Her words pulled Anna from her reverie. At the same time, they reinforced reality. That she had really won. Even though many entrants had gone through formal classes with professionals mentoring them. She realized she was waiting for her to respond, so she used the most appreciative voice she could. "Thank you."

She turned to dart a smile at Anna before turning back to face the front. "Like they say, there's no replacement for natural talent."

"Thanks for those kind words, Claire."

Randy flipped on the radio. As Anna listened to the song on the Christian radio channel, she found herself absorbed in the melody. In her household, there was no radio, of course. But as she listened to the words from "Resurrecting," a sense of calm swept through her until she breathed in and rested her arms over her lap.

Suddenly, tears stung her eyes. But they weren't tears of worry. Instead, they were tears of love for her Lord and Savior.

Thank you, God, for taking over my life and making clear to me what to do. That I belong with Jesse. That

*from this day forward, I will create my own future,
making following You the most important part of it. I
will heed Mamma's advice.*

Claire's cell phone rang, and she answered. She gave
an impatient motion of her hand to her husband to turn
down the radio. Not wasting time, Randy lowered the
volume. Anna leaned forward in her seat as the tone of
Claire's voice turned serious.

As Anna listened to part of the conversation, she
frowned. Apparently, there had been an accident.

Anna put her hand over her mouth and closed her
eyes, continuing to listen to Claire say, "Who?"

Anna sat very still, and there was not a sound inside the
vehicle except for Claire's emotional voice. "Two dead?"

An uneasy sensation swept through Anna's chest until
it ached. As she listened to Claire, Anna's tight chest
made it difficult to breathe. "There was a fatal accident
this morning on County Road 300 East. Two killed."

Dismay edged Randy's voice. "Was anyone we know
involved?"

Claire offered a silent nod. "There were two drivers
from Tuscola, and Jesse Beiler."

As soon as she got home, Anna rushed inside her
house to her parents. Their faces were filled with sadness and concern.

In tears, Anna blurted out, "Jesse . . . is he alive?"

Her parents turned to each other and then to Anna.
Her *daed*'s low voice cracked with emotion. "*Jah*. But
the doctors aren't sure he'll make it."

She caught a breath that was a combination of relief and pain as she started out the door and to the barn to use the phone to call Randy to drive her to wherever Jesse was. "I've got to get to him."

That night, Anna looked down at the man she loved with all her heart in a hospital bed in the ICU unit at Carle Clinic in Champaign, Illinois. His eyes were closed. She took in his pale face. The IV that was taped to his arm. Plastic tubes hung behind him. The smell of antiseptics filled the air.

Slowly, Anna bent forward and planted a kiss on his lips, even though she knew it was not permitted between a single man and woman before marriage. The kiss he'd wanted so badly from her and she'd refused to give him. She frowned at the feel of his cold skin against her lips.

Breathing in, she took his fingers in hers and squeezed them affectionately. A voice from behind her made her turn to a man wearing a white coat. "He had a blood transfusion. It's a miracle he's alive. The drivers of the two cars weren't as fortunate."

A large knot blocked Anna's throat so she couldn't respond. All she did was offer a nod of understanding before immediately focusing on Jesse. She squeezed his hands and prayed out loud. *"Dear Lord, please let Jesse live. And please . . . help me to be a good wife to him and a loving mother to our children. Amen."*

She told him about the contest, even though there was no indication from him that he could hear what she was saying. "You know what I figured out while I was there?" Not expecting a reply, she went on. "I'm Amish,

all the way through. What I would have been if my birth
mamma had raised me doesn't matter. I believe the way
I've been raised by my *eltern*, who love me unconditionally. Who I am doesn't have anything to do with
how I could have been raised. It has everything to do
with how I was molded."

She swallowed. "You know what I've wanted all
along more than anything?" She touched her finger to
his lips. "You. That was what Mamma tried to tell me in
her letter. But I had to go away to come home. And all
the while, you unselfishly supported me."

She paused to keep her composure from slipping. "I
can't believe I almost lost you, Jesse. I took your love
for me for granted. I love you so much."

She stopped a moment to check his reaction, hoping
desperately for some sign that he could hear her. Nothing.

Still, she went on as if he was listening to her.
"You're going to make it. And I'll be your wife. Jesse, I
love your farm. The house we'll live in."

Excitement edged her voice as she squeezed his
hands. "I can't wait to start drawing in our home. With
Pebble Creek in the background. But please, Jesse. Be
there with me."

She sniffed back a tear. "I don't ever want to be without you again. The sketch that won the contest was a
drawing of you. I want it to hang in our bedroom. You
won the contest, Jesse. You won it for me. You are my
inspiration."

She closed her eyes and prayed silently. And when
she opened her lids, he squeezed her hand back.

* * *

Two Months Later

Hand in hand, Anna and Jesse walked alongside Pebble Creek. Anna steadied him with her arm as he limped. This was the very place she'd sketched his picture. Where he'd asked her to be his wife. And where she'd accepted his second proposal. Today.

At the same time, they stopped, and he planted a long kiss on her lips. This time, she allowed it.

"I know this isn't proper, Anna, but now I'm more aware than ever of just how fragile we are. How we can be gone in a snap of the fingers. And every moment is precious." He breathed in and looked up at the cloudless sky before lowering his gaze to hers. "I must be the luckiest guy in the world."

She ran an affectionate hand over the wicked scar on his forehead. "Jesse, I praise God that you made it through that accident. You're right about every moment being precious. I regret that it took me the time it did to figure out what I really wanted. I don't know what . . ."

"Shhh." He pressed his finger gently on her lips. "I'm here to stay." His lips curved in amusement. He winked, and that all-too-familiar, mischievous twinkle in his eyes made her smile. "Now we both have scars on our foreheads."

She grinned.

"And my parents are relieved I'm staying here. To be honest, I feel like I'm getting a second chance at life. Thanks to the doctors. Most of all, thanks to Him." He looked up at the sky.

"And I'm getting a second chance, too."

"You know what I was thinking before the car hit me?"

She lifted a curious brow. "What?"

"It was something I heard a long time ago. I was told that it came from Old Sam. That letting go of earthly possessions lets us take hold of heavenly treasures."

She swallowed an emotional knot. "He let you live."

Jesse nodded. "God's hand protected me."

He stopped and caught an emotional breath. "I'll never forget what unfolded right in front of me. Serene got us both over to the side of the road so the oncoming car would have room to get by. But the driver of a car I couldn't see suddenly passed him, hit me, and knocked me out of the buggy. I learned that the other driver couldn't stop and hit him, and their lives were taken."

She squeezed her eyes closed to maintain her composure. When she opened them, she blinked at the sting of salty tears. "But God let you live." She smiled a little. "And, miraculously, your horse."

"There's something you should know."

"What?"

"When I lost consciousness, I could feel God's presence. I can't really explain it. But it was there, Anna. And it was so powerful, I'll never forget it."

Tears of joy streamed down Anna's cheeks.

Jesse ran a gentle finger to stop one. "Hey, it's okay. God gave us a happy ending." He hesitated before lowering the pitch of his voice. "But Anna, not everyone is so fortunate."

Several heartbeats later, he held her hands and looked into her eyes. "The drivers are dead. And Reuben's mother is about to go to the Lord. He'll need a home."

The corners of Anna's mouth began to curve upward in a hopeful smile. "Could we adopt him?"

Jesse's response was a firm nod. He bent to kiss her. Afterward, he looked into her eyes and pushed back a loose strand of hair that had escaped her *kapp*. "Anna, I would like nothing better than to have a house full of children. And I've always wanted a son. In fact, I can already see Reuben and me fishing together. Working together in the barn. He needs us."

She expelled a sigh of amazement. "It's wonderful how things work out. When I was in St. Louis, I saw an interesting wall plaque that put my priorities into perspective."

"What did it say?"

"Not to try to find your path. To create your own. And when we have children, I want to raise them to be independent thinkers. That it's okay to question things."

Jesse offered a wry smile.

"God has blessed us. And I'm so happy we won't have to wait long to marry. In the next three months, we'll be married church members. And you know what?"

"What?"

"Sometimes, when I'm at Pebble Creek, I imagine Old Sam looking down on me. I know he had a saying about the real secret to happiness. I can't believe I'd forgotten."

"What?"

"The real secret to happiness is not what you give or receive; it's what you share." After a slight pause, she went on. "And when our children are grown, I pray that they'll be as blessed as us. That they'll find love at Pebble Creek."

RETURN TO THE BEGINNING

THE HOPE CHEST OF DREAMS SERIES

Book 1: *Rebecca's Bouquet*

The last thing Rebecca Sommer dreamed her plan to
marry would bring is a heart-wrenching choice. She
thought she and her betrothed, William, would spend
the rest of their lives in Illinois's heartland, raising a
family in their close-knit Amish hometown. But when
he must travel far out of state to save his ailing father's
business, Rebecca braves her relatives' disapproval—
and her own fears—to work by his side. And though
she finds herself ever more in love with the dedicated,
resourceful man he proves to be, William's growing
interest in English ways may be the one challenge
even her steadfast faith can't meet . . .

Book 2: *Annie's Recipe*

Annie Mast and Levi Miller were best friends until his
father was shunned by the church. Now, ten years
later, Levi has returned to Arthur, Illinois, for a brief
visit, and he and Annie discover their bond is as strong
as ever. Spending as much time together as possible,
Annie finds herself dreaming of a future with Levi.
And Levi is soon dreaming of building a home on a
beautiful local hillside—to live in with Annie.
Yet their longings are unlikely to become reality . . .

Book 3: *Rachel's Dream*

Rachel Kauffman and Jared Zimmerman seem to
have nothing in common. She's the outgoing youngest
of a large, close-knit Amish clan, and longs to raise a
brood of her own near those she loves. Estranged from
his family by tragedy, Jared is a young veterinarian
who trusts the animals he heals far more than he
trusts people. However, when Rachel's beloved horse
falls ill, Jared's struggles to save him show Rachel
he's a man who cares deeply. And the respect he
feels for her gentle, warmhearted ways soon
becomes an irresistible bond . . .

Available wherever books and eBooks are sold!

Turn the page for an excerpt from
Rebecca's Bouquet . . .

His announcement took her by surprise. Rebecca Sommer met William's serious gaze and swallowed. The shadow from his hat made his expression impossible to read.

"You're really leaving?"

He fingered the black felt on the brim. "I know what a shock this is. Believe me, I never expected to hear that Dad had a heart attack."

"Do they expect a full recovery?"

William nodded. "But the docs say it will be a while before he works again. Right now, they can't even guess at a time line. In the meantime, Beth's struggling to take care of him."

While Rebecca considered the news, the warm June breeze rustled the large, ear-shaped leaves on the catalpa tree. The sun peeked from behind a large marshmallow cloud, as if deciding whether or not to appear. In the distance, a sleek black gelding clomped its hooves against the earth.

Pools of dust stirred, swirling and quickly disappearing. Lambs frolicked across the parcel of pasture separating the Sommer home from Old Sam Beachy's bright red barn. From where they stood, Rebecca could barely glimpse the orange YIELD sign on the back of the empty buggy parked next to the house.

"I'm the only person Dad trusts with his business." William paused and lowered his voice. "Beth wants me to come to Indiana and run his cabinet shop, Rebecca."

The news caused a wave of anxiety to roll through Rebecca's chest. She wrung her hands together in a nervous gesture. A long silence ensued as she thought of William leaving, and her shoulders grew tense. Not even the light, sweet fragrance floating from her mother's rose garden could take away Rebecca's anxiety.

When she finally started to respond, William held up a defensive hand. "It's just until he's back on his feet. This may not be such a bad thing. The experience might actually benefit us."

Rebecca raised a curious brow. The breeze blew a chestnut-brown hair out of place, and she quickly tucked it back under her *kapp*. Her gaze drifted from his face to his rolled-up sleeves.

Tiny freckles decorated his nose, giving him a youthful appearance. But there was nothing boyish about his square jaw or broad shoulders that tried to push their way out of his shirt. Her heart skipped a beat. She lifted her chin, and their eyes locked in understanding.

William smiled a little. "One of these days, we'll run our own company." He winked. "Don't worry."

She swallowed the lump in her throat. For one blissful, hopeful moment, she trusted everything would be okay. It wasn't those simple two words that reassured her, but the tender, persuasive way William said them.

The low, steady tone in which he spoke could convince Rebecca of almost anything.

The warm pink glow on his cheeks made Rebecca's pulse pick up speed. As he looked at her for a reaction, her lips lifted into a wide smile. At the same time, it was impossible to stop the nervous rising and falling of her chest.

She'd never dreamed of being without William. Even temporarily. At the young age of eighteen, she hadn't confronted such a difficult issue.

But her church teachers and parents had raised her to deal with obstacles. Fortunately, they had prepared her to be strong and to pray for guidance. As she stared at her beloved flower garden, her thoughts became more chaotic.

The clothes on the line rose and fell with the warm summer breeze. Their fresh, soapy scent floated through the air. She surely had greater control over her destiny than the wet garments, whose fate was dependent on the wind. She and William could get through this. They loved each other. God would take care of them, wouldn't He?

She glanced up at William. The way the sun hit him at an angle made him look even taller than his six feet and two inches. He'd always been bigger and stronger than other kids his age.

The gray flecks in his deep blue eyes danced to a mysterious tune as he darted her a grin. When she looked into those dark pools, she could drown in happiness. But today, even the warmth emanating from his smile couldn't stop the concern that edged her voice. "Don't worry? But I do, William. What about . . ."

"Us?"

She nodded.

He leveled his gaze so that she looked directly at him. "Nothing has changed. We'll still get married in November after the harvest."

Rebecca hesitated. She couldn't believe William would really leave Arthur, Illinois. But his reason was legitimate. His father needed him. She wasn't selfish, and asking him to stay would be.

Circumstances were beyond her control. What could she do? The question nagged at her until frustration set in. Within a matter of minutes, her world had changed, and she fought to adjust. She nervously tapped the toe of her black shoe against the ground.

As she crossed her arms over her chest, she wished they could protect her from the dilemma she faced. Her brows narrowed into a frown, and a long silence ensued. She looked at him, hoping for an answer. Seeking even a hint of a solution.

To her surprise, William teased, "Rebecca, stop studying me like I'm a map of the world."

His statement broke the tension, and she burst into laughter because a map of the world was such a far stretch from what she'd been thinking.

"Of course, you've got to help your folks, William. I know how much Daniel's business means to him. You certainly can't let him lose it. I can imagine the number of cabinets on order."

Surprised and relieved that her voice sounded steady,

Rebecca's shoulders trembled as the thought of William leaving sank in. They'd grown up together and hadn't spent a day without seeing one another.

She stopped a moment and considered Daniel and Beth Conrad. Nearly a decade ago, William's mamma had died, and Daniel had married Beth.

He was a skilled cabinetmaker. It was no surprise that people from all over the United States ordered his custom-made pieces. Rebecca had seen samples of his elegant, beautiful woodworking.

A thought popped into Rebecca's mind, and she frowned. "William, you seem to be forgetting something very important. Daniel and Beth . . . They're English."

He nodded. "Don't think I haven't given that consideration."

"I don't want to sound pessimistic, but how will you stay Amish in their world?"

He shrugged. "They're the same as us, really."

She rolled her eyes. "Of course they are. But the difference between our lifestyle and theirs is night and day. How can you expect to move in with them and be compatible?"

William hooked his fingers over his trouser pockets, looked down at the ground and furrowed a brow. Rebecca smiled. She knew him so well. Whenever something bothered him, he did this. Rebecca loved the intense look on his face when he worried. The small indentation in his chin intensified.

What fascinated her most, though, were the mysterious gray flecks that danced in his eyes. When he lifted his chin, those flecks took on a metallic appearance. Mesmerized, Rebecca couldn't stop looking at them.

Moments later, as if having made an important decision, he stood still, moved his hands to his hips, and met her gaze with a nod.

In a more confident tone, he spoke. "It will be okay, Rebecca. Don't forget that Dad was Amish before he married Beth. He was raised with the same principles as us. Just because he's English now doesn't mean he's forgotten everything he learned. No need to worry. He won't want me to change."

"No?"

William gave a firm shake of his head. "Of course not. In fact, I'm sure he'll insist that I stick to how I was brought up. Remember, he left me with Aenti Sarah and Uncle John when he remarried. Dad told me that raising me Amish was what my mother would have expected. The *Ordnung* was important to her. And keeping the faith must have also been at the top of Dad's list to have left me here. Nothing will change, Rebecca."

Rebecca realized that she was making too much out of William's going away. After all, it was only Indiana. Not the North Pole! Suddenly embarrassed at her lack of strength, she looked down at the hem of her dress before gazing straight into his eyes. He moved so close, his warm breath caressed her bottom lip, and it quivered. Time seemed to stand still while she savored the silent mutual understanding between them. That unique, unexplainable connection that she and William had.

"I've always read that things happen for a reason," William mentioned.

"Me too." Rebecca also knew the importance of the *Ordnung*. And she knew William's mamma, Miriam, would have wanted him to stay in the faith that had meant everything to her.

As if sensing her distress, he interlaced his fingers together in front of him. His hands were large. She'd watched those very hands lift heavy bales of hay.

"Who knows? Maybe this is God's way of testing me."

Rebecca gave an uncertain roll of her eyes. "Talk to your aunt and uncle. They'll know what's best. After all, they've raised you since your father remarried."

The frustration in William's voice lifted a notch. "I already did. It's hard to convince them that what I'm doing is right." He lowered his voice. "You know how they feel. When Dad left the faith, he deserted me. But even so, I can't turn my back on him."

"Of course not."

"Aenti Sarah's concerned that people will treat me differently when I come back. She wants to talk to the bishop and get his permission. If that makes her feel better, then I'm all for it."

"If he'll give his blessing."

William nodded in agreement.

"But we're old enough to think for ourselves, William. When we get married and raise our family, we can't let everyone make up our minds for us."

He raised a brow. "You're so independent, Miss Rebecca."

She smiled a little.

A mischievous twinkle lightened his eyes.

"Your decision shouldn't be based on what people

think," Rebecca said. "If we made choices to please others, we'd never win. Deep down inside, we have to be happy with ourselves. So you've got to do what's in your heart. And no one can decide that but you."

The expression that crossed his face suddenly became unreadable. She tilted her head and studied him with immense curiosity. "What are you thinking?"

His gray flecks repeated that metallic appearance. "Rebecca, you're something else."

A surge of warmth rushed through her.

"I can't believe your insight." He blinked in amazement. "You're an angel." His voice was low and soft. She thought he was going to kiss her. But he didn't. William followed the church rules. But Rebecca wouldn't have minded breaking that one.

In a breathless voice, she responded, "Thank you for that."

As if suddenly remembering the crux of their conversation, William returned to the original topic. "I've assured Aenti Sarah and Uncle John that I won't leave the Amish community. That I'll come back, and we'll get married. They finally justified letting me leave by looking at this as an opportunity to explore *Rumspringa*."

Rebecca grinned. "I guess that's one way to look at it." *Rumspringa* was the transition time between adolescence and adulthood when an Amish youth could try things before deciding whether to join the faith for him—or herself. She even had a friend who had gone as far as to get a driver's license.

He paused. "Rebecca, I know we didn't plan on this." His voice grew more confident as he continued. "You've got to understand that I love you more than anything in the world. Please tell me you'll wait for me. I give you my word that this move is only temporary. As soon as Dad's on his feet again, I'll come home. Promise."

As William committed, Rebecca took in his dark brown hair. The sun's brightness lightened it to the color of sand. For a moment, his features were both rugged and endearing. Rebecca's heart melted.

Her voice softened. "How long do you think you'll stay?"

William pressed his lips together thoughtfully. "Good question. Hopefully, he'll be back to work in no time. His customers depend on him, and according to Beth, he has a long list of orders for cabinets to produce and deliver. He's a strong man, Rebecca. He'll be okay."

"I believe that. I'll never forget when he came into town last year to see you." She giggled. "Remember his fancy car?"

William chuckled. "He sure enjoys the luxuries of the English. I wish our community wouldn't be so harsh on him. He's really Amish at heart."

William hesitated. "I used to resent that he left me."

Long moments passed in silence. He stepped closer and lowered his voice to a whisper. "Rebecca, you've become unusually quiet. And you didn't answer my question."

She raised an inquisitive brow.

"Will you wait for me?"

Her thoughts were chaotic. For something to do, she looked down and flattened her hands against her long, brown dress. She realized how brave William was and recalled the scandal Daniel Conrad had made when he married outside of the faith and had moved to the country outside of Evansville, Indiana. She raised her chin to look at William's face. Mamma always told her that a person's eyes gave away his feelings.

The tongue could lie. But not the eyes. William's intriguing flecks had become a shade lighter, dancing with hope and sincerity. His cheeks were flushed.

"William, you've got to do this." She let out a small, thoughtful sigh. "I remember a particular church sermon from a long time ago. The message was that our success in life isn't determined by making easy choices. It's measured by how we deal with difficult issues. And leaving Arthur is definitely a tough decision."

He hugged his hands to his hips. "What are you getting at?"

She quietly sought an answer to his question. What did she mean? She'd sounded like she knew what she was talking about. Moments later, the answer came. She recognized it with complete clarity.

She squared her shoulders. "I promised you I'd stick by you forever, William. And right now, you need me."

He gazed down at her in confusion.

Clearing her throat, she looked up at him and drew a long breath. "I'm going with you."

Inside Old Sam Beachy's barn, Rebecca poured out her dilemma to her dear friend. Afterwards, Buddy whimpered sympathetically at her feet. Rebecca reached down from her rocking chair opposite Old Sam's workbench and obediently stroked the Irish setter behind his ears. The canine closed his eyes in contentment.

Old Sam was famous for his hope chests. He certainly wasn't the only person to put together the pieces, but he was a brilliant artist who etched beautiful, personalized designs into the lids.

Rebecca had looked at his beloved Esther as a second mother. Since she'd succumbed to pneumonia a couple of years ago, Rebecca had tried to return her kindness to the old widower. So did her friends, Rachel and Annie. The trio took care of him. Rachel listened to Sam's horse-and-buggy stories. Annie baked him delicious sponge cakes while Rebecca picked him fresh flowers.

Drawing a long breath, Rebecca wondered what advice he'd give. Whatever it was would be good. Because no one was wiser than Old Sam. She crossed her legs at the ankles. Sawdust floated in the air. Rebecca breathed in the woodsy smell of oak.

When he started to speak, she sat up a little straighter. "The real secret to happiness is not what we give or receive; it's what we share. I would consider your help to William and his parents a gift from the heart. At the same time, a clear conscience is a soft pillow. You want to have the blessing of our bishop and your parents. The last thing you want is a scandal about you and William living under the same roof."

Rebecca let out a deep, thoughtful sigh as she considered his wisdom. In the background, she could hear Ginger enter her stall from the pasture. Old Sam's horse snorted. And that meant she wanted an apple.

Sam's voice prompted Rebecca to meet his gaze.

"Rebecca, I can give you plenty of advice. But the most important thing I can tell you is to pray."

Rebecca nodded and crossed her arms over her chest.

"But remember: Do not ask the Lord to guide your footsteps if you're not willing to move your feet."

Rebecca was fully aware that William was ready to leave. In her front yard, she hugged her baby sister, Emily, shoving a rebellious strand of blond hair out of her face. Rebecca planted an affectionate kiss on brother Peter's cheek. "Be good."

Pete's attention was on Rebecca just long enough to say good-bye. As she turned to her father, the two kids started screaming and chasing each other in a game of tag. Emily nearly tripped over a chicken in the process. Rebecca was quick to notice the uncertain expression on Old Sam's face.

The sweet, creamy smell of homemade butter competed with the aroma of freshly baked bread. Both enticing scents floated out of the open kitchen windows. Tonight, Rebecca would miss Mamma's dinner. It would be the first time Rebecca hadn't eaten with her family.

Her heart pumped to an uncertain beat. But she'd never let her fear show. Ever since the death of her other little sister, Rebecca had learned to put on a brave façade. Her family depended on her for strength.

Rebecca's father grasped her hands and gave them a tight squeeze. She immediately noted that his arms shook. It stunned her to realize that his embrace was more of a nervous gesture than an offer of support. And the expression on his face was anything but encouraging.

Rebecca understood his opposition to what she was about to do. Her father's approval was important to her, and it bothered her to seem disrespectful.

All of her life, she'd tried hard to please him. They'd never even argued. In fact, this was the first time she'd gone against his wishes. But William was her future. She wanted to be by his side whenever he needed her.

In a gruff, firm voice, her father spoke. "Be careful, Becca. You know how I feel. I'm disappointed that William hasn't convinced you to stay. You belong here. In Arthur."

He pushed out a frustrated breath. "But you're of age to make your own decision. We've made arrangements with Beth so that living under the same roof with William will be proper. We trust she'll be a responsible chaperone while you're with the Conrads. Just come home soon. We need your help with chores."

He pointed an authoritative finger. "And never let the English ways influence you. They will tempt you to be like them, Becca. Remember your faith."

Rebecca responded with a teary nod. When she finally faced Mamma, she forced a brave smile. But the tightness in her throat made it difficult to say good-bye.

Mamma's deep blue eyes clouded with moisture. With one swift motion, Rebecca hugged her. For long moments, she was all too aware of how much she would miss that security. The protection only a parent could offer.

Much too soon, Mamma released her and held her at arm's length. When Rebecca finally turned to Old Sam, he stepped forward and handed her a cardboard container with handles.

She met his gaze and lifted a curious brow. "This is for me?"

He nodded. "I hope you like it." He pointed. "Go ahead. Take it out."

Everyone was quiet while she removed the gift. As she lifted the hope chest, she caught her breath. There was a unanimous sound of awe from the group. "Old Sam . . ." She focused on the design etched into the lid. "It's absolutely beautiful! I will treasure it the rest of my life."

"You always bring me fresh flowers, so I thought you'd like the bouquet."

She glanced at William before turning her attention back to Sam. "I'm taking the miniature hope chest with me."

Sam's voice was low and edged with emotion. "I will pray for your safety. And remember that freedom is not to do as you please, but the liberty to do as you ought. And the person who sows seeds of kindness will have a perpetual harvest. That's you, Rebecca."

Rebecca blinked as salty tears filled her eyes. With great care, she returned the hope chest to its box on the bright green blades of grass.

Old Sam's voice cracked. "You come back soon. And if you want good advice, consult an old man." A grin tugged at Rebecca's lips. Sam knew every proverb in the book. She'd miss hearing him recount them.

"Thank you again. I can't wait to start putting away special trinkets for the children I will have some day."

When she looked up at him, he merely nodded approval.

William's voice startled her from her thoughts.

"Rebecca, it's time to head out. It's gonna be a long drive."

Her gaze remained locked with Mamma's. Mary Sommer's soft voice shook with emotion. "This is the first time you've left us. But you're strong."

Rebecca squeezed her eyes closed for several heart-beats.

As if to reassure herself, her mother went on. "We hope Daniel recovers quickly. William needs you. In the meantime, God will keep both of you in His hands. Don't forget that. Always pray. And remember what we've taught you. Everything you've learned in church."

"*Jah.*"

"It's never been a secret that God gave you a special gift for accepting challenges. I'll never forget the time you jumped into that creek to save your brother. You pulled him to shore."

Rebecca grinned. "I remember."

"*Rumspringa* might be the most important time in your life. But be very careful. There will be temptations in the English world. In fact, the bishop is concerned that you will decide against joining the Amish church."

"I know who I am."

A tear rolled down Mamma's cheek while she slipped something small and soft between Rebecca's palms. Rebecca glanced down at the crocheted cover.

"I put together this Scripture book to help you while you're away, Rebecca. When you have doubts or fears, read it. The good words will comfort and give you strength. You can even share them with Beth. She's going through a difficult time. Your *daed* and I will pray for you every day." She paused. "Lend Daniel your support. The bishop wants you to set three additional goals and accomplish them while you're gone. Give them careful consideration. They must be unselfish and important. Doing this will make your mission even more significant."

After a lengthy silence, William addressed the Sommers in a reassuring voice. "I'll take good care of her. You can be sure of that."

Rebecca's dad raised his chin and directed his attention to William. "We expect nothing less."

Long, tense moments passed while her father and William locked gazes. Several heartbeats later, Eli Sommer stepped forward. "I don't approve of my Becca going so far away. I'm holding you responsible for her, William. If anything happens . . ."

William darted an unsure glance at Rebecca before responding. "I understand your concern. That's why I didn't encourage her to come."

Rebecca raised her chin and regarded both of them. "I've given this a lot of thought. I'll go. And I'll come back, safe and sound."

Rebecca listened with dread as her father continued making his case. She knew William wouldn't talk back. And she wasn't about to change her mind about going.

"Daed, it's my decision. Please don't worry."

Before he could argue, she threw her arms around him and gave him a tight, reassuring hug. After she stepped away, William motioned toward the black Cadillac. As Rebecca drew a deep breath, her knees trembled, and her heart pounded like a jackhammer. Finally, she forced her jellylike legs to move. She didn't turn around as William opened her door.

Before stepping inside, Rebecca put Mamma's Scripture book inside the hope chest. William took the box from her and placed it in the middle of the back-seat. Rebecca brought very little with her. Just one small suitcase that her father placed in the trunk.

With great hesitation, she waved good-bye. She forced a confident smile, but her entire body shook. She sat very still as Daniel's second cousin, Ethan, backed the car out of the drive. Gravel crunched under the tires. This wasn't Rebecca's first ride in an automobile. Car rides were not uncommon in the Amish community.

Trying to convince herself she was doing the right thing, she gently pushed the down arrow by her door handle, and the window opened. Rebecca turned in her seat and waved until the sad faces of her family, their plain-looking wooden-framed house built by her great-grandfather, and Old Sam, disappeared.

William turned to her. A worry crease crept across his forehead. The cleft in his chin became more pro-nounced. "Rebecca, your dad's right. I should have made you stay. The last thing I want to do is create tension between you two."

"It wasn't your choice. As far as my father's concerned . . ." She gave a frustrated shake of her head. "I don't like displeasing him either. On the other hand, it's not right for me to stay here and send you off to save Daniel's shop all by yourself." She shrugged.

In silence, she thought about what she'd just said. She nervously ran her hand over the smooth black leather seat.

"You can adjust the air vents," Ethan announced, turning briefly to make eye contact with her.

She was thankful she didn't have to travel to the Indiana countryside by horse and buggy. She rather enjoyed the soft, barely audible purring of the engine.

Next to her, she eyed the cardboard and pulled out the mini hope chest, setting the box on the floor. She smiled a little.

"Old Sam is something else." William's voice was barely more than a whisper.

"*Jah*. I can't wait to tell him about our trip." Rebecca giggled. "I'll miss listening to him grumble while he works in the barn. I enjoy watching him make those elaborate chests that he sells to the stores in town."

William gave a small nod. "He loves you three girls."

"Thank goodness that Annie and Rachel will be around to keep him company."

The three friends had loved Esther. Now they took care of Old Sam. He was like an uncle to them. But Rebecca was leaving the world she knew. Would she fit in with the English?